Eternal Recurrence

Ken Lavacot

CONTENTS

Exhausted, I drifted off to sleep and entered a dream world where I found myself in heaven. As I looked around, I saw all the gods of the world happily playing, dancing, and laughing together. This blissful scene continued for some time until they took notice of me and asked, "We are all friends here, why aren't you?"

INTRODUCTION

Picture this: what if the answers to the myriad questions that mystify us are, in reality, surprisingly simple? What if the solutions have been hiding in plain sight, lurking in the corners of our minds, yet remaining elusive because of our preconceived notions? Some of these answers may challenge or unsettle you, but they are essential to consider nonetheless.

Imagine the existence of two parallel realities. One we can perceive, comprehend, and interact with — the physical world. Beyond this is another realm, hidden from our direct view — whether it be metaphysical, spiritual, or even quantum.

Life is more than mere existence; it's about honing

essential skills. Love and happiness are not mere freebies; they must be nurtured and cherished. Moreover, we should entertain the possibility that our planet Earth is sentient, reacting and responding to our actions, striving to maintain equilibrium when we disturb its natural harmony.

Now, embark on a mental journey and entertain the idea that the ancient Egyptians had mastered interstellar travel. What if they had ventured to distant planets using advanced electro-mechanical mechanisms? Not through miracles or magic, but tangible scientific advancements. An idea so revolutionary that it could reshape our understanding of life on Earth.

True comprehension is a precursor to benefiting from information. This simple yet profound principle can be obstructed by our rigid beliefs or misunderstandings. To truly evolve, we must remain open to new concepts, even when immediate proof is lacking. As Albert Einstein aptly said, "I never came upon any of my discoveries through the process of rational thinking."

Consider the concept of death, or rather, its absence. It's a puzzle that has long bewildered humanity, yet one the ancient Egyptians seemed to grasp.

Many shy away from the idea of rebirth because life's challenges can be overwhelming. The notion of reliving these trials in another lifetime is daunting. However, reincarnation suggests a way for the soul to begin anew, shaped by a different lineage and environment, ushering in a fresh iteration of 'you.'

Envision life as a cosmic school where virtues are rewarded, and transgressions bring consequences. Our actions create ripples in time, affecting those around us. We must find life's meaning; it isn't handed to us effortlessly.

Our solar system, a majestic waltz of celestial bodies around the sun, stands as a monument to eons of scientific discovery. Visualize a cosmic lifecycle where planets are birthed, flourish, and eventually meet their end, influenced by the sun.

When a planet nears the end of its lifecycle, it breaks down into its fundamental elements, regressing to the very gases from which it originated. This cycle is one of the unseen wonders that transform the ordinary into the extraordinary.

I propose that there exist unseen energy rings capable of sustaining a life force or soul. These rings become visible during various stages of a planet's life, each layer teeming with different life forms. As Earth reaches its twilight, a nascent planet emerges, primed to perpetuate the cosmic dance.

What are death and time, if not concepts that both intrigue and terrify us? What if death is not an end but a new beginning? A transition, a doorway to another phase where our life energy prepares for rebirth.

This metamorphosis might present itself as a guiding light, an energetic beacon leading us to our destined path. Our choices, thoughts, and deeds, all meticulously chronicled in the universe's ledger, shape this destiny.

For the ancient Egyptians journeying into the afterlife, time would cease to hold meaning, creating a realm where their life energy temporarily vacates the tangible realm. When the time comes, this energy reincarnates, steered by the cosmic blueprint, eager to embark on another voyage.

Love is the unseen catalyst propelling this eternal cycle, the binding force of this vast cosmic web.

Rest assured, I don't mean to disconcert you. These are mere musings, thoughts to ponder during tranquil, introspective moments. Perhaps on a quiet evening, by the fireplace with a glass of wine, allowing oneself to plunge into the depths of existential wonder. Let this treatise be your invitation to explore the vast expanse of the unknown. For in such explorations, profound truths often emerge.

CHAPTER 1 - THE SURPRISE

As the door slams shut with a resounding boom, memories flood back to Lenny of all the times his parents had been disappointed in him. The 12-year-old boy, sitting fearfully in a kitchen chair, was well-behaved most of the time, but had a tendency to lose control in stressful situations when he felt inferior. It was a defense mechanism he had developed to protect his innermost feelings.

His father, Jason, with a furrowed brow, speaks in a raised voice to instill fear in Lenny, "Do you know why we are so upset?" His mother, Lisa, stands behind him, her face a mask of sorrow. Jason's anguish is palpable as he remembers Lenny's academic evaluations over the years and the familiar event that this was. After a few moments of silence,

Jason looks at his son's face, torn and hurting, and shouts, "Go to your room!" in disbelief and frustration.

Lenny slowly gets up from the chair and drags himself to his room, tears streaming down his face. As he lies on his bed, he looks up at the posters of his idols and the success he dreams of achieving. "I will never be that good!" he sobs, completely humiliated, and turns to the wall, burying his face in his pillow.

Meanwhile, Jason and Lisa exchange worried and doubtful thoughts in the kitchen. "He just has the hardest time reading, and he's not much better in math. What's the problem?" Jason asks, loud enough for Lenny to hear. "He used to be such a good little boy," Lisa tries to calm the situation. "Maybe it's our fault, too soft on him," Jason says, trying to calm down. Suddenly, something changes in Jason's mind, like a key turning in a lock, and he feels a sense of compassion towards his son. He recalls his disdain as Lenny's grades started to slip and his son's social awkwardness darkened his outlook on the next generation of their family. Jason begins to question himself, "Why am I so upset? Why am I doing this?" It dawns on him that he is afraid his son won't be able to care for himself in the world, let alone start a family, and his natural reaction is anger. Remembering what a wonderful boy Lenny was just two years earlier, Jason starts to reflect on what happened. "So the academic community calls my son stupid?!!.... I think they are stupid!!!.... They don't understand my son, so he is dumb! He is a 12-year-old boy, and they can't figure him out? How smart are they? My son is just as important as any person there! What do we call intelligence? The ability to read a book he's not interested in and take a test? My son has more soul than all of them put together!"

Suddenly, Jason hears a knocking and pounding noise, "What is that?" he asks Lisa. Jason hurries up the stairs to Lenny's room and opens the door to find Lenny ripping down his beloved posters and hitting his head against the wall, crying out, "I am stupid!" Jason rushes over to him and holds him in his arms, saying, "You're okay, son. You're okay. I'm sorry, so very sorry."

The next morning, as Lenny sits in the car, broken, Jason gets into the driver's seat and notices the damage on his son's face. He decides to try something different, "I think your school is stupid." Lenny experiences a glimmer of hope as a tiny light returns to his face. "Let's go," Jason starts the car and drives to Lenny's school.

As they walked toward the administration office, the school's slippery floors glistened from the rain. Through the glass, Jason and Lenny observed well-dressed men and women going about their daily duties as they entered the building. Jason felt a sense of determination, like a cowboy walking into a saloon ready for confrontation. He spoke with conviction, his voice ringing out across the office.

"I want you all to listen! I am sick of the pain and destruction you cause with your archaic way of teaching. You blame these kids when it is you who are failing! These are children! How can they be wrong? You pit them against each other in an impossible contest. You break down their self-confidence in a world that does that already! I am an auto mechanic, and even I can see that it's you who are the dumbasses!"

As the spectacle unfolded, a clerk in a rear office reached for the phone to alert the police. The principal and vice-principal entered the area, while Lenny watched as his father defended him.

"How do you expect a maturity level to be consistent across any age group? It's impossible! The school board uses the kids as weapons to push through propositions at election time for more money, which never seems to get to them? I see the new cars you drive and the fancy clothes. We entrust this responsibility to you, the educators, but year after year, kids are flunking out, ending up on the streets or committing suicide. That's all on you."

Other students noticed the commotion and started gathering outside the office as the police walked in through the rear entrance. The principal gestured for the officers to hold up. Standing on a proverbial soapbox, Jason continued his impassioned speech.

"Hey, here's an idea: how about interest-based learning? Tailor the education to the individual and abolish grade levels. They would learn at their own pace and never feel stupid. Think of the self-confidence they would have, think of the improvement in the social dynamic! Drugs and alcohol usage would plummet. They would succeed at anything they wished through natural curiosity. We have the technology, why don't we use it? Too easy? Hello? We need classes about love to avoid the traumatic event of heartbreak with the collateral damage it brings. Let's show them life and happiness and how life ends up if it's done incorrectly. So many of life's hardships can be avoided if we teach them at a young age. Kids know the love of a parent, sibling, or pet, so why not teach them about it? Without these things, what is life for anyway? They don't need to know about Magellan unless the kids want to! You degrade their self-confidence until they lash out, and you wonder why the jails are full? That's your failure! Every criminal has a baby picture they hate looking at! You don't think they cry at night in jail? You are wrong! Passion-based education! All jobs in the world need to be done, and no one should feel bad doing their part. No one person is better than another. A doctor cannot do their job if there is no one to dig the ditch and supply the building with water."

 As the room falls into a hushed silence, Jason's gaze sweeps over the assembled crowd, searching for any hint of reaction, but finds none. His eyes meet Lenny's, who grins with unbridled delight. An air of expectancy lingers, the onlooking children and administrators locked in a wordless exchange. Then, gradually, the commanding officer initiates a round of applause that soon swells into a crescendo. It feels as though a burden has been lifted, and a warm ray of hope pierces the hearts of all who bear witness. In this singular moment, a speech has set in motion the blueprint for a brighter future.

 Jason glides into work slightly behind schedule, finding a car already awaiting his attention in the repair bay. He unlocks his toolbox to begin and, as he slips on his work gloves, notices the manager approaching. "Jason, what's going on? Our customers are relying on us, and Mrs. Brown has to pick up her young children from school!"

 Jason acknowledges, "I know, I know," only to be met with his manager's sharp retort, "If you know so much, why are you late?"

"I encountered an issue at Lenny's school that I needed to resolve, but it shouldn't happen again," Jason explains defensively. The manager, while walking away, mutters under his breath, "Let's hope not. It would be a shame for a pink slip to mar your upcoming vacation."

Elegant gifts of bon voyage adorn Lisa's desk, thoughtfully presented by friends and colleagues as she transfers files to a thumb drive, preparing for potential needs during her absence. As her laptop shuts down, it marks the end of a year-long anticipation to truly live once more. She receives encouraging nods from acquaintances and heartfelt hugs from close friends before leaving the building. Casting a glance back at the AT&T insignia, she offers a farewell wave before heading to her car.

Upon settling into her vehicle, she attempts to start the engine, but to no avail. Lisa considers calling Jason for assistance, but decides to search the internet for a simple solution first. Following a link from 2CarPros.com, she opts to inspect the battery cables beneath the hood. As suspected, the positive cable is loose. Resourcefully, she retrieves napkins from the glove compartment, using them to secure the cable terminal. With the issue resolved, she closes the hood and is ready to embark on her adventure.

"You would have been so proud of me today, my love," Lisa proclaimed to her husband as Jason crossed the threshold of their home. "Oh? What happened?" he inquired. Beaming with pride, Lisa responded, "I repaired my car today! There was a loose battery cable." Jason warmly replied,

"Impressive work, sweetheart."

Jason longed to share the details of his own day, but chose to remain silent so as not to overshadow his wife's achievement. "It's hard to believe we're embarking on our trip tomorrow. It's been a lifelong dream, to say the least," he exclaimed with enthusiasm. Jason and Lisa's love story began in high school, during a history class, and led to marriage in their early twenties. Their union has weathered both highs and lows. Through the tumultuous tempests and strife, they've managed to keep their somewhat lopsided relationship afloat.

As their plane departs from Orlando Airport, the lines on the runway merge into mere dots. Jason and Lisa feel the ascent, knowing that in about ten hours, they'll land in Cairo. An inexplicable force seems to draw them to this destination. "Jason," Lisa interjects suddenly, "it's too cold in here, and I don't want to catch a cold. It would ruin our trip, and you know how much I've been looking forward to it. Could you please ask for a blanket?" With that, she searches for a tissue, as her nose starts to run.

Jason rises from his seat and approaches a flight attendant. "Excuse me, my wife is feeling cold. Could we have something to keep her warm?" he asks politely. The attendant retrieves a blanket from an overhead compartment and hands it to him with a warm smile. "Here you go, this should keep her cozy."

Returning to Lisa, Jason tenderly drapes the blanket over her and retakes his seat. Lisa's excitement shines through as she speaks of their upcoming adventure, "I can't wait to explore Egypt's wonders. I've always been drawn to visit." Just then, a beverage cart rolls by, and Lisa orders a cocktail. As the steward attempts to pass the drink to her, Lisa's grip falters, and the glass topples, spilling its contents on Jason.

Startled, Jason exclaims, "What the—!" and quickly rises to dry himself with a towel provided by the attendant. Lisa chides him, "If you'd help me more, these things wouldn't happen!" Under his breath, Jason mutters, "The glass must have been slippery."

The pilot announces impending turbulence, advising everyone to fasten their seatbelts. Slightly tipsy from a few cocktails, Lisa leans towards Jason and says, "Darling, we've faced so much together, haven't we? The challenges of raising children, striving to keep them content and safe, all while juggling bills and maintaining our own happiness."

Jason nods, replying, "It seems almost insurmountable at times."

Lisa, deep in thought, adds, "And our son – if anything were to happen to us now, would he be alright? We're fortunate to have such a supportive family and trustworthy neighbors. Lenny is at Mike's house, and I'm not worried at all. But will he have the same opportunities we had? Or any child, for that matter? The world they're growing up in can be harsh."

As Jason observes a newfound fear in Lisa's eyes, he reassures her gently, "My love, this trip is meant for us to unwind. Let's not spend it worrying about Lenny – he'll be just fine." He offers an encouraging smile, though harboring concerns of his own.

As the aircraft soars into the eastern skies, Jason and Lisa engage in a heartfelt exchange about their lives, reflecting on the fortuity of their enduring relationship. They acknowledge the contrasting fates of their college and high school friends, many of whom have been beset by the ravages of divorce, the constraints of poverty, or the burdens of both.

In Cairo, a young man's heart shatters as his first love confesses she no longer desires him and has found solace in another's embrace. His chest feels unbearably heavy, breathing becomes laborious, and his head threatens to burst. Sitting on the bed, he curls inward, tears streaming down his face to form small, glistening pools on the floor. Eventually, Duran's gaze meets Anat's unfeeling stare, and he loses control. "How could you do this to me! You said you loved me! I hate you!!!!"

The dispute intensifies as each hurls venomous remarks, exposing the other's flaws. Suddenly, a knock on the door echoes through the room. "Knock Knock! Police, open up!" Anat scampers to the entrance, a subtle grin playing on her lips. Unperturbed by the authorities' presence, Duran cannot hold himself back and is swiftly apprehended. "You deserve everything you're going to get!" Love curdles to hatred as Anat watches, smiling, while Duran is forced into the patrol car.

As the vehicle gradually vanishes, Duran cranes his neck for one final glimpse of his lost love. "I can't believe this is happening! Yesterday everything was fine!" He screams within the car's confines. "Why are you arresting me? You should be arresting her! She is the betrayer!" His face flushed with rage, the tirade comes to an abrupt halt. The officer in the passenger seat turns to assess the situation, finding Duran slumped over, unconscious, his tongue lolling. "Yup! He popped, looks like we have another one on our hands, I'll call it in," he informs his partner.

The police cruiser eases to a halt outside the Central Asylum for the Mentally Disturbed. "It's disheartening to leave him here," one officer remarks, to which the other responds solemnly, "Indeed, love is a peculiar force." Their mutual concern resonates in the air.

Duran remains lifeless as the orderlies delicately

transfer his limp form from the vehicle onto a medical stretcher, fastening restraints around his limbs. As he is wheeled inside, imposing metal doors seal shut behind him, their ghostly groan echoing through the halls. Armed officers observe the scene with calm assurance, their weapons poised to defuse any potential threat.

Meanwhile, distant cries and disjointed chatter, muddled and unnerving, filter through the corridors. Due to Duran's unblemished record, he is placed in a minimum-security ward where he can convalesce under careful monitoring of his vital signs.

As the nurse stood beside Duran, she apprised the newly arrived doctor, clutching Duran's medical records, "He lost consciousness in the back of the squad car, and we're unsure of the cause. The patient had been in a fit of rage following a breakup with his girlfriend. According to the officer, he was incessantly screaming before abruptly falling silent. They then discovered him unconscious in the backseat, but his vitals appear stable."

The doctor, with a puzzled expression, scanned Duran's past records for a moment before remarking, "Interesting. He graduated at the top of his class from the university, has no criminal record... However, there is a mention of Duran experiencing prior episodes of uncontrolled outbursts and aggressive behavior, including a notable event during his Ancient

Egyptian History course at the University of Cairo."

While conducting a brief examination, the doctor observed that Duran remained unconscious and unresponsive. Ultimately, the doctor asserted, "He should be alright. Let's place him in room 101 and monitor his condition."

Escorted into the observation chamber, Duran garners the attention of the medical staff. A nurse, intrigued by his peculiar state, remarks, "In my nine-year tenure here, this ranks among the most baffling cases I've encountered. On the cusp of graduating at the top of his class, and suddenly, he spirals into madness." The attendant replies with a tone of disbelief, "It's certainly strange, to say the least." An intern chimes in, attempting to lighten the mood, "Perhaps his mathematics major contributed to his condition?" The nurse, unamused, rebukes the jest, "That's hardly a laughing matter. I was a math major once!" She punctuates her statement with a playful, yet stern, hand gesture.

Curiosity piqued, she inquired, "How fares your young lad?" As a nurse entered Duran's room after several hours, she observed his labored breathing and fluttering eyelids. Swiftly, she initiated a code blue alert, and the ensuing siren summoned a surge of medical personnel. They flooded the room, swiftly releasing Duran's restraints. Focused intently on the patient in cardiac arrest, they positioned electrodes on his chest and sent an electric current coursing through his body. With a dramatic lurch, Duran's frame arched, and his heart resumed its vital rhythm.

Duran, his conscience now fully engaged, assesses the situation and makes a swift escape, akin to a jackrabbit. In his haste, he tears the IV from his arms and vaults over tables and chairs. Glancing over his shoulder, he spies a clear path to the exit, only for a sizable officer to intercept him unexpectedly. After a brief struggle, Duran seizes the officer's gun and aims it at himself, exclaiming, "Stay back! You're all imbeciles! I can't bear being in this place any longer!" As he flees, the doors of the facility burst open in his wake.

Azure clouds grace Egypt's pristine sky as Lisa and Jason catch their initial sight of the land they have long dreamt about. Looming majestically in the distance are remarkable architectural wonders, which become more prominent as their flight descends into Cairo.

"I know you want to play golf tomorrow, but—" Lisa starts, only to be cut off by Jason, who reassures her, "Don't worry, sweetheart. I can postpone it for a few days." Her concerns were justified, as Jason's recent infatuation with golf had led to occasional disappointments due to his insistence on playing at inopportune moments.

A sudden lurch of the fuselage and the screech of tires against the tarmac signal Lisa and Jason's safe arrival in Cairo. As they make their way to retrieve their luggage, the richness of the local art and culture envelops them, evoking the sensation of discovering a long-lost home.

As the sun casts its final rays upon the trio of pyramid-shaped monuments, the hotel shuttle van comes to a gentle halt. A man alights from the vehicle, extending a warm greeting, "Hello, and welcome to our country. May I assist you with your luggage?" With utmost hospitality, the driver tends to the bags before returning to his seat. The engine hums to life once more, as the shuttle embarks upon the familiar route towards the local hotel.

Jason pressed the bell at the check-in desk, and a vibrant Egyptian woman with a thick accent appeared from around the corner, making her way towards the counter. "May I assist you?" she inquired. Jason then placed his bags onto the gleaming floor and responded, "We would like to check in."

With a warm smile, she greeted them, "Hello, I will be right with you." Shortly thereafter, they were escorted to room 303 and handed the keys. As they entered, Lisa raised her voice in frustration, "I specifically requested separate rooms to avoid your snoring! How am I supposed to sleep?" she exclaimed. Jason calmly replied, "This was the only room available, dear. There must have been a mix-up with our reservations."

Silently, they ascended in the elevator, the view of the Giza plateau giving way to the entrance of their room. Upon opening the door, they were struck by the elegance and immaculate condition of their temporary abode. "This is lovely, but if your snoring wakes me, I'm smothering you with a pillow," Lisa playfully warned. Jason chuckled, "I can hardly wait! Besides, you'd miss it when it's gone, wouldn't you?"

As they unpacked their belongings and filled the closet and dresser, Jason observed Lisa's assortment of gear. "You seem prepared for anything," he remarked, noticing her hat, eyewear, and footwear. Lisa grinned, "If I find a secret passage, I'm all over it! Just think about Howard Carter—discovering Tutankhamun's tomb in 1922. You can't tell me keeping your eyes peeled doesn't pay off!"

Arm in arm, they stand by the hotel window, gazing at the Giza Plateau as the sun dips below the horizon, casting a sublime backdrop for a selfie they'll cherish in their photo album for months to come. "I'm going to hit the shower," Jason declares to Lisa before vanishing into the bathroom. Lisa can hear the water running and Jason's comically off-key singing as she flips on the TV in search of the news.

A knock at the door interrupts her channel-surfing,

and she opens it to find their busboy, smartly dressed in his uniform. "I have a delivery for you, madam. Would you like it over here?" he inquires, wheeling a trolley cart across the door's threshold with a rhythmic clacking sound. Lisa tips him generously, and he departs with a grateful gesture.

As if on cue, Jason emerges donning a plush white robe. "I see my special delivery made it," he grins. Displayed on the cart are a delicate lotus flower, flickering candle, a bottle of fine wine, and an assortment of hors d'oeuvres.

Lisa slips into the bathroom to prepare for bed, while Jason meanders to the bedside, adjusting the mood lighting. Shortly after, she emerges to find Jason reclining in bed, cradling a bottle of wine in one hand and a pair of glasses in the other. "You... I knew you had an ulterior motive," Lisa teases, happily settling into bed. The fragrant scent of the bouquet envelops the room as Jason uncorks the wine and begins to pour.

"Dinner was amazing; I think I liked your dish even better than mine," Lisa muses playfully, accepting her glass. "So, what's on the tube?"

Jason grinned as he shared a mixed bag of news. "I discovered a travel channel that offers previews of our destination, a little appetizer before our arrival. But unfortunately, I can't comprehend a single word they're saying." Lisa inquired about their tour tickets for the following day. Excitedly, Jason confirmed their plans, "Yes, I've booked them. We'll start at the Museum and allocate roughly four hours for the rest of the tour."

As the evening unfolded, Jason and Lisa reconnected, reigniting the passion they had initially felt for one another. Liberated from life's pressures, they gazed into the vast desert sky and fell into a tranquil slumber.

The next morning, Jason awoke to the invigorating desert breeze. He took a deep breath, glanced at the clock, and realized he had overslept. Silently cursing, he dressed hastily, trying not to disturb Lisa. He quietly slipped out of the room and dashed toward the elevator. As the doors were about to close, he leaped inside just in time.

Upon reaching the breakfast area, Jason swiftly grabbed a coffee and a buttered croissant with jelly on the side for Lisa, along with a bowl of Cheerios for himself. With their breakfast in hand, he hurried back to the room, ready to begin their day.

Lisa's eyes brighten as a tray laden with breakfast treats and steaming coffee enters the room. "Just as you like it, honey," Jason declares cheerfully. "I hope it's hot... you really shouldn't have let me drink all that wine," Lisa admits, clearing her throat. "Rise and shine, sleepyhead. We need to get moving if we want to make the tour on time," Jason urges, hastily gathering his hat, sunglasses, lip balm, and water bottle. As the bus fills with eager tourists, Jason and Lisa dash through the hotel's entrance, panting. "Wait, wait! You have two more!" Lisa calls out to the shuttle driver. Upon boarding, they weave their way to the only vacant seats towards the rear.

"What's that?" Lisa inquires, noticing a police barricade and a queue of halted cars and trucks. Red and blue lights flash at the checkpoint, while squad cars stand poised for action. Sensing the bus slowing down, Jason prepares to investigate, but is jolted as the vehicle comes to an abrupt halt. The doors swing open, admitting two police officers who scrutinize the passengers closely. After a thorough inspection, one officer departs, while the other shows the driver a photograph of a man named Duran. "He's on the run, heavily medicated, armed, and dangerous. If you see him, contact us immediately!" The officer casts a final, wary glance at the travelers before stepping off the bus and signaling the inspection crew to let them pass.

The bus hesitates for a moment before resuming motion. The driver and attendant's raised voices catch Jason and Lisa's attention, only to abruptly cease. "What do you think that was about?" Lisa inquires. Jason, clearly agitated, replies, "I have no idea... I can't stand when this happens!" Lisa responds stoically, "Unfortunately, that's the world we live in."

Determined to enjoy their vacation, the couple pushes the incident aside. Gradually, their anticipation for the marvel they are about to witness rekindles. Lisa gazes in awe at the Giza plateau through the bus window, noting, "It looks so much bigger in person." The bus meanders through the small loop inside the Plateau's parking area, providing visitors with a panoramic vista before decelerating to a stop.

Enthusiastic travelers disembark the bus, faces beaming with delight and hearts yearning for adventure. "You're not wrong, it's incredible! So, this is the seventh wonder of the world... I can't wait to see what's inside," Jason exclaims with excitement.

As the eager tour group assembled at the base of the majestic pyramid, an animated tour guide began with an enthusiastic address: "Welcome everyone, I'm Tamer, your guide for today's unforgettable experience. Prepare to be spellbound by the wonders that await you – sights that will leave a lasting impression for a lifetime! Even after 12 years working here, I still discover something new with each visit. Now, let us embark on a fascinating journey into our ancient past, starting with the enigmatic Sphinx enclosure. Please, follow me."

With a graceful wave, Tamer ushered the group along

the path towards the temple of the Sphinx, his captivating narration continuing: "These awe-inspiring monuments were constructed by the great Egyptian civilization approximately four to five thousand years ago, using simple tools such as copper chisels and hammers. Wooden sleds were employed to haul massive ten to twenty-ton stones, while lubricating the ground to minimize friction. Some theories propose that sound harmonics or even an anti-gravity device, similar to those described by Nikola Tesla, were utilized to assist in lifting the stones. Others have written about the possibility of polymer aggregate stones being poured into molds, yet this seems implausible to me, as each stone is a unique size. Nevertheless, it's this sense of mystery and personal interpretation that make our explorations all the more intriguing!"

As Jason observes the group's footsteps falling in sync, Tamer proceeds to share fascinating facts about the ancient pyramids. He explains that Radiocarbon dating, which dates the pyramids to around 4,000 BC, is based on organic materials such as charcoal and reeds found within the pyramid's construction. Intrigued, Jason raises an eyebrow and points out the conundrum: if the established pyramid construction timeline is flawed, so too is the foundation for Radiocarbon dating. Tamer nods in agreement, indicating that this journey would be a captivating learning experience, sparking the crowd's imagination.

The tour soon arrives at the majestic Sphinx, where
Tamer delves into recent debates surrounding its
chronological timeline. Experts like Dr. Karman
Butler and Graham Hancock contest the traditional
dating, citing the alignment of Orion's belt with the
Sphinx around 10,500 BC. The late archaeologist
John Anthony West even posited that these structures
could be over 35,000 years older, a staggering two
precession cycles ago. West argued that 13,000 years
ago, Earth experienced numerous catastrophes, such
as the Ice Age, which would have made constructing
colossal monuments like the pyramids a monumental
challenge.

As the group gathers around the Sphinx's enclosure
walls, Tamer highlights the unusual wear patterns
etched into the stone. He points out the vertical
fissures and circular erosion, explaining that most
experts concur that such marks can only result from
water currents flowing over the rock for centuries.
This intriguing detail lends credence to the alternative
dating theories proposed by Butler and West, as it
suggests that the Sphinx may have been built before
the Ice Age, also known as the Younger Dryas
Cataclysm. The revelations shared by Tamer captivate
the group, immersing them in the enigma of these
ancient wonders.

With a graceful sweep of his hand over the
weathered stone, Jason remarks, "Notice this wear

pattern—evidence of water erosion. It's hard to believe, but it must have been underwater." Lisa, captivated, agrees.

As they marvel at the Sphinx, Tamer delves into its intriguing history: "The Sphinx's head was likely re-carved to resemble a pharaoh, explaining its disproportionate size. The original visage may have been a Pharaoh Hound or a lion. The statue, now unrecognizable, is believed to guard scrolls of knowledge beneath its front paws, and perhaps, a secret entrance resides on its back."

Jason, contemplating the massive figure, compares it to their loyal dog Penny, who waits patiently by the stairs for their return. Lisa finds this parallel touching, musing that perhaps the Sphinx, too, waits for long-lost loved ones.

The group moves on to the Pyramid of Menkaure, the smallest of the three, marred by glaring damage above its entrance. Addressing the question of a curious visitor, Tamer explains that in 1197 AD, Quand Melic-alaziz Othman ben damaged the structure in a misguided quest for something hidden. Many lives were lost in the futile effort, and the fallen rock still litters its base—a testament to human folly.

As they crouch and descend into the pyramid, Tamer reveals the layout of antechambers and a master burial chamber. They marvel at the empty granite sarcophagus and speculate on the reasoning behind such an immense undertaking.

Emerging from the pyramid, a young woman inquires about the directional orientation of the shafts. Tamer confirms that most Egyptian pyramids feature north-facing shafts, with the notable exception of the Great Pyramid, which also possesses southern-facing ones. The tour continues, leaving the group to ponder the enigmatic wonders they've just encountered.

The eager tour group congregated at the rest area nestled between the enigmatic Menkaure and Khafre pyramids, pausing to catch their breaths and exchange animated musings about the mysteries of the past and potential revisions to our understanding of history. Sensing the electric anticipation of what awaited them, Tamer observed the crowd's excitement begin to ripple. They soon found themselves ascending the eastern slope of Khafre, marveling at the historic Causeway that once linked the monumental edifice to the distant Nile River.

As they walked, Tamer postulated, "The Causeways were constructed to transport something, or perhaps someone, from the waters of the Nile to the base of the eastern slopes and into what we now call Funerary Rooms. Much of our knowledge, however, is mere speculation." Upon reaching the entrance shaft of Khafre, Lisa chimed in, "But the Nile is nowhere near the Causeway entrances now?"

Tamer acknowledged the conundrum, "That's another issue. Geologists posit that the Nile shifted eastward over a vast expanse of time—a subject still fraught with controversy. It's fascinating to consider the names we attribute to these structures, particularly since many ancient Egyptian texts mention discovering and adopting them as a form of inheritance. Khafre could simply be the last Pharaoh to claim the title. There's even evidence of Ramses II's cartouches being overwritten and transposed onto older works of questionable origin—perhaps he claimed them as his own and branded them with his name. Intriguingly, these inscriptions are of lesser quality when compared to the sophisticated craftsmanship exhibited in the statues and monuments they adorn."

The journey once more gracefully descends the slope, leading into a sepulchral chamber at the heart of the pyramid on the ground level, where an awaiting granite receptacle lies. The primary chamber is securely sealed, devoid of any shafts or alternative passageways; it is immaculate and robust, boasting a portcullis stone mechanism designed to obstruct the passage and deter potential intruders.

"I feel it's important to note that not a single corpse has been discovered within any pyramid, although remains have been found in the mastabas surrounding the area," Tamer shares. He then presents a fragmented piece of pottery, which exhibits "machine grooves" crafted using a lathe machine. He permits the tour participants to handle the relic, while informing them, "Observe the remarkably consistent machine grooves, uniformly spaced apart, as well as the precision of the circular base and top lip. This artifact was collected from the subterranean tunnel complex within the Bent Pyramid of Dahshur; indeed, there are hundreds of such pieces simply strewn about down there. It is evident that advanced technology was employed in the creation of this pottery."

"Why don't we witness these machines or sophisticated equipment?" Lisa inquires. "An excellent question... and one I can only address by referencing the time just prior to the Younger Dryas. We have discovered tools purported to have been instrumental in accomplishing the task, such as Diorite pounding stones or copper chisels. However, the issue is that it would be virtually impossible to execute this level of work; in fact, even in modern times, no one has successfully replicated the final product using these methods. The esteemed Flinders Petrie examined a core sample he obtained, which displayed unmistakable machining cut marks produced at a speed far exceeding what we can achieve today, even with our state-of-the-art equipment. So, to answer your question, evidence of the machines and tools must have been swept away by the flood. Nevertheless, we did uncover irrefutable evidence, though no one has pieced it together yet - the discovery of the Antikythera Mechanism," Tamer declares.

"Why does a discrepancy exist in the historical timeline?" a tour member inquires. "I believe it is a simple misunderstanding, as it is incredibly challenging to grasp such a vast array of information, particularly when the technology may be far superior to our own. We are just now beginning to comprehend our own history and the worldwide events that have transpired. The mathematical complexity alone is astonishing, particularly when considering the astrological alignments with our celestial heavens. In fact, there are over 100 pyramids in Egypt with varying quality and size, and they all share a common feature: they all possess entrances facing the North Star," Tamer responds.

Departing from the monument of Khafre, the tour group engages in animated discussions as they proceed toward the grand Pyramid. "There's evidence suggesting that the pyramids, like the Sphinx, were once submerged, as indicated by the heavy salt deposits that had to be removed prior to opening them to the public. Some claim it's a natural excretion of the rock, but early photos might lead one to think otherwise," Tamer explains while guiding the group along the eastern face of the Great Pyramid. A noticeable change in temperature heralds the sun's impending zenith, as Jason and Lisa buzz with enthusiasm, moving toward the entrance of the Pyramid.

Jason ventures a hypothesis to the group: "So the Younger Dryas could have created a gap between two distinct, yet similar civilizations." Tamer replies, "I'm inclined to believe that around 13,000 years ago, a truly advanced society thrived just before the last ice age, which persisted for about 1,000 years. Vestiges of their knowledge endured through stories and communication among survivors. When the icy conditions relented, these people returned to Egypt and attempted to recover their lost civilization. Despite retaining some abilities of their ancient predecessors, the scope of their talents and skills had waned. To me, it seems plausible that the construction of these magnificent structures was separated by the Younger Dryas."

Lisa inquires, "Wouldn't the mortar alongside the stones have been washed away by the flood?" Tamer responds, "Not if the casing stones were in place, which were only removed in more recent times." As they approach the monument, Jason and Lisa are once again struck with awe by the splendor and grandeur of humanity's most remarkable feat. Brimming with anticipation, the tour reaches the entrance of the Pyramid of Khufu, now standing before them.

"Now, we have arrived at the main attraction," Tamer announces. "I prefer to save this pyramid for last due to its advanced technology, especially when compared to the interior architecture of the Menkaure and Khafre pyramids."

"Kindly gather around in this vicinity, everyone," Tamer proclaims from the entrance of the pyramid. "I appreciate your cooperation. Before we venture inside this magnificent structure, there are several essential points to bear in mind. Although the passageways are illuminated, some may be constricted and lengthy. Do not hesitate to take your time and seek assistance if required. We request that you refrain from touching anything within the pyramid to help preserve it for future generations. The entrance at which we now stand was fortuitously discovered by Al-Ma'mun and his laborers circa 820 AD while employing a battering ram to shatter the granite blocks inward. This entranceway is also referred to as the 'Robber's Tunnel,' a nod to Al-Ma'mun's intentions." Tamer gestures toward the original opening of the pyramid, near the assembled group. "Observe how the original entrance was fully sealed by these colossal blocks, ingeniously crafted to blend seamlessly with the original facade. Contemplate this remarkable feat as you immerse yourself in the experience, and kindly follow me," Tamer beckons the tour group inside, with Lisa and Jason trailing closely behind.

"Be cautious with your footing, dear," Jason cautions his wife. "Thank you, sweetheart," Lisa responds, embarking on their expedition into the pyramid. They navigate a rocky corridor, and after a brief stroll, the path takes an upward turn into a slender passageway leading to the Queen's chamber. "This is utterly astonishing!" Jason exclaims with a level of zeal that makes Lisa uncomfortable. "Lower your voice, people are observing you," Lisa chides. "It's nearly unfathomable that people from so long ago possessed such advanced knowledge. Consider our current altitude – they hoisted these massive blocks all this way? I remain in disbelief. Observe the precision with which the stones are cut and assembled, and the sheer quantity of them – how on earth did they accomplish this?" Jason marvels.

The tour group reaches the base of the majestic gallery, where two stairways gracefully unite before rising towards the King's Chamber. Nestled between the stairs lies the entrance to the Queen's Chamber passage, demanding a hunched posture for entry. Although slightly uncomfortable, the sensation dissipates as the passage unveils the Queen's Chamber, featuring a central stepped cathedral recess that culminates in a saddle vault ceiling. As everyone gathers inside, Tamer resumes, "Welcome to the

Queen's Chamber, situated beneath the King's Chamber and perfectly centered within the structure."

He continues, "One captivating feature of this room is the presence of these small square passageways on each side." Tamer gestures towards two square shaft openings on opposite ends of the chamber. "Initially believed to serve as air vents, subsequent investigations by the University of Leeds Engineers Scoutek and Dassault Systems, creators of a diminutive remote-controlled robot, found the passages obstructed by three-inch-thick plugging stones. Undeterred, the ingenious team attached a drill to the robot, only to encounter another plugging stone beyond the initial one. Observe the pristine condition of the air shafts, seemingly untouched by time. While no sarcophagus has been conclusively proven to reside here, some accounts suggest it once existed, but was dismantled to fit through the passage."

Tamer goes on, "The construction methods and purpose of these enigmatic structures have long been debated. Only recently has Jean-Pierre Houdin postulated a plausible explanation, proposing an ingenious internal ramp system. A sub-density test performed by a French team of scientists in 1986 provided vital data to support Houdin's remarkable hypothesis. In fact, from the pyramid's exterior, you can discern two distinct 7% grade indentations along the sidewalls that lend credence to his theory."

With great enthusiasm, the tour group listens intently as Tamer proceeds, "Other theories suggest that water ramps might have been constructed alongside the pyramid, facilitating the placement of the massive stone blocks by utilizing wooden gates as locks and air-filled animal skins tied securely to them. These stones, quarried near the Nile, would have floated downstream, transported through covered causeways, and subsequently moved onto vertical ramps up the pyramid's smooth surfaces. While there is much speculation about the method used to build the pyramid, the true purpose behind such a monumental undertaking remains shrouded in mystery. Although this particular pyramid bears the name of Pharaoh Khufu, who ruled during the first half of the Old Kingdom, the evidence supporting this claim is far from conclusive." Animated chatter fills the air as the group members exchange thoughts and opinions on the enigmatic motivations and various aspects behind the pyramid's design and construction process.

"If there are no further inquiries, let us proceed to the King's chamber," announces Tamer, as he guides the tour down the corridor leading away from the Queen's Chamber and back towards the grand gallery. The group spontaneously splits into right and left contingents, and they start ascending the grand staircases of the gallery. The long, smoothly cut stones that stretch from one end to the other remind Jason of a concert hall. Suddenly, he begins to hear something faint yet distinct. "Do you hear that?" Jason asks Lisa with curiosity. "Hear what?" she responds, turning to him. "It sounds like a sort of singing, are you sure you don't hear it?" he exclaims with bewilderment. "Hush, people will think you're losing your mind," Lisa whispers cautiously.

"Excuse me, but when we were near the Sphinx, what exactly did you mean by 'precession'?" Lisa inquires of Tamer, as she trails closely behind. "Ah, I appreciate your curiosity. The precession of the equinoxes refers to Earth's 26,000-year wobble, similar to a spinning top that oscillates over thousands of years. Plato referred to this cycle as the Great Year. Numerous ancient civilizations, such as the Inca, Maya, and Egyptian societies, made reference to this time cycle. Intriguingly, the ancient cultures of India and Islam share the exact same long count calendar. They called this cycle a Baktun, and it is believed that the state of humanity follows its course, from the top of the wobble to the bottom. Their comprehensive timeline consists of thirteen cycles and is interconnected, which, quite remarkably, concludes this very month. Thus, your presence here is rather courageous," Tamer adds with a light chuckle. "Oh, goodness! I wasn't aware that it's happening this month!" Lisa exclaims, turning to Jason. "Indeed, that's quite a coincidence, but let's remain calm, my dear. It's not as though extraterrestrials are about to abduct us or anything," Jason assures her. "Well, you don't know that!" Lisa retorts, taking a deep breath.

As they approach the King's Chamber, Tamer pauses at the top of the grand stairwell, looking up and declaring, "The design and purpose of this hallway have been the subject of considerable debate. As you can observe, these inverted ledges or corbelled vaults form a sort of upside-down staircase." Glancing downward, Tamer elaborates, pointing out the evenly spaced holes on both sides of the stairwell running the entire length of the chamber. "These cavities flanking the stairwell have been widely speculated upon and generally accepted as aids in the pyramid's construction. By inserting dowels, the large stones of the King's Chamber would be held in place while workers took a respite between their efforts. Supporting this notion, you can see scrape marks on either side of the runways." Tamer goes on to explain, "These monuments align with the stars in the constellation Orion's Belt. Much like the Sphinx, this reveals that something was occurring far earlier than what our present academic community initially thought. In my opinion, it's an outdated perspective," Tamer chuckles. "Why are you laughing?" Lisa inquires. "It seems almost absurd that we've advanced so significantly with modern technology, yet our understanding of these awe-inspiring structures remains limited. Few are willing to think outside the box or entertain novel ideas." Jason interjects abruptly, "I've heard outlandish theories suggesting that aliens provided assistance?" Lisa shoots Jason a sideways glance as they proceed to ascend the grand stairwell. "Let's keep moving, everyone," Tamer encourages, noticing guests falling behind while guiding them through the gallery. The singing that Jason had heard earlier gradually subsides and ultimately ceases. "That was certainly bizarre," he remarks. "Was it the singing stopping that you found strange, you oddball?" Lisa teases playfully. "I thought I might be losing my mind," Jason responds with a smile.

Brimming with excitement for his tour group, Tamer steps into the King's Chamber, closely followed by the rest of the visitors. "Please proceed into the King's Chamber and be mindful of your footing," he advises. The group files into the majestic room one after the other. "Welcome, everyone, to the King's Chamber. This enigmatic space has arguably been the subject of the most heated debates in history. Numerous well-educated professionals have pondered its purpose without reaching definitive conclusions." Murmurs ripple through the tour group.

"We just entered through a doorway that was originally sealed by four massive portcullis stones, each weighing several tons. Modern work crews took months to breach this barrier – clearly, someone didn't want anyone entering this chamber. Now, let me share a few intriguing facts about the ancient Egyptians. They utilized more than 4,000 hieroglyphic characters for communication, yet none were specifically designated for death. Furthermore, fascinating mathematical discoveries have been made regarding ancient monoliths worldwide, involving the Great Pyramid of Khufu as the prime meridian instead of our contemporary Greenwich. These discoveries link the monoliths through geomathematics. Mathematical formulas such as Pi and its various forms have been identified by several people, including the late, brilliant mathematician Carl P. Munck. He examined these structures from an unconventional perspective, unveiling specific equations that correlated with the geographic location of each monument."

Lisa interjects, "What do you mean by 'unconventional ways,' if you don't mind me asking?"

Tamer replies, "Certainly. Munck detected particular design features of each structure and ingeniously crafted mathematical equations around them. The results revealed geodetic coordinates for specific structures' locations on Earth's surface, along with supplementary mathematical directions for identifying significant sites in other locations globally – a clear indication of communication. He dubbed his method

'The Pyramid Matrix'." Another tour member inquires, "I was taught in school that slaves built these pyramids, but then later heard it wasn't true. Is that correct?"

Tamer responds, "Although certain aspects of Egyptian culture might appear to be slave-driven, recent evidence suggests this simply wasn't the case. The remarkable level of perfection achieved in the construction of these pyramids bears testament to the builders' deep love and commitment to their work. These awe-inspiring structures have withstood the test of time for thousands of years, thanks to that very devotion."

An elegant rectangular stone box resides at the chamber's far end, with one corner entirely absent and numerous nicks along the top edges. Lisa catches sight of Jason tracing his fingers over the container's stone surface and approaches him. "Jason! What are you up to? They explicitly said not to touch anything!" Lisa chastises as she playfully swats his hand away. Jason chuckles quietly, "I'm amazed that you always manage to catch me doing things I shouldn't be."

Tamer strolls over to Jason's position, drawing the tour group's attention, and gestures toward the worn and fractured corner of the solid granite vessel. "This level of damage suggests significant use during the era of the Pharaohs, and Jason, please refrain from touching," he remarks, prompting laughter from the group. He elaborates, "We're unsure whether this is truly a sarcophagus or what it was referred to in ancient times."

Tamer gestures towards two shafts on opposing sides of the chamber, "These air shafts vary slightly in size, one being marginally larger and not perfectly square, but both extend to the pyramid's exterior unlike those found in the Queen's Chamber. Originally thought to facilitate air or food transport, their alignment with the stars in Orion's Belt and Polaris suggests a more spiritual purpose. One notable feature is the scorched appearance of the shafts' openings, hinting at the passage of intense heat."

Lisa tells Jason, "This experience exceeds my expectations; I'm glad we decided to come." Jason replies, "It's an unforgettable sight I've always dreamt of witnessing. The presence of those who've been here before is almost palpable." Lisa responds, "It's a bit eerie." As Tamer continues, he mentions George Sandys, the archbishop of York's son, who described the shafts in 1610 as "Not large enough to be crept into, also sooty within, as if created by a flame of fire that darted through it." He adds that traces of burnt ash can still be seen. Intrigued, Jason shines his phone's light into the shaft, exclaiming, "Look, honey! I can see it up there!" Lisa peers inside, spotting the black and gray marks, and wonders aloud, "So strange, could it have been fire?"

Tamer gestures toward the sky in a diagonal trajectory, remarking, "There's an intriguing aspect to consider: the same robot that explored the Queen's chamber also ventured through these shafts, discovering a sequence of four bends in the north-facing shaft. Some have speculated that this could represent an intentional design to circumvent a hidden chamber or an as-yet undiscovered internal feature." Tamer gracefully returns to the entrance, inquiring, "Does anyone have questions they'd like to pose?"

Without hesitation, Jason raises his hand, "Why are there no hieroglyphs visible in this area?"

Tamer acknowledges the frequently asked query, explaining, "Although numerous hieroglyphs adorn the smaller structures throughout the Plateau, it is indeed puzzling that none can be found inside or on any of the Giza pyramids. We are left without a definitive explanation, but one plausible theory is that the Egyptians who constructed the Giza Plateau pyramids exhibited a more methodical approach, whereas their Dynastic counterparts displayed greater artistic prowess. This distinction may account for the abundance of intricate carvings gracing the exterior temples and courtyards, while the pyramids' interiors remain devoid of such adornments."

At a distance of half a mile, law enforcement officers feverishly transcribe a panic-stricken call from a woman amidst the bustling downtown market. "He appears deranged, his eyes wild... it's the man from the television! Duran!... Please, I have children!" In response, the police hastily dispatch three patrol units in a frenzied manhunt for the notorious Duran. As the piercing wail of sirens draws nearer, an air of anticipation fills the city streets.

One patrol unit finally spots a visibly distraught Duran, trembling uncontrollably and his expression a mixture of rage and fear. Like two wild beasts locked in a primal standoff, they exchange tense glares before Duran suddenly bolts, setting the adrenaline-fueled chase in motion.

Tires screech, and officers spring from their cars, shouting at the top of their lungs, "Stop, police!... Stop!" Duran's defiance only intensifies as he darts toward a busy intersection. Spotting a motor scooter idling nearby, he unceremoniously shoves its unsuspecting rider aside. Consumed by blind fury and a powerful determination to escape, Duran guns the throttle and executes a daring wheelie, evading the pursuing police and their hail of gunfire as he speeds toward the Great Pyramid.

Panting officers radio ahead, urgently requesting a strategically placed blockade to halt his escape. In a desperate bid for freedom, Duran veers onto a pristine golf course, weaving through the 18th green as terrified golfers scatter in his wake, their tranquil afternoon shattered. Hurtling through the air, he brings the scooter to a screeching halt in the visitor parking lot of the majestic Plateau.

Wielding his weapon menacingly, he shoves people aside, his breaths short and rapid as he charges toward the entrance of the Great Pyramid. With determination, Duran ascends the grand stairwell leading to the enigmatic King's Chamber.

Unbeknownst to Tamer, calmly answering questions from his captivated audience, chaos is about to erupt behind him. Duran bursts onto the scene, bellowing, "GET OUT!" as he aims his gun at Tamer's head, the tension in the room palpable. A young girl's scream pierces the air, "HE'S GOT A GUN!" Tamer, realizing the gravity of the situation, bellows, "HE IS CRAZY... EVERYONE GET OUT!" Lisa, aghast, recognizes the madness in Duran's eyes, her heart pounding in her chest.

Frantically waving his weapon, Duran yells again, his voice cracking with desperation, "GET OUT NOW!" as the remaining chamber occupants flee in terror, their once-in-a-lifetime experience forever marred by the terrifying intrusion.

Gripping Lisa's hand tightly, Jason expertly guides her down the shadowy stairwell, his body shielding her from any potential gunfire. As they descend, Lisa stumbles at the sudden shift, her ankle twisting painfully beneath her. Instinctively reaching for Jason, he hoists her into his arms, and one by one, they make their way out of the enigmatic pyramid. Lisa, Jason, and Tamer are among the last to exit, stepping into the chaotic aftermath.

A throng of people has amassed outside the pyramid, their curiosity piqued by the commotion, as they attempt to console the distressed tour group members. "That was insane! What just happened? Are you alright, honey?" Jason exclaims, concern etched on his face. "I'm okay," Lisa replies, her voice quivering from the intensity of the encounter.

As the wail of approaching police sirens amplifies, the gravity of the situation dawns on everyone. They hastily seek cover behind the massive stones scattered nearby, while patrol cars screech to a halt and officers sprint towards the pyramid entrance.

Inside, beads of sweat trickle down Duran's face as he painstakingly climbs into the sarcophagus. Lying atop the cold, unyielding stone, he positions the weapon against his heart, barely able to maintain his grip as the barrel grazes his chest. Meanwhile, the police inch closer to the entrance, their determined strides echoing through the chamber.

Outside, bystanders are struck by the surreal sight of numerous birds circling the pyramid's peak, their feathers generating a haunting harmony. Abruptly, the birds disperse as an enormous wave of electromagnetic energy envelops the pyramid. It knocks everyone off their feet, distorting the fabric of reality around them, before coming to an abrupt halt.

Jason is the first to regain his footing, his eyes darting from his wife to the now eerily silent pyramid. With a mixture of bewilderment and fear, he demands, "WHAT THE HELL JUST HAPPENED?"

CHAPTER 2 – THE LESSON

(Story continues in Ancient Egypt at the time of construction of the Great Pyramid. Words translated to English)

Under the serene veil of the night, two majestic vessels adorned with intricate Egyptian artwork stand ready to embark on remarkable voyages. Their holds are brimming with supplies, meticulously packed for the long journeys ahead. Departing from the enigmatic Giza Plateau, the crews of these stately boats are divided into small, focused groups, each with a unique and vital role to play.

Their destinations are ancient sites steeped in mystique and wonder. One sets sail for the shores of Southampton, England, with the enigmatic

Stonehenge as its ultimate goal. The other, bound for the awe-inspiring Göbekli Tepe in the heart of Turkey. These places, erected in distant epochs, share a common purpose: serving as observatories for celestial contemplation. Each site was painstakingly constructed in their respective hemispheres, designed to reveal the secrets of the heavens from unique vantage points.

These journeys are not merely expeditions of discovery but a quest to unravel the essence of human aspiration, our innate longing to understand the cosmos. By exploring these sacred sites, the intrepid voyagers seek to bridge the chasm between ancient and contemporary knowledge. In their pursuit, they hope to uncover lost wisdom and reconnect with the spirit of our ancestors, who, like us, yearned to comprehend the universe that stretches out before us in all its majesty and complexity.

As the vessels gracefully traverse the serene waters, their sails swelling beneath the tender touch of the breeze, they bear the aspirations and dreams of countless souls driven to decipher the mysteries of antiquity. Compelled by an unquenchable thirst for knowledge, they seek to unravel the enigmas of our world and explore the celestial realms beyond.

Hepu, the second-born son in his family, is a tall, slender young man with dark brown hair and dusky skin. He walks in his father's footsteps as he trains diligently at the local metalsmith shop. Hepu's wife, Alara, is the first daughter of Mahu and Bunefer, respected educators within the community, teaching valuable life skills and fostering love and personal growth. Expecting their first child, Alara's heart brims with affection as she and Hepu embark on their journey as lifelong soulmates.

Under the moonlit sky, sails ripple gently in the evening breeze, with a large sail anchored at the vessel's center and a smaller one adorning the front. As the crew meticulously inspects the rigging, final preparations are made before embarking on their voyage. Mitry, Khamet, and Hepu join a six-person expedition, led by Djoser, Hepu's father, who will guide them into the unknown, driven by the timeless allure of discovery.

The primary objective of this voyage is to join forces with the esteemed surveyors at Stonehenge in order to obtain supplementary insights that could prove invaluable in the construction of the Great Pyramid. Moreover, the mission also entails providing the mathematicians at Stonehenge with an update on the ongoing progress at the Giza plateau.

Djoser, the custodian of the magnificent pyramid design scrolls, carefully guards these precious documents stored within an ornate gold-covered container. As one of his men stumbles while handling the heavy cargo, Djoser promptly steps in, assisting in carrying the precious load onto the vessel. These periodic mathematical exchanges play a crucial role in honing the pyramid's structural features, refining its conceptual blueprint, and offering confirmation to the Stonehenge astronomers.

A palpable sense of anticipation permeates the atmosphere as relatives and friends eagerly assist in preparing their loved ones for the journey ahead. Djoser stands on the deck, his gaze sweeping across the moonlit Nile River, as memories of a similar expedition with his father many years ago flood his mind. His initial delight in reminiscing soon transforms into a deep sense of responsibility, as he recalls the profound wisdom and enlightenment his father had imparted upon him. This voyage signifies much more than a mere expedition; it represents an annual rite of passage, a cherished tradition during which ancient knowledge is passed down and preserved for future generations.

With an air of anticipation, Djoser implores, "Come now, we are prepared to embark on our journey." His tone conveys urgency as Hepu bids farewell to his beloved wife, Alara. They embrace tenderly, and Hepu whispers, "I love you, my dear." Alara's voice is gentle as she replies, "I'll miss you, Hepu," while offering a warm smile and a wave goodbye.

As the final provisions are secured aboard the vessel, the command is given to release the rope. The crew steadily guides the boat away from the riverbank, and the vast expanse of the Nile opens up before them. Hepu casts a lingering glance back at Alara, who remains steadfast at the dock, her hand raised in farewell. The half-constructed Great Pyramid glistens in the distance, casting its ancient aura over the scene.

The night sky stretches above them, laden with possibility, while the wind gently propels the boat from the dock. The river currents work in harmony, accelerating the vessel as it travels northward and out of sight, bound for the Mediterranean gulf. The flickering lights from accompanying boats serve as a beacon, and the men's spirits are lifted by laughter and camaraderie as they embark on their adventure. The soft splashing of waves against the boat's bow punctuates their conversations.

With a deep, purposeful breath, Djoser addresses the crew from the helm, "I imagine you all must be curious as to the purpose of our voyage to Stonehenge." Mitry responds, "We aim to gather celestial data and verify the accuracy of our mathematical equations, right?" Djoser nods, "That is one objective, but there is another." His face, etched with concern, falls silent as moments pass.

Regaining his composure, Djoser continues, "This journey will not only take us across the seas, but it will also transport us into the future. I will share with you the fate of our world beyond our time and the purpose of our existence in this era. My father once passed this wisdom onto me aboard this very vessel."

As the night sky unfurls its vast expanse, a gentle breeze ushers the boat onwards, harmonizing with the river's current to propel the vessel swiftly northward until it vanishes from view. Aboard the boat, Hepu and his companions maintain a cautious silence, uncertain of the journey ahead. Djoser, their leader, exudes an air of quiet determination as he steers the craft with unwavering focus. Time ebbs away as the crew labors diligently, securing ropes and adjusting sails under the soft glow of lantern light.

Eventually, the winds relent, prompting Djoser to direct the boat towards shallower waters. He commands the crew to drop anchor, announcing that the spot is perfect for their much-needed rest. The moon's tender beams play across the deck, illuminating the restless rustling of crew members as they attempt to find sleep. Meanwhile, the captains from each vessel exchange final thoughts, preparing for the uncharted waters ahead.

Beneath the deck, two distinct rooms offer respite. The larger one accommodates the weary crew, their hushed murmurs and rustling betraying a collective anxiety. The smaller chamber serves as Djoser's sanctuary, where he pores over maps and contemplates the voyage's uncertainties. Despite his fatigue, sleep eludes Hepu. Tossing and turning, he eventually rises and ascends to the deck.

There, he discovers solace in the mesmerizing, harmonious ebb and flow of the water's surface. This rhythmic dance of darkness and light unlocks the depths of his memory, permitting him to journey through recollections of his father and the wisdom he imparted. Hepu, immersed in nostalgia, strolls alone upon the deck as the moon sinks into the western horizon. A smile graces his lips as he remembers the carefree days of his youth, and, for a brief moment, he finds respite from the weight of the present.

The ancient door to Djoser's chamber creaks open, revealing an eager and anxious Hepu standing in the doorway. "Father, I'm truly exhilarated to embark on this remarkable journey with you. Is this our navigational guide?" he asks, focusing on the intricate maps meticulously laid out on the expansive table.

Djoser, brimming with fatherly pride, commences the briefing: "Once we leave the mighty Nile behind, we'll chart our course west, steering our vessel towards the bustling port city of Tripoli. From there, we'll skillfully navigate around the point, setting sail for Algiers before venturing into the vast expanse of the Mediterranean Sea, through a strategic gap between the landmasses. As we journey through uncharted waters, we'll keep close to the coastline for our safety, prepared to confront any challenges we may encounter along the way."

His finger traces their intended route on the map, ultimately landing on their destination. "Once we arrive here, we'll secure our trusty boat and prepare ourselves for a monumental meeting with the enigmatic celestial architects at the legendary Stonehenge. Hepu, this once-in-a-lifetime experience will undoubtedly leave an indelible mark on our lives."

Though Djoser senses his son's trepidation, he remains steadfast in moving forward. "Fear not, Hepu, for your nerves will subside after just a few days at sea. This voyage serves as a vital rite of passage; the wisdom and strength you gain from it will empower you to become a dependable and nurturing partner and father to your future family."

Drawing in a deep breath, Hepu embraces his father, whispering, "Thank you." As their eyes meet, Hepu searches for the reassuring gaze that has been his guiding star throughout his life. Djoser, fully aware of the gravity of their impending journey, offers a warm, supportive look in return, instilling Hepu with the confidence he needs.

As they stand together, embracing the unknown that lies ahead, both Djoser and Hepu recognize the transformative power of the adventure they are about to undertake. Though Hepu's nerves initially clouded his anticipation, there is no turning back now. With each passing day, this epic voyage will test their resilience, strengthen their bond, and ultimately, mold Hepu into the man he is destined to become.

As dawn broke, the winds gracefully embraced a westerly course, propelling the vessel effortlessly from the Nile's embrace into the welcoming arms of the Mediterranean Sea. The ship's crew, brimming with excitement, bade farewell to their sister vessel, which embarked on a southeastward journey towards Port Said before veering northeast to Ashdod, and ultimately reaching its final destination at Iskenderun. Steeped in history, Iskenderun—once known as Alexandretta and Scanderoon—lies nestled within the picturesque Hatay Province along Turkey's sun-kissed Mediterranean coast.

The crew, a tapestry of anticipation and determination, worked in harmonious unison, casting the sails to harness the capricious gusts. Djoser, a seasoned navigator, confidently manned the rudder, his eyes tracing the familiar landmarks that adorned his childhood memories of voyages with his father. Though Djoser was no stranger to the ebb and flow of the sea, the uncharted waters ahead brought a palpable sense of trepidation to the less experienced crew members.

Underneath the celestial canopy, the stars offered guidance and solace as Djoser imparted the invaluable lessons he had learned from his father. With a knowing smile, he directed the crew's gaze to the heavens and began his instruction. "Behold, the unwavering North Star—the sole constant in our ever-changing night sky. The remaining constellations dance around us, composing a symphony of celestial navigation that is our key to traversing these expansive waters."

A slender, perpendicular mast of about five feet in height majestically towers at the heart of the vessel, casting its long shadow across the deck. "I possess an innate understanding that during this particular season, determining our orientation relies on aligning the boat with these two distinct points in the celestial canopy above. With careful precision, we must align the boat's hull with this prominent mast, utilizing the hull as a reliable reference point to gauge the course we embark upon. Throughout our nautical journey, intermittent land formations shall serve as invaluable aids in steering us on our path, providing reassurance and guidance amidst the vast ocean".

Djoser gracefully kneels behind the mast, his gaze locked onto the glimmering North Star and the boat's starboard side, searching for the perfect alignment. Drawing his knife with a steady hand, he etches a discreet mark onto the hull, forever marking their current trajectory. "We've now ascertained our bearing," he announces with confidence. "Maintain this alignment with the North Star as we venture forth into the unknown waters until land reveals itself to us, offering a welcoming embrace."

The subsequent evening proves less strenuous as they arrive at a quaint village near the site of Tripoli, its warm lights twinkling in the distance. A dock has been thoughtfully established to accommodate their needs, making it the ideal location to restock provisions and brace for the more extended leg of their daring expedition. Here, they replenish their supplies with fresh water, nourishing sustenance, and invigorating wine, providing the energy required to face the challenges ahead.

The hospitable villagers offer comfortable accommodations to the weary travelers and host a grand feast in honor of the intrepid crew. Huddled around a roaring fire that flickers against the night sky, they exchange captivating tales of their diverse backgrounds, delving into the enigmatic riddles that life presents. As laughter and camaraderie fill the air, the crew feels a renewed sense of unity, bolstering their spirits for the adventures that lay before them.

As dawn's first light graced the horizon, the intrepid crew embarked on their journey, determined to conquer the capricious seas once more. Sailing steadfastly, they traversed the vast expanse of the North Atlantic Ocean, skirting the coasts of the lands we now recognize as Morocco and Spain. The ocean's temperament grew increasingly volatile, warning of the approaching tempest that lay ahead.

The crew braced themselves for the impending storm, courageously following Djoser's command. "Prepare for a rough ride, my friends... Stay steadfast as we navigate these treacherous swells." His voice echoed through the vessel as waves crashed over the deck, cascading back into the sea's unfathomable depths.

Deep within the ship's hull, Mitry tirelessly pedaled an ingenious bilge system, tirelessly transporting buckets of seawater from the vessel's bowels to the ocean outside. His fellow sailors, resilient and unwavering, adjusted the rigging and performed vital repairs as they confronted the storm.

Unflinching, Djoser grasped the rudder firmly, guiding the ship through the raging waters. Rain streamed down his face, veiling his true emotions of profound exhilaration amidst the tempest.

At long last, the harrowing ordeal subsided, and Hepu's exultant cheer heralded the first sight of their destination. Djoser, too, was filled with a sense of accomplishment as the familiar shapes of the landscape and shoreline came into view - the shores of what is now known as Southampton, England.

With hearts filled with joy and relief, the crew was warmly greeted by the people of Stonehenge. Laughter and camaraderie filled the air, painting a stark contrast to the perilous scene of mere hours ago. The crew's unbreakable spirit had prevailed, forging a bond that would forever unite them in their shared adventure.

As the boat gently came to a halt, workers diligently secured it, their efforts ensuring the safety of the weary crew who had braved the wrath of the sea. Exhausted, the sailors ambled from the vessel and stepped onto the welcoming embrace of the dock. The kind-hearted locals greeted them with warm meals and the promise of soft, fresh beds in which they could recuperate from their arduous journey.

After a night of peaceful slumber, the crew awoke to the enticing aroma of a hearty breakfast prepared by their gracious hosts. While the sailors enjoyed their meal, the boat received the tender attention of local craftsmen, who diligently carried out minor repairs.

With their spirits lifted, Mitry, Khamet, Hepu, Djoser, and their companions were led to an entourage of supply-laden wagons, patiently waiting to accompany them on the final leg of their grand adventure. For seven days and six nights, the crew and their equine companions journeyed towards the enigmatic Stonehenge.

Stonehenge, a mysterious cosmic map, was a wondrous monument consisting of thirty upright lintel stones supporting thirty massive sarsen stones, as well as an inner horseshoe arrangement of ten vertical stones, which held up an additional five sarsens. These stones were meticulously aligned, providing an ancient mathematical key to pinpoint Earth's location within the universe's intricate cosmic framework.

As the travelers journeyed onward, questions about the Great Pyramid poured forth, fueled by insatiable curiosity. As more members of the convoy joined in the conversation, the atmosphere became lively, brimming with laughter and personal anecdotes. The sharing of stories about their families and life experiences drew the two parties closer, forging friendships as they ventured together towards their enigmatic destination.

As the weary, sea-worn crew disembarks from their vessel, diligent workers rush to secure the boat to the dock. The gracious locals, delighted by the arrival of these newfound acquaintances, offer the exhausted sailors nourishing meals and freshly-prepared beds for a well-deserved rest. With a night of rejuvenating slumber behind them, the crew awakens to a hearty breakfast as the village's skilled boat makers tend to their vessel, carrying out minor repairs with practiced expertise.

Mitry, Khamet, Hepu, Djoser, and the rest of the crew are then led to a well-appointed entourage: wagons brimming with supplies and sturdy horses ready to accompany them on the final leg of their epic

journey. A seven-day, six-night trek lies ahead, guiding
the intrepid travelers to their ultimate destination –
the enigmatic Stonehenge. As the convoy progresses,
a torrent of inquiries about the legendary Great
Pyramid pours forth, with curiosity infecting
additional members of the party.

In no time, laughter and camaraderie fill the air as
both the crew and their local companions exchange
heartwarming tales of family and life experiences. The
jovial atmosphere fosters an unbreakable bond, as
they forge ahead, united in their shared quest towards
the mysterious and awe-inspiring Stonehenge.

With a sense of purpose, they traversed the path to
the nearby settlement of Stonehenge, guided by
Intef's steady stride. As the door swung open, they
were greeted by a vast, well-lit chamber bustling with
activity. Fifty tables stood strong, supporting the
weight of over two hundred dedicated individuals
tirelessly working on complex mathematical
equations. The tables were adorned with an intricate
maze of maps and diagrams, illustrating the enigmatic
expanse of the universe, spreading out in every
conceivable direction.

An unmistakable air of urgency permeated the room.
Parchment was filled, crumpled, and discarded,
frustration etched upon the faces of the weary math
smiths. Intef, visibly concerned, addressed Djoser and
Hepu, "We have encountered a troubling issue in the

past few weeks. It pains me to say this, but... an anomaly has been discovered in our conclusions. One of our esteemed elders found it."

Djoser's face paled, his voice trembling as he replied, "That can't be... the design... it's flawed?" His gaze sought solace in Intef's eyes. Meanwhile, Hepu, unable to comprehend the conversation fully, felt a foreboding sensation gnawing at his gut.

"But the construction... it's already halfway completed! This is disastrous!" Djoser exclaimed, a deep exhale betraying his inner turmoil. Hepu's intuition had been accurate - the Great Pyramid was indeed plagued by an issue, and it was far from trivial. The gravity of the situation loomed over them like a dark cloud, casting shadows upon their uncertain future.

Constructed on a loft of land Intef had walked up to the Constellation Design Room which sat above the large work room with Djoser and Hepu close behind. The Constellation Room was a marvel of mathematical and astronomical expertise. Located within a sacred temple, it featured a domed ceiling adorned with intricate representations of celestial bodies. This room was specifically designed to align with the stars at key moments in the Egyptian calendar. Skilled astronomers and mathematicians used this celestial map to track the movement of constellations, predict seasonal changes, and establish a connection between the divine realm and earthly events. The Constellation Room not only served as a hub for intellectual inquiry but also reinforced the Egyptians' profound reverence for the cosmos.

Twelve large thin gold plates glowed with one star constellation mapped out on each of the metallic surface with a fundamental mathematical equation inscribed below. "Here, look over this to see this mapping equation of the twelfth constellation. This is where the anomaly exists". Twelve large thin gold plates, meticulously crafted by skilled artisans, lined the walls of the ancient Egyptian Constellation Room. Each plate showcased a specific star constellation, painstakingly mapped out with precision and detail. Below each celestial representation, a fundamental mathematical equation was inscribed, reflecting the Egyptians' remarkable understanding of astronomy and geometry.

"You stand as the most esteemed mathematician on this earth, and I beseech you to deliver a solution to this most vexing conundrum," implored Intef, his voice trembling with urgency. Djoser's eyes roamed over the gleaming gold plates, each one presenting a complex puzzle. Recognizing the magnitude of the task at hand, he replied, "I shall require ample time to unravel this enigma," before departing the room and disappearing into the embrace of the starry night.

Hepu, with worry creasing his brow, inquired, "Why

is my father so distraught? Has a problem arisen?"
Intef sighed deeply, weariness etched into his features,
and began to explain the significance of their task.
"When your father and grandfather last graced this
room, they were the driving forces behind the
creation of the equations for the tenth and eleventh
constellations. You must understand, my young
friend, that the universe is akin to a harmonious
mathematical music box, playing its symphony
through the twelve constellations of the zodiac."

He paused, gathering his thoughts before continuing,
"We hold the belief that half of the stars symbolize
the essence of life, while the remaining half signify the
inexorable passage of time. Our future, as a species,
hinges on the accurate deciphering of these celestial
enigmas. To ensure that life will continue to flourish
and evolve for generations to come, we must solve
these cosmic puzzles and uncover the hidden
knowledge within. This, Hepu, is the burden your
father now bears, as he endeavors to bring light to the
secrets of the stars."

Hepu nodded solemnly, his understanding of the
situation deepening, as the profound importance of
their work settled heavily on his young shoulders.

Star constellations have a rhythm and harmonic
which cause them to group together and it's up to us
to figure out what that frequency is and to put
together the pieces of the puzzle through

mathematics. This is the reason behind Stonehenge's developed, it's locates our position in the cosmos.

Follow me Hepu I want you to see something". Intef and Hepu then walk under a star lit night to the inner circle of Stonehenge. Stars are clearly visible through every air gap passage made by the giant monoliths. Intef begins, "As our earth travels through its yearly cycle around the sun we set our base using the northern star.

A particular logic starts to unfold using the reminder of the stars as the variables. Through many years and thousands of equations rigid patterns emerged which we will now call constellations. Within these set patterns other mathematical constants and variables become apparent, it's how we determine our position in the universe and more importantly where we will go next."

"The constellations in the night sky possess a unique harmony and rhythm, enticing celestial bodies to cluster together. It is our responsibility as curious minds to discern this hidden frequency and assemble the enigmatic puzzle through mathematical expertise. Stonehenge, an ancient and storied monument, stands as a testament to our ancestors' relentless pursuit of understanding our position within the cosmos and their desire to decipher the patterns formed by the celestial orchestra above. Come with me, Hepu, there is something I want you to witness," said Intef, leading his apprentice beneath the starlit night sky towards the inner circle of Stonehenge.

The heavens above shone brightly through the gaps created by the towering monoliths. The monument was a sacred space, where countless generations had gazed skyward, seeking wisdom and inspiration from the stars. Intef explained, "As our Earth journeys through its annual orbit around the sun, we anchor our observations using the unwavering Northern Star. A particular order begins to manifest when we examine the remaining stars as variables. Our predecessors have observed the skies, documented their movements, and engaged in a myriad of calculations. This rigorous process has led us to uncover the fixed patterns we now call constellations."

"Within these established formations," he continued, "other mathematical constants and variables reveal themselves. These secrets of the universe unveil not only the intricate cosmic dance that unfolds above us but also the celestial connections between the heavens and Earth."

"It is through this process of observation, computation, and analysis that we come to determine our position in the universe and, more crucially, to envision where we might venture next," Intef concluded. With a sense of awe and wonder, Hepu realized that he was now part of an enduring legacy, one that bridged the gap between the ancient wisdom of the past and the boundless possibilities of the future.

For several days, Hepu had not laid eyes on his father. Enchanted by the constellations, he dedicated countless hours to the design room, captivated by the shimmering gold plates and, more significantly, the intricate equations that formed the foundation of mathematical law.

On one such evening, Mitry and Khamet strode into the room, cradling a flask of fine wine. "Hepu, it's time for a well-deserved respite," they gently coaxed. "We're well-aware of the daunting problem that plagues your thoughts. However, relentlessly pursuing the answer will not yield the solution you seek. Join us in a moment of reprieve." Their words rang with sincerity and concern, resonating within Hepu's heart.

Reluctantly, Hepu accepted the offer, and Mitry poured him a glass of the rich, crimson liquid. Together, the trio ventured from the confines of the design room and into the lively streets of the bustling city. A vibrant tapestry of people indulged in a feast for the senses, partaking in delectable dishes and swaying to the rhythm of the night.

The air was thick with melodious tunes, a harmonious symphony that beckoned the mind to release its grip on worries and surrender to the soothing embrace of relaxation. The infectious atmosphere enraptured Hepu, reminding him of the importance of balance and the need to occasionally step back from life's challenges in order to truly appreciate its beauty.

In the midst of the swelling crowd, the trio found themselves enveloped within an assemblage of individuals who seamlessly melded together, as the pulsating music reached crescendo after crescendo. An ethereal connection materialized, dissolving the boundaries between the attendees and fostering a united, vibrant energy. A glistening speck of light, akin to molten chrome, emerged at the nucleus of the human vortex, which steadily spun in harmonious unity.

The wine flowed generously as the gathering's fervor intensified. Mirroring a metamorphosis, the chromatic light evolved into a mesmerizing, conical rainbow that spun in a counterpoise to the people. Its enchanting dance boasted vibrant hues of red, blue, and orange interwoven within, as it expanded in size with each new soul that was drawn into its embrace.

This synesthetic experience transported the congregation into an entrancing, collective journey, delving into the depths of the subconscious while simultaneously traversing new realms of consciousness. The exquisite amalgamation of sight and sound, color and energy, continued to grow and captivate until, in a sudden instant, the music ceased and the dazzling light vanished.

Astonished by the surreal encounter, the crowd erupted in applause, jubilant cheers, and heartfelt embraces. They had shared a transcendent moment, binding them together in a profound and unforgettable experience.

Hepu couldn't quite articulate his thoughts, yet he possessed an inkling about the issue at hand. Traversing the corridors, he returned to the chamber where his father, Djoser, stood with a contemplative air. "Father, I believe I've discerned the root of the problem," Hepu confidently declared.

Perplexed, Djoser inquired, "What do you mean, Hepu?" Hepu approached the diagram of the twelfth constellation, his eyes studying the intricate mathematics that governed its celestial pattern. The room held its breath as Hepu's finger traced the problematic section of the equation. "Here, this argument. It should have been one-third the radian, not one half. That modification would resolve the issue, Father."

Djoser's eyes widened in realization, and he hastened to a nearby table to rework the equation. At that moment, Intef entered the room. Hepu stood silently, sensing the positive energy beginning to materialize. Djoser scribbled on parchment, while Intef beckoned three additional scholars to lend their expertise.

Intef joined the collaborative efforts, merging the equation's definition and outcome. One by one, the scholars handed their work to Intef, who assimilated their contributions and presented the final version to Djoser, who was still engrossed in calculations. The room remained hushed, save for the scratching of a solitary quill perfecting the revised equation.

Suddenly, Djoser leaped to his feet, exclaiming, "YAAA HAAA! It works! Hepu, you're a prodigy!" Overcome with pride and gratitude, Djoser enveloped Hepu in a warm embrace. Together, they presented the refined constellation equation to Intef and the other scholars, their faces alight with the excitement of discovery.

In a moment of pure serendipity, they settle down to verify the final star's position within the freshly revised constellation. Intef gradually lifts his gaze from the work table, beaming at Hepu with a mixture of astonishment and pride. "He's right, isn't he?" Djoser exclaims with unrestrained enthusiasm, "I can scarcely believe it, Djoser! Your son has untangled the intricate enigma!"

Intef signals for the others to spread the incredible news throughout the city. "Truly, the wisdom of the young is astounding. If anyone were to find the solution, it should have been your prodigious son,

Djoser," Intef utters, his voice laced with excitement. The melodious sound of cheers and laughter reverberate in the background as the triumphant announcement sweeps through the bustling city.

"Well, this certainly means our architects and structural engineers will face a monumental challenge with the Great Pyramid," Intef quips, chuckling lightly. "Indeed, but it's far better than uncovering such a complication after its completion," Djoser responds, his eyes gleaming with excitement.

Throughout the jubilant celebration, Hepu remains silent, unable to fathom how he arrived at the crucial insight. He simply knew it felt right. As the trio - Intef, Djoser, and Hepu - depart the room, they feel as though their lives and those of everyone they have ever known have transformed irrevocably. They merge into the throng of ecstatic people, the city itself a vibrant tapestry of music, food, drink, dancing, laughter, and resounding cheers that soar into the night sky until darkness gives way to the golden dawn.

Djoser, unable to contain his joy, hugs his son tightly, as the most glorious sunrise they have ever witnessed unfolds before them. "I love you, Dad," Hepu whispers, his heart swelling with love and pride.

The first light of dawn bathed the landscape in a warm glow as the caravan bustled with activity, diligently packing food and supplies for the long journey home. Intef bade farewell to his family and friends, as he prepared to accompany Djoser, Hepu, and their comrades on the return expedition. With the latest scrolls safely tucked in Djoser's satchel, the group set forth, their faces beaming with confidence and high spirits.

As the caravan leisurely traversed the verdant, undulating hills separating the enigmatic Stonehenge people from the harbor, their vessel - rejuvenated and primed for the voyage - awaited their arrival. Gradually, the caravan diminished from sight, melding into the vastness of the rolling terrain.

"It's fortunate that Intef is joining us on our return," Hepu remarked to Mitry, who responded with a knowing smile, "It couldn't possibly be because he wants to spend more time with us, could it?" Mitry paused for a beat before continuing, "What transpired back there was nothing short of miraculous."

Hepu beamed, humbly deflecting the praise, "What I did was a result of our collective efforts. No one can truly take credit for an idea; they just appear. But I'm incredibly grateful it all worked out." The camaraderie and shared anticipation for the forthcoming journey home brought a sense of lightness to the group. Hepu, unable to contain his joy, performed a playful jig, eliciting hearty chuckles from his companions as they continued onward, filled with hope and anticipation for the adventures that lay ahead.

Under the spell of a mesmerizing twilight sky, Djoser's voice rang out with conviction, "This enchanting locale shall serve as our haven for the night." As the sun gracefully bowed out, leaving behind a trail of hues, the camp swiftly materialized with an array of tent-style dwellings and a crackling campfire at its heart. A gentle breeze whispered secrets through the trees on the ridge, while Intef found solace in the fire's embrace.

A sense of warmth and camaraderie enveloped the group as they shared a delectable meal, sipping on fine wine that flowed as generously as their high spirits. The atmosphere was undeniably lively, filled with laughter and conversation, a testament to the bond they had forged.

Amidst the revelry, Mirty observed Intef, who appeared to be swaying ever so slightly, his gaze firmly anchored on the hypnotic dance of the embers. A serene expression washed over his face, reminiscent of a meditative trance, which Mirty recognized as the prelude to the transmission of ancient wisdom. Such moments were rare, and they signified the passing of knowledge from one generation to the next.

Sensing the significance of the impending discourse, Mirty discreetly motioned to the others, urging them to turn their attention towards Intef. As the chatter subsided, an air of anticipation settled upon the camp, each member eagerly awaiting the pearls of wisdom that were about to be bestowed upon them.

His words gracefully glided through the air, enveloped in a melodious timbre, captivating all who listened. "Humans are the guardians of time... Without them, time ceases to exist, and the universe manifests as a symphony, oscillating between night and day, as the celestial bodies weave their eternal dance."

Intef, now gazing at the heavens, continued with a profound intensity, "Unleash the potential within by embracing positive energy, thus achieving an equilibrium of the mind. Life propels you on a path of its choosing; resisting it only exacerbates your struggle."

His eyes rolled upward, lids gently falling shut as he entered a deeper meditative state. "The mind is a vault of memories, safeguarding the essence of our aspirations and inspirations—unique treasures that can never be replicated or artificially forged. Evolution abides by the beat of precession, with the Earth gracefully waltzing back and forth in accordance with the cosmic waves. Stagnation is but an illusion, for change fuels the universe's eternal engine."

Intef continued, "And within these transformations, cycles emerge—patterns that echo throughout the cosmos." Abruptly, his words ceased as a serene energy suffused the surroundings. Intef's gaze returned to the fire, where he drew a deep, purposeful breath, and exhaled slowly, surrendering to the enigmatic dance of the flames.

Intef and Djoser, both wise and experienced, recognized that the younger generation possessed immense potential to reshape the world. However, without proper guidance, they understood that this unbridled energy could lead to irreversible mistakes, leaving a lasting, detrimental impact on generations to come. As the night unfolded, the fire blazed steadily, casting a warm glow on the eager faces of the young tribe members who absorbed the pearls of wisdom bestowed upon them.

It was a night filled with hope and promise, and as it reached its zenith, the tribe laid down to rest beneath the inky, star-studded sky. The celestial canopy shimmered with possibilities, inspiring each of them to ponder the enigmatic path that lay ahead, filled with both challenges and opportunities.

When dawn broke, the sky was a vast canvas of clouds, with fleeting glimpses of the sun peeking through in transient, golden rays. Amidst this atmospheric tapestry, Hepu assumed his position on the wagon's perch, gently steering the horses along a narrow, winding trail. A cooler, eastward breeze stirred memories of his homeland, evoking a deep longing for his beloved Alara. Despite the distance and the journey's uncertainties, his love for her remained unwavering, fueling his determination to carry forward the wisdom and legacy of his ancestors.

As Djoser gazed at his crew, his eyes radiated warmth and his smile gleamed with infectious optimism. "My friends," he announced in a buoyant tone, "this is a journey that will be etched into your memories for the remainder of your days." With that, he pivoted back and led the men along the serpentine path that would take them downward into the valley. There, their vessel laden with supplies eagerly awaited their arrival. Though a day's journey still lay ahead, they settled down for the night, making camp and readying themselves for the morrow.

During the process of setting up camp, Hepu approached Djoser with a sense of caution. "I've been pondering what we're doing and its significance, but I'm struggling to grasp the wisdom Intef shared with us. What did he mean by 'the cycle'?" Hepu observed a shift in his father's countenance, a rare expression of concern and desolation. "I'm pleased you asked, my son," Djoser replied. "What I must disclose to you and the others may be somewhat more disconcerting than Intef's teachings." He paused, then added, "Tonight, as we gather beneath the starlit canopy, you will come to understand."

In his words, Djoser carried the weight of responsibility and knowledge, determined to enlighten his crew about the mysterious cycle. He knew that as they embarked on this extraordinary adventure, they would not only be shaping their own destinies but also uncovering secrets that could alter the course of history. His determination to see their mission through only grew stronger, fueled by the bonds he shared with his crew and the unwavering support they showed for one another.

On their final evening in the Stonehenge continent, a sumptuous feast awaited the group, their anticipation filling the air. The fire's spirited crackle and roar accompanied the hushed tones of conversation as they sat around the blazing embers. An air of anxiety enveloped the gathering, particularly the younger members of the caravan, who sensed something momentous on the horizon, though they could not quite place their fingers on it. Intef, seated beside Djoser, felt a quiet contentment, recognizing that his role in that moment was to listen and absorb.

As the night unfolded, Djoser assumed command, drawing the gaze of all those present. He began, "The vast expanse of the universe holds within it all knowledge, accessible to those who seek it. Our Earth undergoes transformations so extreme that our verdant paradise will one day be rendered a barren desert."

Drawing closer to the fire, Djoser picked up a small stick, sketching a sinuous waveform in the sand -

cresting at the top, dipping to the bottom, and rising again. He placed the stick atop the first peak and continued, "In this moment of time, we revel in the knowledge and wisdom bestowed upon us by our ancestors." Djoser paused, allowing the gravity of his words to sink in before exhaling deeply. "Yet, many years hence, the tides will shift, and the decline will begin."

Djoser traced the stick along the downward arc of the waveform, emphasizing, "Inevitably, when we reach the pinnacle, the only path is downward, and conversely, so goes the ebb and flow of the Earth's natural cycles, to which we all are subject. Future generations may deem themselves intelligent, but in truth, they will be found wanting. They will struggle to grasp the essence of humanity's purpose and fail to comprehend the significance of the legacy we leave behind. Therefore, we must take precautions to preserve and protect ourselves and our knowledge."

With an air of solemnity, Djoser glides the stick downward along the line before pausing. "Here is where a profound shift will occur. The people of this era will learn to manipulate one another, prioritizing self-interest over the welfare of their loved ones and fellow inhabitants of the world." Hepu and the others exchange puzzled glances, unsure of what to make of these forebodings.

Djoser continues gravely, "Once this transformation

begins, it will not cease, and I fear it will instill terror in your hearts." As Djoser recounts these memories, he is engulfed by a wave of unwelcome negativity that seems to erode a fragment of his life force.

"Violence and cruelty will proliferate as they annihilate one another in unimaginable ways. Mothers and wives will bid their sons and husbands farewell, never to lay eyes on them again as they perish in great multitudes." Hepu and the others watch in horror as Djoser elucidates, "Their concept of love will be distorted. Although they possess the capacity for affection, many will struggle to harness it or remain unsure of its significance. Love will often manifest as an unguided, capricious force, wreaking havoc and chaos for all involved."

He adds, "Moreover, their perception of death will diverge from ours. They will view it as a conclusion, rather than a new beginning. They will experience the anguish of loss, but only if they held a genuine attachment to the departed." After unburdening himself of this disheartening information, Djoser takes a moment to exhale and regain his composure.

Hepu, in a state of disbelief, could not help but interrupt his father, "How could they be so blind? When they witness the miracle of a baby's birth, do they not comprehend the source of that life? Are they incapable of understanding the connections between past and future lives?" To this, Djoser calmly replied,

"They will experience the joy of birth, but it will elude them to see the grander tapestry that ties everything together."

Hepu's voice trembled as he barely whispered, "How can this be... this sounds like a cruel deception. Please tell me this is not the truth." Djoser, understanding the weight of the revelation, continued, "It is challenging to divulge this information, but it is necessary to grasp the reality of our predicament. At present, we exist in a harmonious state, devoid of negativity in thought or deed. We, as a people, are acutely aware that our future hangs in the balance.

In our time, love and relationships are explored and taught in school, fostering a sense of natural progression. However, the future will be starkly different. Learning will become a contest, with few reveling in success while the majority languishes in despair. This practice will divide those who excel academically and those who thrive in hands-on learning, giving rise to distinct subcultures within their society.

Mass communication tools will keep them preoccupied as they inadvertently brainwash themselves in the pursuit of selling happiness. Material possessions will be sought to provide fleeting moments of joy, resulting in a perpetual competition between individuals. This unsustainable cycle will deprive them of true happiness, leaving them utterly confounded as to the reason behind their dissatisfaction."

In an elegant display of disbelief, Intef covers his ears as he gazes at Mitry, while Khamet shields his eyes and Hepu clasps his hands over his mouth.

In a subdued tone tinged with frustration, Hepu inquires, "I fail to comprehend the allure of material possessions. What exactly are they?" Djoser responds, "In essence, they amount to mere trinkets—shiny rocks and metal objects, often infused with a touch of electricity. While these resources are abundant on Earth and belong to all, many still fervently desire them." Hepu probes further, and Djoser elucidates, "Their allure lies in the illusion of control. These material things ultimately hold no true value and may even prove detrimental, yet their significance often only becomes apparent when life has run its course."

In this world, individuals known as "crooks" and "leaders" wield power over others, inadvertently perpetuating a cycle of suffering that spans millennia. Guided by the erroneous belief that amassing possessions and admiration places them ahead in life, these individuals lose sight of the essence of life energy: the quality of one's character, rather than one's possessions.

As a consequence, they exist in a negative vibrational state, which manifests as incurable diseases leading to agonizing deaths. The Earth, too, senses this energy, responding with uncontrollable pestilence and upheaval. Although these individuals may possess mathematical abilities, they will become reliant on machines for solving complex problems, never achieving the intellectual heights that we know today. The invaluable knowledge we currently hold will be obscured by the passage of time.

Djoser concludes his somber account, describing a world vastly different from their own, despite sharing the same planet. As he catches his breath, the weight of the negative energy in his words leaves him momentarily depleted.

Despair tugged at the edges of their hearts as Khamet beseeched Djoser with urgency, "Is there no glimmer of hope for the days to come?" Intef interjected, his voice heavy with wisdom, "Indeed, there are noble souls wielding power, striving to channel the virtuous energies of our time. Alas, they are far outnumbered."

The fire's hypnotic dance intensified, its crackles and pops resonating with the night's somber atmosphere. Embers spiraled upwards into the dark sky as more logs fed the flames. Djoser collected himself, while Hepu and the rest stared, still reeling from the harrowing vision of the impending era they had just witnessed.

Intef's voice carried a solemn weight, "This revelation is for us alone. The knowledge we now possess bears the potential to reshape the world. We are the chosen few who can see the future. Treasure this foresight, and share it only with those whose hearts are resilient enough to withstand its truth." As Intef concluded, his gaze returned to the fire, searching for answers within its flickering depths.

The once jubilant gathering had taken an ominous turn, leaving each individual grappling with the heavy shadows that now clung to their souls. The fire blazed, mirroring the haunting images of the gruesome future etched in their innocent minds. Paralyzed, they could not even exchange glances. Gradually, one by one, they retreated from the fire's glow, leaving Intef and Djoser behind.

"Well done," Intef whispered, offering his hand to Djoser in quiet acknowledgment of the shared burden they now bore.

With urgent determination, the footsteps of Doser, Intef, Hepu, Khamet, Mitry, and the others thundered upon the wooden dock like a charging stampede. Now, fully aware of the gravity and significance of their mission, the men swiftly boarded the boat. As they scanned their surroundings, they observed that every task on board had been executed with impeccable precision and unwavering attention to detail. The vessel had been prepared to perfection, eagerly awaiting its crucial journey back to Egypt.

Djoser, his heart heavy with responsibility, cautiously entered his quarters, the updated scrolls gripped tightly in his hand. Carefully, he stowed them securely within the travel box, his mind racing with anticipation. Though exhausted, he found himself invigorated by the thought of seeing the great pyramid once more and witnessing the transformative changes that now had to be made.

With a solemn air of finality, the boat cast off from the port, the crew waving their farewells to the supportive comrades left behind. Few words were exchanged as the ship cut through the waves in a southerly direction, but the unspoken gravity of their mission was evident in the determined expressions on each crew member's face. They sailed tirelessly, taking turns at the helm, their focus unwavering as day gave way to night.

A spark of excitement flickered in Djoser's eyes as he recognized the landmark signaling the boundary where the mighty Atlantic Ocean yielded to the tranquil waters of the Mediterranean Sea. A sense of relief washed over him, for he knew they were now halfway home. The enormity of their mission weighed heavily upon their shoulders, but with renewed vigor, they pressed on, their hearts filled with a sense of duty and the knowledge that the fate of their beloved homeland rested in their hands.

Fatigued from the taxing sail, and approaching the end of their journey, the vessel gracefully glided into the harbor at Algiers. As if guided by a sixth sense, the locals had prepared for their arrival with food, wine, and immaculate beds. Weary from their confrontations with the capricious sea, the crew disembarked and found solace in the nearby homes of the welcoming port town.

A festive celebration commenced, with the crewmembers as the distinguished guests of honor. Melodious tunes enlivened the atmosphere as the sailors were lavished with scrumptious fare and delectable wine. The evening brought respite and a chance for the crew to regain their strength. The locals exchanged tales of their lives and customs with the sailors, fostering a sense of camaraderie between the two groups.

Following a rejuvenating night's sleep and preparing the boat for the final leg of the journey, Hepu and Djoser found themselves in a serene moment, sitting in solitude by the flickering fire on the second night. "We will be home by tomorrow," Djoser proclaimed with a faint smile, observing Hepu's reaction closely. He could sense that something weighed heavily on Hepu's mind. "What is it, Hepu?"

Hepu hesitated, his voice faltering, "What you've told us... this journey we're on... so much has happened... I never expected any of this." He appeared overwhelmed by the revelations and the responsibilities now resting upon his shoulders.

Djoser, ever the wise mentor, gently offered his counsel. "Visionaries rarely know what awaits them. It is both a blessing and a curse. The path is arduous, but necessary." He paused, his gaze drawn towards the stars and the crescent moon adorning the cool night sky. "Our solar system holds the key... and the universe... the lock. Your actions at Stonehenge were nothing short of miraculous... and they will forever alter the course of our history."

Hepu managed a smile as Djoser continued, "Alara and your children will herald the dawn of a new generation, prepared for the completion of the Great Pyramid. Your progeny, my dear grandchildren, represent the hope for our future. It is your duty to guide them beyond their formal teachings, to help them grasp the dangers of this world and the benefits of positive chi. Only the most exemplary individuals will be permitted to accompany our pharaoh into the new world."

The fire's glow illuminated their faces, as both men contemplated the magnitude of their roles in shaping the future. As the night grew deeper, their conversation delved into the intricacies of their mission, discussing the importance of preserving their culture, the impact of their discoveries, and the challenges that lay ahead.

They spoke of ancient prophecies and the convergence of celestial events, pondering the mysteries of the universe and their place within it. As the embers in the fire began to fade, a profound sense of purpose enveloped them. United by their shared vision, Hepu and Djoser were determined to secure a brighter future for their people and fulfill their destiny.

With renewed vigor, they faced the final leg of their journey, knowing that their actions would echo through the ages, leaving an indelible mark on the sands of time.

As the first rays of morning sun illuminated the horizon, the vessel gracefully departed from the shore. With a now rejuvenated crew on board, they eagerly set sail for their homeland and the Giza plateau. As excitement swelled within their hearts at the thought of reuniting with loved ones, they skillfully adjusted the sails to harness the power of the easterly wind. The boat seemed to come alive, dancing with each gust, as if called homeward by the warmth and affection of the community awaiting their return.

By nightfall, the vessel had gracefully entered the mouth of the Nile River, embarking on the final leg of their journey. The gleam in Djoser's eyes inspired the crew to smile as they expertly adjusted the sails, maximizing their speed under the moonlit sky. It was as if the boat itself was instinctively aware of the path that led to its home.

As they continued on their course, a ship from Göbekli Tepe suddenly emerged along the shore. Contrasting the jubilant mood on Djoser's vessel, the captain and crew of the other ship appeared worn and fraught with anxiety. Djoser, knowing that their journey was shorter and that they were due to return days earlier, felt a sinking suspicion that they needed to confer before completing their mission and delivering the updated mathematics to the builders and architects of the great pyramid.

"Ahoy!" Djoser bellowed as his boat drew nearer to the distressed vessel. Crew members from the Göbekli Tepe ship hastily cast ropes, securing the two boats together as they mingled to exchange their thoughts and experiences. It didn't take long for Djoser and the others to realize that both crews had encountered the same unresolved dilemma.

"I see you have discovered the issue with the construction, much like we did," Djoser began. "But I am here to tell you that we have found the solution to the mishap." The atmosphere aboard the two vessels transformed instantaneously. Cheers, whoops, and hollers filled the air as the weight of uncertainty was lifted, replaced by a newfound sense of camaraderie and shared triumph. Together, they would return home, united by their collective success, ready to complete the magnificent project that awaited them on the Giza plateau.

The recent revelations instilled a sense of trepidation within the crew, yet in spite of their weariness, they persevered with a growing anxiety. The arduous voyage had taken its toll, but the promise of homecoming and reuniting with their cherished ones provided solace and fueled their determination. As the sun's first golden rays pierced the remnants of the starry night, the ships glided gracefully into the harbor.

Fishermen, embarking on their daily ventures, paused to marvel at the sight of the weary yet triumphant sailors. Their silhouettes danced upon the water's shimmering surface, creating a mesmerizing scene. The vessels approached the dock, and with great haste, ropes were thrown and secured to ensure the ship's safe mooring.

A collective sense of accomplishment washed over the crews as they exchanged proud glances. Eager to return to their loved ones, they disembarked with knapsacks filled with clothing and tokens of their journey. Their hearts swelled with anticipation, longing for the warm embrace of their soulmates.

Alara, gently awakened by Hepu's tender kiss, found herself wrapped in his loving arms. Overwhelmed with emotion, she whispered, "I missed you so much,

Hepu." He replied with equal affection, "I missed you too, sweetie." As the sun ascended over the Egyptian city, they remained entwined, savoring the precious moments of their reunion.

Though the expedition had been fraught with challenges, the crew had emerged wiser and more resilient. They recognized the value of the hardships they had endured, understanding that the pain and struggle were essential elements of their growth and personal transformation.

CHAPTER 3 – THE BIRTH

As the sun descends towards the horizon, its warm hues softly envelop the half-built Great Pyramid, casting a golden glow on the scene below. The air is filled with the sound of laughter and the exuberant energy of children at play, as if the day was not merely a workday but a jubilant celebration shared among friends and family. Stories of the day's events are exchanged, with each person reveling in the amusing anecdotes of their children's antics, their joy magnified by the happiness they find in the experiences of others.

This harmonious atmosphere extends throughout the expansive families residing in open-style dwellings, where insects are scarce and harsh weather is a distant memory. This idyllic climate is the result of diversified weather patterns influenced by the earth's optimized axis—a testament to the profound transformation of the world.

People now live in a state of absolute peace and tranquility, their lives resonating with positive energy and the short-wave vibrations emanating from such a serene existence. The earth spins in perfect harmony with its equinox, a far cry from the dark age that occurred thirteen millennia earlier when human civilization teetered on the brink of extinction due to ignorance and dissolution.

With the remnants of that tumultuous past now a faint whisper in the annals of history, mankind has emerged into a lighthearted existence focused on the bright future that lies ahead. The collective attitude of the people has shifted, and they have left behind the destructive vibrations that once threatened their very survival. In their place, a newfound sense of unity and hope has blossomed, shaping a world where individuals work together to create a better tomorrow for themselves and generations to come.

As the day draws to a close, the sun's lingering rays continue to bathe the majestic Great Pyramid in a gentle, golden light. The people gathered around it— united in laughter, love, and a shared sense of purpose—stand as a testament to the incredible journey of human civilization, a beacon of hope and a symbol of the limitless potential that lies within us all.

The cityscape unfurls before the eyes, adorned with ornate planters and exquisitely sculpted pottery brimming with a vibrant tapestry of flowers in red, yellow, blue, purple, pink, and white. Flora of every kind embellishes the streets and the facades of buildings, transforming them into living art. Rich green shrubs and a diverse array of trees intertwine, weaving through polished basalt floors, which are themselves meticulously arranged in striking geometric patterns and styles. The city is a harmonious blend of nature and human ingenuity, a testament to the beauty of coexistence.

Majestic sculptures of pharaohs, both past and present, stand sentinel throughout the city, watching over the inhabitants with serene, peaceful smiles. As the sun dips towards the horizon, casting a warm golden glow, couples stroll hand-in-hand, their love infusing the cityscape with an intimate, enchanting ambiance. Simultaneously, a group of men skillfully ignite the city lights with gold scepters, generating sparks of static electricity that awaken the fire within the fixtures. These luminous beacons radiate a vivid glow, illuminating the night in all directions.

The denizens of the city, dressed in immaculate white cotton linen, gather together in clusters, their laughter and camaraderie painting a picture of unity, peace, and harmony. Children's giggles echo through the air, their youthful energy contagious as they play and learn life's lessons from the wisdom of their elders. The atmosphere is invigorating, the air cool and crisp, with a gentle breeze that whispers through the leaves of the trees, adding a soothing melody to the urban symphony.

As twilight envelops the city, the first glimmers of starlight punctuate the midnight blue sky. People pause in their activities, their eyes drawn upwards, captivated by the celestial dance unfolding above them. The city, bathed in the soft light of the stars, takes on a mystical quality, as if suspended in time, the perfect fusion of nature's splendor and human ingenuity. It is a place where the past, present, and future coalesce, a living testament to the power of love, unity, and the indomitable spirit of the human heart.

Amidst the bustling city, the enchanting melody of gentle music casts its spell, as the hypnotic rhythms of an Egyptian-style guitar and deep bass intertwine with captivating singing. The harmonious atmosphere washes over the city, captivating its residents in its embrace. Swells of people move together in a mesmerizing dance, their bodies swaying gracefully to the entrancing rhythm, as if under the spell of a master sorcerer.

As the sun sets, the anticipation of a sumptuous nightly feast grows. Marble countertops, layered with elegance, become the canvas upon which a cornucopia of fresh fruits, vegetables, breads, fish, and meats are laid out. The fires from numerous dome ovens erupt in a symphony of flames, signifying the commencement of a culinary masterpiece.

The kitchen transforms into an arena of love and skill, where fathers, uncles, grandfathers, and great-grandfathers take their positions as artisans, crafting a meal that will satiate and delight all who partake. Mothers, aunts, grandmothers, and great-grandmothers join this dance, preparing the bread, fruits, vegetables, fruit juices, milk, and wine with practiced hands and nurturing hearts.

A tantalizing aroma wafts from large sheets and skillets, where fresh fish and meat are being cooked to perfection, adorned with the finest spices. The irresistible scent beckons to those fortunate enough to be downwind, drawing them closer to the epicenter of this magnificent feast.

The kitchen buzzes with lively conversation and laughter, as the family members share stories of the day, their voices filled with life and love. Soon, the time arrives for the meal to be unveiled. Presenters hoist large trays laden with delectable delights, entering the dining hall as hungry guests eagerly anticipate the feast before them.

Families, friends, and newfound acquaintances gather around long tables, their hearts warmed by camaraderie and the promise of a satisfying meal. The applause erupts as the food servers enter, and the eager diners express their gratitude for the bountiful spread.

The feast continues until every guest has had their fill, the atmosphere reverberating with the sounds of contentment and joy. Upon completion, the talented chefs emerge from behind the kitchen, met with resounding applause from the grateful crowd. Beaming with pride, the family takes a bow, their hearts overflowing with the love and appreciation they receive from those they have nourished and united through this shared experience.

In this enchanting evening, the true essence of human connection comes alive, as the simple act of breaking bread transcends the mundane, transforming into a celebration of life, love, and the magic that lies within each shared moment.

In the heart of a grand ancient city, majestic stone partitions stretched from the floor to the ceiling, their surfaces adorned with exquisite carvings and enigmatic hieroglyphics. These imposing walls encased a vast and luxurious bathing complex, where the city's inhabitants could cleanse themselves after a day's labor.

As twilight descended, casting a gentle glow upon the cityscape, families eagerly anticipated their nightly ritual of warm showers. The crystalline water cascaded forth, its soothing flow a testament to the architects' ingenious design. Vast sections of the bathing facility featured an array of individual stalls, each equipped with a steady supply of hot and cold water. This life-giving elixir was meticulously filtered and heated by gleaming, solid gold tanks, a symbol of the city's prosperity and technological prowess.

Upon entering the stalls, visitors would discover scented soaps nestled within elegant stone dishes. The fragrant cleansing agents were crafted to rejuvenate the body and spirit, washing away the day's toils and leaving the bather feeling refreshed and invigorated. The thoughtful design of the facility ensured that every need was catered to, providing an oasis of comfort and relaxation for the city's denizens.

Upon exiting the showers, guests were greeted with plush towels, still warm from the sun's embrace. Neatly folded, clean garments awaited them, a visual reminder of the thoughtful consideration that permeated every aspect of this ancient civilization. As families gathered to bid each other goodnight and exchange wishes of pleasant dreams, the air was filled with an atmosphere of contentment and gratitude.

Retreating to their homes, the people of this remarkable city would find themselves enveloped in an atmosphere of serenity and repose. Within each dwelling, pristine white linens beckoned, draping down feather mattresses that seemed to promise the most blissful slumber. The immaculate blankets, pillows, and sheets stood as a testament to the city's culture of care and attention to detail, ensuring that every member of the community was well-rested and ready to face the new day.

In this extraordinary city, the people's nightly routine of bathing and restful sleep was more than a mere necessity; it was a cherished ritual that bonded the community together. The intricate stonework, ornate hieroglyphics, and luxurious amenities of the bathing complex bore witness to a civilization that valued cleanliness, comfort, and the fostering of strong familial ties. As the stars above began their nightly dance, the city's inhabitants would slumber, secure in the knowledge that they were part of a society that understood the importance of nurturing both body and spirit.

As dawn's first rays gently illuminate the morning sky, Hepu is roused from his slumber by the tender voice of Alara, his loving wife. "Awake, my dear, for your father eagerly awaits you," she whispers, her delicate touch massaging his back. Slowly rising from his bed, Hepu gazes out the window, taking in the picturesque view and reflecting on the beauty of the life he has built. The air is filled with the inviting scent of freshly brewed tea and warm, fruit-filled pastries, delicacies delivered to each household throughout the city.

"Make haste and consume this on your journey to work," Alara urges, pressing a pastry into Hepu's hands as she ushers him out the door.

Hepu and his father are integral members of a large metallurgical enterprise, situated at a distance from the city. Working alongside a team of over fifty men, they skillfully forge gold, silver, and iron elements, contributing to the construction of the magnificent pyramids as well as the intricate moldings and fixtures that adorn the cityscape. Moreover, their craftsmanship extends to the creation of vital tools required for quarry work. An accomplished sailor, the elder Djoser is also renowned for his expertise in

mathematics, a knowledge that he generously imparts
to the apprentices under his tutelage.

As Hepu hastily devours his breakfast, a neighbor
catches sight of him and calls out jovially, "Hepu, my
friend, it appears you're running late! Thank you for
addressing our issue, but now you must hasten!" With
a hearty laugh, the neighbor watches as Hepu
vanishes from view.

Despite the urgency of the situation, Hepu cannot
suppress the broad grin that stretches across his face,
a mixture of both pride and unease. He has worked
diligently to master his craft and contribute to the
thriving city, and his efforts have not gone unnoticed.
As he traverses the bustling streets, he feels a deep
sense of gratitude for the life he shares with Alara, the
warmth of their home, and the camaraderie of his
fellow artisans.

Yet, the pressures of his profession weigh heavily on
his shoulders. The meticulous nature of his work
demands exactitude and precision, as the fate of
monumental structures and the very fabric of the city
depend on the quality of the materials he and his team
produce. As he strides purposefully towards the
metallurgy shop, Hepu acknowledges the magnitude
of his responsibility, even as he takes pride in his
achievements.

This delicate balance between pride and humility is a

constant companion in Hepu's life, shaping his approach to his work and his relationships with others. As he greets his colleagues with a warm smile, he resolves to continue honing his skills and embracing the challenges that lie ahead, ever mindful of the remarkable life he has built and the people who support him on his journey.

Within the brilliantly illuminated metal workshop, an array of tables are laden with newly crafted tools, meticulously designed for cutting through even the hardest of rocks. These gleaming instruments eagerly await their forthcoming delivery, as nearby sand molds stand prepared to receive the searing flow of molten metal. A prominent feature of this bustling workspace is a sophisticated hydro-electrical generator, fashioned from shimmering gold and embellished with copper windings. This impressive device is connected to reservoirs filled with a unique liquid solution, employed in the electrolysis process for producing exquisite gold-layered headdresses and masks.

The artisans' latest masterpiece—a remarkable creation intended for a pharaoh—sits prominently upon the foremost table. This exquisite sculpture showcases a serene countenance skillfully fashioned from solid gold, with rays of sunlight emanating from its core. As a symbol of eternal love, the radiant beams embody the spirits of cherished relationships from the past.

At the back of the workshop, domed furnaces burn fiercely, emitting an intense, rumbling roar that speaks of the raw power harnessed within. The steady cadence of hammers striking metal resounds throughout the space, echoing the dedication and expertise of the craftsmen at work. The sounds begin with a gentle hum, gradually evolving into a symphony of metallic tones that celebrate the essence of human endeavor. This harmonious melody grows in intensity, swelling in volume as more artisans join the chorus of creation.

When Hepu entered the busy workshop, Djoser quickly spotted him from his peripheral vision, observing Hepu's attempt to sneak in unnoticed and late yet again. An undercurrent of irritation colored his voice as he spoke to his son, "Hepu, why this delay once more? Don't you realize how much this upsets me?"

"Sorry, Father," Hepu replied sheepishly.

Djoser's disappointment grew more palpable, "Apologies alone won't suffice for the fourth time. I'm proud of your accomplishments, but don't let them inflate your ego. You should know better!"

With a radiant grin that he couldn't suppress, Hepu admitted, "I know, Father, but I just can't help it. I solved the problem!"

The previously restrained shop workers, now captivated by Hepu's dramatic entrance, spontaneously burst into applause. Their clapping quickly escalated into a thunderous roar, as Hepu, basking in the adulation, indulged in a theatrical bow.

Djoser, attempting to maintain his composure,

simply shook his head and returned to his work. As he labored on, he couldn't help but feel a mixture of pride and concern for his son. Although Hepu's achievements were commendable, Djoser couldn't ignore the growing arrogance that seemed to be taking root. He hoped that, in time, his son would learn the value of humility and punctuality, to ensure that his talents were not overshadowed by an inflated sense of self-importance.

In the heart of a thriving agricultural community, vast fields teem with life as men, women, and young adults diligently tend to the land, harvesting an abundance of fruits and vegetables destined for their evening meals. Meanwhile, the elderly observe with pride and contentment as their families contribute to the community's ongoing prosperity and sustenance. Fathers and sons can be found further afield, nurturing herds of animals in the nearby hills and erecting wooden fences, all the while preparing the soil for the forthcoming planting season.

The successful harvests are stored in sizeable grain containers, meticulously filled and sealed by an industrious workforce. These abundant yields are then transported to distribution centers, where they are systematically divided and allocated to individual households within the network, ensuring equal access to sustenance for all. Amidst the rural landscape, the rhythmic clatter of textile gins punctuates the air as they tirelessly produce a wide array of garments and linens. Shirts, pants, towels, blankets, and sheets are woven and stitched together with remarkable precision, destined for the community's bathing and clothing supply stations.

Across all age groups, smiles serve as a universal symbol of joy and camaraderie, as teachers and students alike fill the classrooms with an atmosphere of support and encouragement. In these nurturing environments, children progress in their education without fear of judgment, fostering a sense of belonging and a shared passion for learning.

Meanwhile, the city undergoes a vibrant transformation as skilled landscapers meticulously update the floral arrangements that grace the pots and planters. A captivating blend of orange, purple, and white flowers heralds the arrival of the earth's new equinox, breathing fresh life and energy into the urban landscape.

In the vicinity of the city, a symphony of industry unfolds as logs are harvested from the nearby forest and transported to a bustling wood processing station near the Nile. Taking advantage of the abundant water currents, the station efficiently mills the logs to precise dimensions, ready to serve as the backbone of new architectural projects.

One such endeavor is the construction of a cozy,

welcoming home, diligently crafted by a team of dedicated workers. This new dwelling will soon be filled with the laughter and love of a growing family, as they eagerly await the birth of a precious new member. The anticipation of this joyous event serves as a poignant reminder of the importance of community, love, and the unwavering power of the human spirit.

In a realm where hierarchies of men preside, numerous rock quarries bustle with activity as dedicated specialists meticulously extract soft limestone from the bedrock. These skilled artisans carefully shape and measure the stones to conform to the precise requirements of the Great Pyramid. The master builders, an elite committee composed of astrologists, architects, and structural engineers, determine the intricate stone measurement formulas that guide their work.

Once the stones have been cut to perfection, they are loaded onto specialized transport sleds, ready to embark on their journey. Human steeds replace the sleds, shouldering the immense burden of these stone behemoths as they ascend the causeway and approach the loading ramp. As each stone nears its final resting place, it is meticulously maneuvered into position using pilings, achieving a remarkable tolerance of merely a millimeter.

Any stones of irregular size find their purpose as

filler material, strategically placed behind the casing stones to support the next ascending level of the pyramid. This intricate dance of stone and human effort is a testament to the indomitable spirit of those who labor tirelessly, driven by an innate will to survive. Their interdependence weaves a bond of unity and determination, as they rely on one another for their very existence.

In this grand endeavor, the Great Pyramid stands as a symbol of human tenacity and the power of collaboration, a monument to the achievements of those who dared to reach for the stars and leave a lasting legacy for generations to come.

Composed of delicate papyrus, an array of mathematical scrolls is spread out before Djoser as he diligently carries out complex calculations for his thesis. His work focuses on the adaptations required to accommodate the innovative chamber and shaft designs of his time. As he labors on his calculations, Djoser notices Hepu fully immersed in his most recent project. A friendly grin lights up his face as he calls out, "Hepu!" in a cheerful tone.

Hepu, momentarily distracted from completing a finely crafted tool for the quarry, returns Djoser's grin and inquires, "Yes?" With a sense of urgency, Djoser rolls up his meticulous work and hands it over to Hepu. "Could you please deliver these documents to Isidorus and Intef in the Conclusion Room?" he requests.

Without hesitation, Hepu darts out of the room, clutching the scrolls, and makes his way down the bustling street. Despite his strong work ethic, Hepu finds it difficult to resist the temptation of engaging with others as he carries out his tasks. He is well-aware that the completion of his duties often leads to chance encounters, fostering connections with fellow humans.

These interactions bring Hepu immense satisfaction, as he revels in the opportunity to strike up lively conversations and inadvertently bask in the warm glow of appreciation for his achievements. Unbeknownst to him, his dedication to his work, combined with his affable nature, not only endear him to those around him but also contribute to the success of the projects he is involved in. As Hepu makes his way to deliver Djoser's scrolls, he carries with him an air of enthusiasm that is both infectious and inspiring.

Nestled within sand-washed rock walls, a myriad of window openings invite gentle sunlight to permeate the chamber, casting a warm glow upon the enigmatic hieroglyphs that chronicle the evolution of human intellect and behavior. The grandeur of the room is accentuated by its soaring thirty-foot high ceilings and lustrous, polished floors. Adorning the walls are three magnificent, gossamer-thin gold plates, each standing twenty feet tall and spanning thirty feet in length.

An industrious group of individuals busily ascend and descend ladders, diligently etching intricate mathematical equations into the plates with a flat punch and small hammer. When necessary, they skillfully erase errors by flattening the gold surface once more. These equations represent a celestial tapestry, weaving together the twelve constellations in a precise analytical map of the universe, derived from the scrolls crafted by a distinguished committee.

Hepu, captivated by the awe-inspiring sight before him, surveys the plates with a mixture of amazement and satisfaction. Conscious of the time, he realizes they are behind schedule and proceeds towards the Conclusion Room. As he approaches, the sound of applause crescendos signaling his presence, Hepu raises both arms aloft, fingers outstretched towards the heavens as he assumes a triumphant, hero-like stance, basking in the admiration of his peers.

With an exasperated tone, Isidorus called out, "Hepu! Please come in here!" Hepu entered the room, where papyrus scrolls littered the tables, quills dancing frantically as they recorded astronomical data. Intef and Isidorus, along with other structural engineers, gathered around a circular table, working tirelessly to perform mathematical equations. Their goal: to provide the necessary information to update the Great Pyramid's construction design. These diligent minds meticulously reviewed observations collected by universe surveyors and astronomy groups from Stonehenge and Göbekli Tepe, making sure no detail was missed.

Isidorus rose from the table, leading Hepu away from the others to avoid being overheard. Frustration laced

his voice as he inquired, "What are you doing?"
Confused, Hepu replied, "What do you mean?"
Isidorus continued sternly, "Don't let your recent
success go to your head. Yes, you found a solution to
the problem, but that doesn't make you extraordinary.
You're merely a man who had a thought. Everyone
appreciates your contribution, but don't let it inflate
your ego."

Hepu nodded in understanding, accepting Isidorus's
words. Eager to change the subject, Isidorus held out
his hand expectantly. "Now then, the scrolls from
your father, please." Hepu handed him the scrolls,
and Isidorus couldn't help but express his admiration.
"Your father is one of our finest engineers. It's no
surprise that his son has surpassed him. This will be a
crucial adjustment to our calculations." Offering
Hepu a nod of approval, he dismissed him. Hepu
exited the building, his thoughts turning towards
home and his awaiting wife.

Alara, a petite young woman adorned with dark
chestnut locks and captivating brown eyes, emanated
an effervescent charm that Hepu found irresistibly
enchanting. Her presence radiated a warmth and
vitality that was nothing short of magnetic. As their
eyes met, Alara's face lit up with an electric smile, and
she hurried towards Hepu, wrapping him in a tender
embrace.

"Hi there," Hepu greeted her affectionately. "You're
absolutely radiant today, my love. How do you feel?"

"I'm doing well," Alara replied, her voice filled with a
mixture of excitement and anticipation. "I can sense
that the time is drawing near. The baby is quite active,
kicking and moving around quite a bit." She shifted

her position, seeking a more comfortable posture as she took a seat.

Moved by his wife's resilience and the miracle of life unfolding within her, Hepu placed his hand gently over Alara's womb, feeling the baby's movements for himself. "This entire journey is simply astounding," he murmured softly. "I'm so incredibly proud of you, my love. I cherish you more than words can express."

Alara's eyes shone with affection as she responded, "I love you too, Hepu. I'm thrilled about the life we're building together, and I eagerly anticipate the joys and challenges of raising a family with you. I hope this child is the first of many that we'll bring into this world."

The couple shared a heartfelt embrace, holding each other tightly for a moment that seemed to stretch on forever. Eventually, they exchanged an intimate, knowing smile before departing from their cozy abode. Arm in arm, they ventured into the evening, eager to share a leisurely meal and enjoy the vibrant nightlife in the company of their dearest family and friends.

As Alara and Hepu meandered hand in hand past her parents' home, she couldn't help but notice her father's loyal canine companion nestled by the front door. "There's my dad's dog again, perpetually in the same spot, waiting for his return," Alara observed, her voice tinged with both amusement and admiration. Hepu nodded, adding, "He finds comfort in his vigil, eagerly anticipating the moment he can shower your dad with affection as he himself is adored. I'm certain he would wait a lifetime if necessary."

Alara's gaze lingered on the faithful animal, and she couldn't help but draw a parallel between their lives. "It's remarkable how animals often seem to understand love better than we do. We've certainly learned a thing or two, but the mistakes we make in our relationships leave such lasting scars. Regret doesn't fade with time; rather, it intensifies, looming larger in our memories," she mused, a wistful note in her voice.

Noticing a tear escaping from Hepu's eye, Alara instantly regretted her words. "I'm so sorry, sweetheart. I didn't mean to hurt you," she whispered, her heart aching at the pain she'd inadvertently caused. Overcome with emotion, Hepu chastised himself, vowing through his tears, "It will NEVER happen again. The pain in my soul from hurting you is almost unbearable."

Hepu paused their leisurely walk, pulling Alara into a tight embrace as they shared their sorrow. In a gentle voice, Alara reassured him, "It's okay. We're only human. We learn from our experiences and move forward." As Hepu tenderly wiped away her tears, he made a solemn promise. "I should have listened more attentively to those who tried to teach me. I will ensure our children heed my words and the wisdom of their teachers. I promise you, Alara. I love you more than I ever have."

With a playful grin, Alara sought to lift their spirits. "You better!" she teased, the corners of her eyes crinkling with mirth. Their laughter mingled with the lingering traces of tears, a testament to the resilience of their love. Embracing each other for a brief moment, they then exchanged tender glances before resuming their stroll, hand in hand, into the future that awaited them.

Hepu, noticing the stylish transformation in Alara's hair, gently compliments her, "I admire the change you've made to your hair; it looks stunning." Eager to distract her mind from the past, Alara beams in response, "Thank you, I was hoping you'd like it. My friend began experimenting with this style and encouraged me to try it, so she assisted me in achieving it."

Hepu warmly acknowledges the significance of her friendships, "It's wonderful that you have such a supportive network of friends; it truly enriches life." As Alara gracefully twirls, Hepu's heart swells with affection, forging a vibrant connection between them that eternally intertwines their souls.

As they conclude their leisurely walk, the night sky unfurls its dark, velvety expanse above them. Hepu and Alara find themselves entering a grand, dimly lit cathedral stadium, buzzing with activity. A sizable gathering of elegantly dressed attendees mingles, while mellifluous music plays and spirited conversations fill the air.

Center stage, four empty chairs await their occupants, subtly bathed in the glow of a spotlight. The backdrop is adorned with stars, enhancing the celestial ambiance of the event. A melodious chime resounds, prompting the crowd to hush and take their seats.

Leaning towards Alara, Hepu softly whispers, "I am truly proud of those who will soon grace those chairs." The anticipation in the air is palpable as they eagerly await the arrival of the distinguished guests.

In the heart of the city, the inhabitants cherished their connection to nature and the creatures with whom they shared their world. They dedicated themselves to understanding the habits and behaviors of various species, from the humblest of dogs and cats to the majestic horses, bulls, camels and lions that roamed the land. Through keen observation, they discovered the nuances of each animal's mannerisms, witnessing the subtle differences in their responses to various situations.

These people came to appreciate the unadulterated honesty in the way animals interacted with one another and with humans when unencumbered by fear. They recognized that every action these creatures took was rooted either in their instinct for survival or their innate capacity for love. As they deepened their understanding of the natural world, they began to notice a profound connection between the cycles of celestial bodies and the emotional lives of both humans and animals.

They called this concept "biorhythms" and meticulously documented the correlations they observed. The people found that individuals born during specific times of the year often shared traits with certain animals, whose behaviors, in turn, shifted with the Earth's rotational cycles.

With reverence for this intricate web of existence, they wove these observations into the fabric of their society, immortalizing their discoveries in the creation of a calendar. This wheel of life did more than simply measure the passage of time; it served as a reminder of the harmonious rhythm of the universe to which all living beings were intrinsically connected. By honoring this sacred knowledge, the people found themselves in tune with the great cosmic dance that bound them, and all creatures, together.

The arena was enveloped in darkness, leaving only the celestial radiance of the stars to cast their ethereal glow. A symphony of enchanting melodies filled the air, and, as if summoned by the music, beams of light began to illuminate the chairs on stage one by one. The curator's voice reverberated through the space, a warm and commanding presence.

"Welcome, dear friends. We are a people of understanding, living in harmony with the energies of our environment. We alone, as a species, have the choice to coexist with one another in peace or discord."

As he spoke, men and women gracefully ascended

the stage and took their places in the illuminated chairs. The curator's voice carried on, undeterred.

"The bond we forge with the creatures of the earth enriches both our lives and theirs. We have tamed the wild within them and earned their trust, while they, in turn, have given us their unwavering loyalty. This profound connection is a treasure beyond measure, and we are grateful to share this planet with such remarkable beings."

Gesturing towards the dogs, cats, and birds meandering through the audience, the curator continued. "These loyal companions offer us protection and comfort when we need it most. Though their lives may be fleeting, the love we share with them is eternal. As we grieve their passing, their spirits find their way back to us in new forms, carrying with them the love we once knew. Gaze into their eyes, and you will see the familiar warmth of affection."

"The individuals seated before you have embraced a unique philosophy. They have dedicated their hearts and minds to understanding the essence of a specific creature, seeking to embody its attributes and wisdom." As if on cue, birds of every species soared gracefully above the audience, filling the air with a cacophony of melodious calls and raucous cries. Cats and dogs weaved through the crowd, bestowing their affection upon unsuspecting spectators, a living testament to the bond between humans and animals.

The curator's voice resonated with a profound wisdom as he continued, "When we peer into the eyes of an animal, we are granted a glimpse into the realm of the subconscious mind. These creatures exhibit a remarkable range of cognitive abilities, their brains fine-tuned to discern the subtle fluctuations of energy present in all living things. It is their unwavering dedication to this understanding that has honed their subconscious and made them worthy recipients of the accolades we bestow upon them today."

From the shadows behind the curator emerged a table adorned with four magnificent animal headdresses. He approached the table with purpose, his hands deftly lifting the first headdress. "The Falcon," he declared, "bestows upon its bearer a keen eye, lightning-fast reactions, and an uncanny ability to remember." He gently placed the headdress upon the head of the first awardee, a young man who stood tall with pride.

"The Lioness," the curator continued, "symbolizes a tender heart and the delicate balance between strength and vulnerability." With great care, he crowned two women with the regal headdresses, their faces alight with honor and gratitude.

In that moment, the mighty head of the Sphinx was illuminated, emerging from the darkness like a beacon. The colossal statue sat serenely, the proud Lion pointing toward the stars of Orion's belt. "The Lion," the curator proclaimed, "embodies unrivaled strength, swiftness, and power. As the pinnacle of the array, its existence relies upon the presence of all other levels within it." The final headdress found its place upon the last awardee's head, as the audience rose to their feet, erupting in heartfelt applause.

"That was extraordinary," Alara whispered to Hepu, her eyes shining with admiration. "It's heartening to witness the fruits of their labor recognized in such a manner," Hepu agreed, his voice filled with pride. The honorees stood tall, basking in the adulation of the crowd as they clapped and cheered.

As the audience members began to disperse, they engaged in animated conversations with the awardees, now donning their newfound identities to be worn during future social events. Alara and Hepu, too, prepared to take their leave. Suddenly, Alara doubled over, a gasp escaping her lips as the baby kicked. "Oh my," she exclaimed, her hand pressed to her abdomen. Hepu smiled knowingly, his heart swelling with anticipation as he realized the moment they had been waiting for was drawing near.

As dawn begins to bleed into the velvet blanket of the night, Hepu and Isidorus find themselves perched atop a cresting hill, their eyes locked onto the spectacle below. Approximately two hundred figures, swathed in white robes that billowed like ethereal spectres against the morning breeze, were congregated in an open expanse. Known as the Electrolytes, these individuals were renowned for their profound cognitive capabilities and adept mastery over their energy.

Possessing an uncanny ability to voluntarily slip into a trance-like state of heightened consciousness, these gifted individuals were said to access the seldom-trodden realms of the right-brained psyche. On this particular morning, the assembly of Electrolytes was slowly configuring themselves into a wide, harmonious circle around an expansive pit, their hands interlocked as if they were a single, unified entity.

Simultaneously, their heads were raised in a silent homage to the waning stars above, their faces bathed in the cool, pre-dawn light. As if initiated by an invisible signal, they plunged into the depths of their collective mind-state. A tangible sensation of static electricity began to dance around their feet, their eyelids twitching sporadically as if choreographed by static electricity.

In the depths of their minds, a brilliant light was birthed, drawn from the infinite energy of the cosmos, signaling their connection to the abundance of positive energy from the Van Allen radiation belt. Then, with an abruptness that echoed the silence before a storm, they released their hands. The ground beneath them shivered, the once-darkened expanse blooming into a vibrant blue glow that encased the circle.

With startling suddenness, a lance of electrical

energy, akin to a lightning bolt in its breathtaking intensity, plunged from the heavens. It was drawn towards the gaping chasm, a thirty-foot pit where several gold spikes jutted out like teeth in the gaping maw of some ancient creature. This raw energy alchemized the metal, transmuting it into one of the hardest substances on earth, capable of cleaving through Andesite, one of the densest and most resilient terrestrial rocks known to mankind.

"I never tire of witnessing this miracle," Isidorus murmured, his voice barely audible against the hum of energy. Hepu nodded in silent agreement, "It's astonishing they can harness such power. The mind is a formidable tool, more potent than most could ever conceive."

Isidorus offered a gentle chuckle, his eyes twinkling with warmth. "I'm delighted you could witness this, Hepu. I'm aware of your struggles with punctuality, so it's quite an achievement for you to be here," he teased lightly.

Hepu returned his gaze to the spectacle, his mind churning with thoughts. "I always knew such power existed, but seeing it harnessed live... It's humbling to realize it's there for us to tap into," he said.

Isidorus nodded sagely, "The entire universe is interconnected by magnetism and alternating electrical currents. We've scratched the surface with our applications, but the potential for its usage is infinitely larger... vastly larger." He turned to Hepu, his voice dropping into a whisper, "You should leave now, your father will be expecting you."

In the soft light of the early morning, Hepu severed

the ties with his mentor Isidorus and ventured towards the grandeur of the rock quarry. Here, patiently awaiting his arrival, was Djoser, his father, flanked by a battalion of stone workers. Together they surveyed the forthcoming harvest, a vast procession of rock, broken from the bosom of the earth by the diligent hands of their workmen. These fragments of nature, untamed and raw, lay sprawled in orderly lines, ready to be transformed into the bedrock of civilization.

Hepu and Djoser, bound by blood and shared craft, observed with satisfaction the efficacy of the tools they had forged together. Pride swelled within their hearts, not just for the artistry they brought forth in their workshop, but also for how their creations played an integral part in this symphony of creation.

In the midst of their silent reverie, Djoser turned towards his son, a glint of paternal admiration in his eyes, "Hepu, our cooperation has borne a fruitful enterprise. I am deeply proud of you, my child." Hepu, touched by his father's words, responded with a warm smile before transitioning the conversation onto a question that had been bothering him.

"Dad, I've been meaning to discuss something," Hepu began, his tone marked by hesitance.

Djoser, however, cut off his son's contemplative stance quickly, his hands halting Hepu's meditative gestures. "Survey our surroundings, my son. Look at our abode, at our kin. Observe the happiness that engulfs their souls. We are part of a favorable flow of time, assisting one another without bias. We are genuinely fortunate," Djoser's voice reverberated around the quarry, his profound insight echoing through the surroundings. Then, as if the breeze swept away the weight of his words, his voice faded, softly ending their impactful conversation.

As the morning sun started to gently heat the sand beneath their feet, Hepu and Djoser left the busy work site, their day's work calling them to the city center. Their workshop, tucked within the city's maze-like streets, awaited their skilled touch. But a well-trodden path branched off towards Hepu's home, a detour he often preferred to take. "Wait for me, father!" Hepu called out, his voice echoing through the narrow streets as he veered off towards his home, leaving Djoser to continue on alone.

Upon entering his home, the sight of Alara, his beloved, filled his eyes. She was diligently fashioning a small, comfortable space for their unborn child. Positioned beside their joint bed, it represented their expanding family and the affection between them.

Catching sight of Hepu, Alara's face brightened. "Oh, darling, do you see the bed for our little one?" she asked, her voice filled with warmth and anticipation.

Hepu responded with a smile, his eyes fixed on the tiny bed, "It's beautiful, love." Understanding and compassion flooded Alara as she moved closer to him. She wrapped her arms around Hepu, holding him close, her heart beating in tandem with his. "It will be alright, my love," she murmured into his ear, her voice a balm to his troubled soul, knowing well the ghosts of his past that continued to haunt him.

Hepu leaned into her comforting embrace, his voice a whisper, "Every action of mine ripples through the lives of others. When I err, I know it wounds those I hold dear and even those unknown to me."

Alara tightened her embrace, her heart aching for his torment. "We all stumble, Hepu," she gently reassured him. "It's the sting of our mistakes that etches lessons into our hearts. As long as we learn, the pain is not in vain. Remember, my love for you is eternal."

The room was filled with a silence that was both comforting and healing. Alara's strength seeped into Hepu, her unwavering faith in him soothing his troubled mind. They remained intertwined, sharing a moment of profound understanding and love, until Hepu's spirit was calmed. Their lips met in a tender kiss, a silent promise exchanged - a shared smile painting their faces with renewed hope and love.

As the dusk began to settle, Hepu, the young apprentice, turned his steps toward the shop where his father, Djoser, was waiting with the habitual patience of a seasoned craftsman. Hepu found himself drawn not only to the familial bond that tethered him to the place but also to the camaraderie that existed amongst his fellow workers. Each day, he would absorb the tales woven from their diverse lives and experiences, like threads in a rich tapestry of shared existence.

Upon entering, Hepu was met with the sight of his father, Djoser, framed by the bustling backdrop of the workshop. His voice cut through the harmonious din, "Let's get to work, Hepu. We need those rails completed for the sleds and the handles for the observatory markers."

Without missing a beat, Hepu replied, "Okay, father, I'm on it. I'll have them done by tomorrow." He knew he was slightly behind schedule, but he also understood the importance of maintaining focus and staying committed to the task at hand.

He made his way to his work table, the comforting weight of the hammer fitting perfectly in his hand. As he joined the ongoing work song, the rhythm of his labor intertwining with the melody, he realized the beautiful truth that lay within the boundaries of the shop. Lives matured and blossomed in this shared crucible of sweat and steel, each day offering new insights, shortcuts to wisdom that recorded lessons could not impart.

The sun grew weary in the sky, heralding the close of the day. Hepu was tidying his workspace when an unexpected visitor entered the workshop, striding purposefully toward him - a messenger with news that promised to disrupt the comforting rhythm of their routine.

The messenger burst through the door, panting as he delivered his joyous news. "Alara, your wife, is with child! You must go to her!" His words rippled through the room, echoing in the ancient stone hallways. Hepu's face broke into a radiant smile, his heart pounding with a fervor that spoke of anticipation and elation.

His father, Djoser, watched with pride-filled eyes, a nostalgic smile playing on his lips. The sight of his son's joy mirrored the emotions he had experienced upon Hepu's birth, a thrilling wave of emotion that had felt like the first sunrise of a new world.

"My wife bears my child!" Hepu's voice echoed through the corridors as he bolted from the room. His words were carried on the wind, reaching the ears of the townsfolk as he sprinted towards the town center. The medical building, a symbol of hope and life, was positioned there, and it was to this structure that Hepu felt an irresistible pull, akin to a compass needle drawn to magnetic north.

He burst into the building, his heart throbbing in rhythm with the waves of tension that filled the room. Alara was there, lying on a padded table, surrounded by a ring of medical personnel who moved with the precise and practiced grace of seasoned professionals.

Her anguished screams punctuated the heavy silence, each one growing in intensity as her contractions quickened. The room was an orchestra of preparation, instruments gleaming under the focused light, medicines neatly arranged, a testament to the impending miracle of birth. Hot water steamed in a bowl, clean linens were folded in readiness, and freshly scrubbed hands poised in anticipation.

The birthing coach led the concert, her voice a soft, soothing mantra guiding Alara as the waves of labor propelled the unborn child further down the birth canal. "Push, Alara! Push!" Hepu echoed her words, his voice a cheer of encouragement amidst the storm.

But then, something peculiar happened. Time seemed to constrict, the room's sounds growing faint as if submerged under water. A dizzying sensation washed over Hepu as a brilliant golden light enveloped the room, bathing everything in its warm, ethereal glow. It felt as if life itself had condensed into this radiant light, infusing the room with the raw, potent energy of a new existence being ushered into the present timeline.

Hepu paused, absorbing the surreal beauty of the transformed room. He felt drawn to Alara, his feet carrying him to her side. His hands found hers, their fingers intertwining in a silent promise of shared joy and support.

"Are you okay, my love?" he asked, his voice a soothing whisper amidst the symphony of birth. "Our child... our baby is coming. I can't begin to express my exhilaration." His words were a soft-spoken testament to the profound joy that he was feeling, a sentiment that resonated in the ethereal light-filled room.

A piercing cry once again filled the room, the melodious symphony of life's hardest struggle echoing within the walls. "This is the hardest thing I have ever done in my life!" Alara shrieked as the waves of contractions, now merely five minutes apart, swept over her like relentless tides.

Her determination, as unyielding as the ancient bedrock, was met with nods of approval from the medical staff. They, the silent observers of this primal dance of creation, were awed by Alara's resilience. The doctor, a woman of striking competence, took her position at the foot of the bed, her nurse shadowing her, ready to assist with any medical exigencies.

Freshly sterilized linens, pristine as the first winter snow, were handed to the doctor. A gasp echoed in the room as the baby's head became visible, a tiny promise of new life emerging. "Summon your strength, Alara! Your child is at the threshold of life!" one of the nurses cried out, her voice tremulous with anticipation.

With a final, guttural roar, Alara drew from a

reservoir of strength she never knew she possessed, and the baby was born. A wave of relief, potent and pure, washed over her as the pain ebbed away, replaced by an overwhelming love so profound it was almost tangible. The room was filled with the sweetest sound—the baby's first breath, a whisper of life that heralded his arrival.

"It's a boy!" the doctor announced, her voice a triumphant fanfare that stirred joy in the hearts of Alara and Hepu. The newborn's name was Adeem, a symbol of their love and unity.

As the commotion gradually ebbed, individuals began to withdraw from the room, leaving Alara, Hepu, and little Adeem bathed in the soft glow of the moonlight, their silhouettes creating a tableau of newfound familial bliss. The medical attendees lingered discreetly, ready to offer assistance with sustenance or fresh garments should the need arise.

The world outside the medical center came alive as news of Adeem's arrival spread, the quiet night disrupted by the cacophony of joyous revelry. People filled the streets, their bodies swaying rhythmically in celebration, their laughter and tears flowing freely as food and drink were shared. The city, enlivened by the music of life, rejoiced at the birth of a new life.

With the celebratory echoes wafting through the window, Hepu gathered Alara into his arms, his voice barely a whisper as he declared, "I'm so proud of you, my love." Eyes sparkling with unshed tears, Alara looked at him and their newborn son, Adeem, and whispered back, "We did it... We did it, Hepu." The birth of their son was not just the commencement of new life but the beginning of a new chapter in their lives, one woven with love, strength, and hope.

CHAPTER 4 – THE WORKDAY

As dawn etches the Egyptian skyline, the first tendrils of sunlight reach out, gently caressing the land with a spectral golden touch. The city stirs, its heartbeat echoing in the soft rustle of the wind through the date palms and the distant murmur of the Nile. In the heart of the city, Alara and Hepu awaken, cradled by the day's nascent light that infiltrates their humble abode, bathing everything in a soft, warm hue.

Their bond, already strong, is deepened by the new life that lays nestled between them. Their baby boy, Adeem, a beacon of hope and joy, stirs softly in the dawning light, a cherubic smile playing on his lips. The profound connection that has blossomed through Adeem has interwoven Hepu and Alara's souls, creating an unbreakable tapestry of familial love.

Every touch, every glance exchanged between the pair carries an unspoken promise of forever. Each embrace lingers a little longer, every kiss imbued with more sentiment than the last. This new life, their precious Adeem, has organically drawn them closer, magnetizing their hearts in a way they never knew possible. The birth of Adeem, innocent and pure, has ignited a novel flame of love in their hearts, a flame that burns brighter and fiercer than their very existence.

As Adeem blinks his eyes open, revealing the world behind those sparkly orbs, Alara and Hepu melt. The possibility of who he could become, the promise he holds in those innocent eyes is overwhelming. A wordless understanding passes between them: they are guardians to this little soul, ready to sacrifice all for his happiness.

Preparations for the day unfold amidst soft chuckles and adoring glances. The air is filled with the exhilarating happiness of becoming new parents, their hearts swaying to the rhythm of this newfound love. Their playful banter, the sweet, silly pet names they coin for their little bundle of joy, paints the morning with an extra splash of happiness. In the mirror of their eyes, they see their future, their legacy in Adeem's soft coos and giggles.

Swathed securely in his mother's sling, Adeem nestles against Alara's chest, lulled by the familiar rhythm of her heart. They step out into the day, hand in hand, carrying the weight of their newfound joy with pride. Comfortable and secure in his cocoon, Adeem rides the waves of life, cradled in the comforting sway of his mother's stride. This day, like every day henceforth, is a testament to their unyielding love, a love that binds them together in an ethereal dance of parenthood.

Immersed in a symphony of sensory delight, the group was basking in the comforting aroma of breakfast wafting from the nearby kitchens as they claimed their space in the bustling food court. A convivial gathering of friends and family was encircled around the table, their eagerness for the day was nearly tangible. At the heart of the group, Djoser, a venerable figure of solid and stoic strength, sat with patient anticipation, waiting for the morning's conversation to unfold.

"How did you find your first night with your new life?" he gently prodded Hepu, the youthful vigor of a newly minted father reflected in his eyes. A gust of excitement infused Hepu's words, "Beyond anything I could have dreamt of, we are destined to create a family as large as our hearts can hold. I am on tenterhooks, envisioning a brood to carry on our legacy."

Alara, his radiant wife, overheard the conversation while engaging in hushed murmurs with her mother Bunefer. She chimed in, a playful edge to her voice that belied a sagacious undertone, "But, my love, not too soon," she concluded, her laughter tinkling around the group like a bubbling brook.

Adeem, the tiny catalyst of their joy, was passed around like a treasured artifact, each pair of hands cradling him. As if following a sacred rite, the infant eventually ended up in Djoser's embrace. "My grandson, my first," he murmured, gazing into the infant's eyes, twin mirrors of innocence that pulled a tear from the wellspring of Djoser's emotions, causing it to trail down his weathered cheek.

Caught off guard, Hepu asked, concern tinging his voice, "What's the matter, dad?" Djoser fought back the deluge of emotion threatening to spill over, replying, "He reminds me of my mother," the words punctuated by a hesitant smile, quickly replaced by fresh tears.

Observing the poignant tableau, Henite, Hepu's gentle mother, moved towards Djoser. She radiated a maternal warmth, comforting in its familiarity. "It's hard to hold him, isn't it?" she cooed, her arms tenderly enveloping the large man and the baby nestled against him. Djoser whispered a soft, "...yes," the word barely escaping his lips. "Here, let me take him," she offered, but Djoser clung to the infant, his voice filled with a profound longing, "No, please... not yet. I have been waiting... what seems like forever," his words trailing off as more tears made their pilgrimage down his cheeks.

In the throbbing heart of the city, the day begins in earnest. Massive cauldrons of fresh fruits – pomegranates bursting with ruby seeds, figs sticky with nectar – are rolled out onto the bustling streets, while rows upon rows of pearly eggs, bread that's soft as spun gold, and plump breakfast meats of the choicest variety are piled high. Together, they paint a vibrant mosaic of nourishment for the expectant workforce. At the same time, towering stacks of gleaming plates and finely crafted eating utensils are swept up in a whirlwind of activity, each one soon to be laden with mouthwatering sustenance.

Mirth and anticipation hang heavy in the air, punctuated by the rhythm of laughter and earnest conversation. Blueprints for grand structures are unfurled, the focus of intense discourse as plans for the day's construction work take shape. These shared moments culminate in the communal clearing of dishes, which are meticulously washed, dried and stored away like valuable relics, ready for the next meal. As this morning ritual concludes, the townsfolk disperse like a well-orchestrated dance, each one slipping away to their predetermined duties, their movements tuned to the symphony of productivity.

All around the city, this same rhythm echoes. The residents work in harmony, their voices lifted in song, a sweet serenade to their dedication. Groups of eager children, guided by young adults, are herded to schools, their young minds thirsty for knowledge.

Nestled near the languid flow of the Nile, Alara, cradling her infant in her arms, embarks on her daily endeavor – the washing of clothing and linens. Fresh water, drawn from the river, courses through a labyrinth of carefully engineered channels, feeding into mammoth drums. Heated by the ambient temperature and agitated by fulcrum handles, the drums replicate the ebb and flow of the river, cleansing the fabrics entrusted to them.

The landscape is a ballet of billowing laundry, stretching as far as the eye can see. The women, their tasks entwined with one another, exchange stories and laughter, their camaraderie making light of their labour. They joyously share their gratitude for life's bounties, their words lifting like incense to the clear sky. The air, playful as it cavorts through the drying clothes, whispers its own spell, stripping away moisture from the fibers, leaving behind the scent of the river and sunshine. Amidst this sea of linen, they celebrate Alara and her infant, their praises a testament to the beauty of motherhood, the depth of love and the bonds that tie them as a community.

The instant Hepu stepped into the lively workshop, a burst of cheers and elation echoed through the room, reminiscent of the vibrant energy of a bustling market. Surrounding Hepu were heartfelt hugs and enthusiastic praises, much like the warm embrace of old friends meeting after a lengthy separation.

Djoser sauntered through the workshop, his steps imbued with a boyish bounce, a jovial tune dancing on his lips. Today wasn't merely an ordinary day. It was a sacred reunion, the tapestry of time stitching together the cherished fragments of past and present. "What a splendid day to reminisce and rekindle familial ties!" he declared with infectious enthusiasm.

His attention then fell upon a relic from a bygone era – a weathered, four-wheel chariot once owned by a Pharaoh, echoing tales of majestic parades and royal excursions. A mischievous spark twinkled in his eyes, "Prepare yourself for a bit of excitement," he pronounced, his hands dancing over the chariot, making swift modifications - a removed railing here, an added bottom pan there, et voila!

A fervent call to gather ropes and trail him echoed through the workshop, effectively draining it of its occupants. The growing excitement was palpable as the unusual procession made its way towards the River Nile, the lifeblood of their civilization.

Anxiety swirled amongst the spectators at the sight of the river's tumultuous currents and the steep descent. Undeterred, Djoser asked, "Who will be the first brave heart?" Seeing the hesitant faces, he decided to showcase his idea, pointing the chariot downhill.

Mounting his renovated chariot, he issued a simple command, "Give me a push!" His words barely settled when the chariot took off, speeding downhill amid a thunderous uproar of cheers, spurring him on. A victorious yell, "Ya! Phenomenal, yes!" boomed over the din as he soared through the air, finally splashing down into the river's welcoming embrace.

From the river, Djoser beckoned for the rope, ready to hoist the chariot back to its starting point. From the crowd emerged a proud voice, Hepu, eager anticipation sparkling in his eyes, "That was a thrilling spectacle, father!" It was evident, he yearned to experience the exhilarating ride himself.

In the heart of an ancient civilization, a chariot, drenched in the cool water from the Nile, sits at the crest of a great hill. Hepu, youthful and vibrant, pulls himself onto the wooden carriage. Anticipation surges within him as he pushes off, his journey down the hill starting with an exhilarating rush of wind against his skin. A powerful, jubilant cry escapes his lips, "Exhilaration! This is divine!"

The chariot's momentum picks up, the wheels spinning ever faster over the dry, cracked earth. The air about him tingles with a vibrant energy, and with an unexpected jolt, he finds himself catapulted high into the air. "Marvelous!" He exclaims in awe before he descends into the crisp, waiting waters below, creating a fantastic spectacle of a splash. He emerges, triumphantly pulling the chariot from the river, amid rousing cheers and clapping from onlookers.

The glistening water splashes and laughter ripple through the city, attracting the curiosity of its inhabitants. They venture towards the spectacle, their intrigue piqued. Soon, a procession of other four-wheeled vehicles starts making their way to the hill, each looking for a taste of the thrill. Djoser, his heart bursting with pride, watches the scene unfold. The joy and laughter, the newfound tradition sparked by the birth of his grandson, Adeem, had inspired this spontaneous festival.

On the horizon the Pharaoh and his regal silhouette noticeable even from afar, moves toward the hill. His loyal entourage trails behind him, casting an intimidating shadow over the festivities. The previously vibrant hill falls into a hush as they approach. Djoser, still brimming with excitement, readies himself for another ride. But the Pharaoh intercepts him, his face stern and noble, his voice echoing across the silent crowd. "What is the purpose of this spectacle?"

With his heart pounding, Djoser replies, explaining the celebration of his grandson's birth and the inception of this spontaneous, joyous activity. A transformation takes place on the Pharaoh's face. His stern demeanor softens, and a rich, hearty laugh escapes his lips. "This looks delightfully amusing. May I partake?"

Djoser, visibly relieved, hands over the chariot to the Pharaoh. Osiris, shedding his royal headdress and the strictures of his position, boards the wheeled sled. An uproar of cheers and laughter erupts from the crowd, and the Pharaoh is given a ceremonious push down the hill. "How delightful!" He cries out as the chariot bolts down the slope, throwing him high into the air. "This is magnificent!" He roars, before plunging into the cool water below. Surfacing, he exclaims with a wide smile, "Such a joyous occasion indeed!" The crowd roars in approval, the echo of their laughter resonating across the ancient city.

In the midst of the amicable pandemonium of the day's festivities, the sands of time gradually sifted, the afternoon tapering off into the hushed serenity of the evening. The citizens of the majestic Egyptian city took full advantage of the dwindling daylight, relishing their final activities before the cloak of nightfall prompted them to bid farewell to their friends and families.

The glistening hills of Egypt resonated with the echoes of their laughter and merriment, slowly succumbing to the encroaching tranquility as the populace gradually dispersed to the comfort of their homes. Amidst the departing crowd, two figures were conspicuous by their dedication, their forms silhouetted against the fading hues of the horizon. Djoser and Hepu, dutifully engrossed in their task, diligently amassed the abandoned carts and ropes to return them to their rightful places.

The work was tedious, but the underlying satisfaction of having contributed to such a joyous day provided a sense of accomplishment. The Pharaoh's voice rose above the rhythm of their labor, admiration evident in his tone, "Djoser, your dedication was the catalyst for today's festivities. I am intrigued to meet Adeem; a boy capable of igniting such a day must indeed possess a remarkable spirit."

Subsequently, the Pharaoh and Djoser, were among

the last to abandon the hillside, their footsteps echoing in the silence as they followed the trail back to the city. As they navigated the path, the lingering feeling of euphoria clung to their souls, a souvenir of a day dedicated to joyous liberation. As they parted ways, the Pharaoh bestowed words of admiration upon Djoser, "Your presence is a beacon of hope, Djoser. I eagerly anticipate our next encounter."

The city's Contemplation Natatorium came alive as twilight wrapped the cityscape in her violet embrace. The subtle, dim glow reflected on the walls, animated by the delicate ripples that graced the water's surface. The natatorium was a sanctuary, a haven where adults found solace in meditative reflection, while the younger generations partook in the harmonious symphony of musical instruments.

Glistening pools of thermal water overflowed into the gargantuan elliptic basins hewn from the finest quartz. The water cascaded down a series of stone platforms, creating a grandiose auditorium bathed in the gentle luminescence of the moon. This water was meticulously filtered and preserved in colossal boilers of pure gold, intricately engineered to amalgamate hot and cold to the user's preference.

Djoser and Hepu, exhausted from the day's exhilarations, found their way to one of the pools positioned atop the arena. The soothing embrace of the warm water was a balm for their tired bodies. Luxuriating in the thermal water, with goblets of rich wine held in hand and a sigh of relief echoing their contentment, they savored the serenity of the moment.

The curvature of a meticulously crafted backrest

offered the ideal posture for contemplation, seamlessly merging comfort with functionality in a grand display of ancient Egyptian workmanship. Ensconced in the gentle embrace of the nocturnal warmth, the harmonious ebb and flow of nearby Nile tributaries orchestrated a soothing lullaby.

As they bathed in the velvety expanse of the evening, the celestial bodies above mirrored the boundless mysteries of the cosmos, kindling a meditative trance. The stark lunar brilliance and the shimmering tapestry of countless stars held their gazes, inducing a ripple of visceral energy that wound up their spines. With their eyelids gently lowered, the palpable pulse of the earth served as the sublime conduit, interweaving their consciousness with the ethereal universe.

A nebulous radiance began to illuminate their minds, an echo of cosmic energy seeping into the labyrinth of their subconscious. This spectral pulse birthed an extradimensional vortex within their psyche, its raw potential stirring an unspoken awe. Pulled inexorably towards this singularity of boundless curiosity, the threads of connection twitched with inspiration, pulsating ideas into the tapestry of their imagination.

Abruptly, the tranquil hum of introspection escalated into a deafening roar as the tangible world surged back into their awareness. Loosened by the cathartic journey, their tongues took to conversation with an uncharacteristic openness. Djoser, his gaze unfathomable as the mysterious Sphinx, initiated the dialogue.

"You now grasp the sacred essence of fatherhood, Hepu. The golden illumination you perceived at Adeem's birth signifies a beacon, a promise of a lost affection finding its way back to your heart."

Hepu, taken aback by Djoser's insight, could only muster a faint, "How did you know?" His mentor's knowing smile was timeless, "I, too, have witnessed this radiant vision with each of my offspring," Djoser replied, his voice as serene as a placid desert oasis. "Love is the unchallenged sovereign of all cosmic forces, an eternal flame that neither the sands of time nor the tumultuous tides can extinguish. We imbibe this truth in our learning halls, but it isn't until we taste its sweet nectar... well..."

Djoser's voice trailed off into the warm night, leaving Hepu to ponder the profound truth enshrined in his mentor's words. His mind teeming with thoughts, he found himself awash in a newfound understanding of love and its imperishable force.

Cloaked in the whispering echoes of ancient whispers, Hepu, wearing the mantle of a young seeker, released a breath that bore the weight of many unanswered questions. "Never before in the span of my life," he confessed, "has any experience echoed with such profound resonance. The sensation... it lingers still."

In response, Djoser, a sage worn by the sandstorms of time, looked at his young companion with an air of aged wisdom that shimmered in his dark eyes, devoid of any reference to Ra's golden chariot. He transported them both to a memory etched into their hearts, one that was bathed in sorrow, "Recall, Hepu, the day we said our final farewell to your revered grandmother. The pain, a testament to our shared affection, permeated the air around us. Her vibrant life essence wove itself out of the tangible thread of our shared existence. We mourned, for it felt as though the love we had cultivated was a river whose source had dried."

"But," he added, the corners of his eyes crinkling like aged papyrus, "with the emergence of a newborn, the river surges forth once again, replenishing our love in a heartbeat, it's a rejuvenation, swift and immediate."

Djoser's voice then took on a more solemn tone, the timbre resonating with the lessons he had gleaned from his long journey. "The reins of your emotions, the wisdom you impart to your offspring, these factors will shape their perception of our world. It is through this lens that they will expand their understanding and learn lessons of their own. As a mentor, you will strive for perfection, yet the winds of error will occasionally find their way into your sails."

"But how can I discern the righteousness of my actions?" Hepu interjected, uncertainty casting a shadow on his youthful visage.

The older man responded, his voice carrying a comforting calm, "You can't always be certain, Hepu. Your compass is your heart and your best intentions. Our actions ripple outwards, creating a distinctive energy. This energy, shaped by countless sunrises and sunsets, shapes who you are, who your children will evolve into. Life is like a mosaic, every piece holds significance, contributing to the grand spectacle of existence."

Djoser emptied his goblet, the remnants of the sweet Egyptian wine clinging to the rim. He filled it once more, settling back into his seat, the flickering flames from the oil lamps painting intricate shadows on his weathered face.

"You see, I am but a guide on your journey," he assured, his gaze steady on the younger man, "I can offer insights, drawn from my past experiences, though they may not be a mirror to your own. Your path is yours to traverse, your decisions yours to make. However, my wisdom can serve as a beacon, aiding you in times of uncertainty."

A soft pause settled between them, a comfortable silence that spoke volumes. "Keep your heart at the forefront of all your endeavors," Djoser advised, a tender earnestness in his voice, "then you will find that there are no errors in this dance of life, only different steps that lead to varying paths, each of them carrying lessons of their own."

In the cool, verdant shadows of a moonlit evening, under the heavenly glow of a thousand stars, Hepu beckoned to Djoser, urging him to replenish his chalice with the fragrant crimson wine. Djoser complied with a genial nod, pouring the nectar with practiced grace. As the wine shimmered like liquid rubies in the soft lunar light, Djoser continued his narrative, his voice carrying across the tranquil sounds of the gentle liquid cascade that surrounded them.

"These emerald pools, my son," he said, his voice rumbling like distant thunder, "are where you seek solitude when the weight of grave decisions rests heavily upon your shoulders. The path of truth, although it may scar you, will always lead to a righteous end. For it is in adversity where wisdom is garnered, much like the sharp edges of a stone are smoothed by the persistent flow of the river. My father once imparted to me that pain is the cruelest yet most effective tutor."

Hepu, absorbing his father's words, took a thoughtful sip of his wine, his eyes reflecting the wisdom in Djoser's advice. "So, fatherhood won't exactly be a walk through the papyrus fields, will it, Dad?" Djoser, his lips pulling into a wistful smile, responded, "Far from it... You've done the easy part already," His laugh, hearty and full, echoed off the rippling waters.

As their laughter melded with the gentle lapping of the pools, more figures began to emerge from the cover of darkness, drawn by the allure of the moonlit springs. Among them were two familiar silhouettes; Khamet and Mitry, their arrival punctuating the serenity of the night with a welcomed liveliness.

"Friends, have you space for two more in your lunar soiree?" Mitry queried, a playful glint in his eye. With a broad grin, Hepu extended his arm, "Of course! Join us, the water's embrace is as warm as Ra's favor."

No sooner had Khamet and Mitry slipped into the warm, welcoming water, they produced vessels of wine, already looking quite inebriated with the charm of the night. "Nothing quite matches the serenity of these hot springs after a day of labor and merriment," Khamet sighed, his satisfaction almost tangible as he moved to refill the depleted cups of Djoser and Hepu.

Underneath the twinkling firmament, Mitry gestured towards a particular constellation, his eyes filled with wonder, "Behold, the constellation of Osiris, watching over us from his celestial throne." As if in reverence, he tipped his cup towards the constellation, taking a sip from his wine.

Khamet, his gaze drifting across the numerous merry-makers gathered around the springs, remarked, "Indeed, these blessed waters seem to attract mirth and joy, a testament to their inherent magic."

Concurring with a hearty nod, Mitry added, "It provides a well-deserved respite from our building project. But truth be told, I can't help but long for the satisfaction of the work. Tomorrow, we will proudly place the 54th layer's cornerstones, a monumental step in our grand design." His words, laced with an unmistakable pride, hung in the air, a testament to their unwavering dedication and passion.

"A splendid endeavor, comrades, truly heartening to witness our united effort in building this colossal monument of our civilization," Hepu's voice echoes in the air, his words gilded with pride. The grand edifice towers above them, an embodiment of their collective will, an emblem of their era. The stone silhouette, illuminated by the soft glow of evening, whispers stories of labor and dedication, resilience and cooperation.

Khamet interjects, his voice steady and authoritative, "Indeed, we've been met with technical dilemmas during the process, but our architects and engineers have it all under control. Our plan requires a massive chamber with an intricate series of supporting lentils to hold the upper chamber in place... Ignoring the previous miscalculation could have been disastrous. We owe you a debt, Hepu." As Hepu nods in acknowledgement, a warm smile spreads across Djoser's face. He takes pride in his son's humility, an essential virtue for a leader.

"The other day, I had the chance to visit Alara and see your newborn, Hepu," Khamet changes the subject, a touch of melancholy in his voice, "Such a blessing, indeed. My wife and I have been trying, but we haven't been blessed with progeny yet." Noticing the wistful look on Khamet's face, Djoser offers gentle words of reassurance, "In due course, my friend. Every event has its appointed time in our lives."

The conversation is soon shrouded by the entrancing rhythm of music that wafts in from the outside, overpowering the soothing trickle of the nearby waterway. Hepu, lulled into tranquility by the melodious symphony, leans back, eyes closed, "What an extraordinary composition," he murmurs, savoring the harmony crafted by his favored musicians stationed just outside the grand plaza.

Inebriated and deeply pensive, Mitry suddenly breaks the silence, "But why does music speak to us? I comprehend our affinity, yet the rationale eludes me." To this Djoser, ever the wise, replies, "Music catalyzes creativity. It relaxes the right hemisphere of the brain, facilitating unhindered communication with the left, while concurrently providing inspiration. It is not simply heard, but felt. It invigorates us, soothing and motivating us simultaneously. A truly unique medium that transcends barriers, unifying us all."

Pausing for a moment to savor his wine, Djoser further elaborates, "Its essence lies in the same realm as that of dreamers, those who dare to envision. It echoes in our minds just before we slip into slumber, or upon awakening, or during repetitive tasks, for it is then that our imagination is unshackled, communicating freely with our conscious selves. Inspiration is a spontaneous gift, it simply happens." Hepu grins knowingly at Djoser, the twinkle in his eyes reflecting an understanding of the depth of his words.

"Djoser, his voice carrying the cadence of an ancient oracle, delved further into the mystery of emotion. "What is this ethereal energy that breathes life into our feelings? Just because its form eludes our eyes, many dismiss its existence. But in every furrow of a brow, every spark in a gaze, there's a narrative spun, etched deep with the hues of joy or sorrow. This is Chi, the very essence that pulses through our veins. Mastering the chakras is the sacred journey to harness this vibrant energy."

Hepu, his voice a gentle whisper on the wind, shared his perplexity, "When my anger flares towards Alara, it weighs heavy on my spirit. It's as if she's oblivious to my turmoil."

Djoser, his countenance like a timeless sphinx, imparted his wisdom. "Indeed, she is oblivious. Understand this, Hepu. Men and women are bestowed with unique minds, each adorned with their own distinct jewels of wisdom. In her own ways, Alara shines just as you do. The frustration you feel is undoubtedly mirrored in her. Yet, her mastery over her emotions may well eclipse yours," Djoser's words sparked laughter in Mitry and Khamet.

Hepu, his curiosity ignited like a flame in the night, asked, "Is it this dance of disagreements and understanding that weaves the fabric of love?"

Djoser, with the wisdom of countless moons in his

eyes, responded, "Navigating through the storms of disagreement can often lead to the calm shores of love."

The playful exchange drew to a close as Khamet noted their skin, bearing the evidence of long immersion in the spa. "I propose we seek out the revelry of a celebration," he suggested. Climbing out from the comforting warmth of the spa, Hepu's curiosity sparked once more. "Which festivity shall we honor with our presence?" Djoser, ever the pacifist, merely stated his universal appreciation.

"Let us be guided by the celestial orchestra tonight. The Star Party, beneath the quilt of constellations, is a spectacle to behold," Khamet suggested as they shook off the water and began to attire themselves.

As they journeyed away from the glittering city, the moon's silver glow erased the faint twinkle of distant stars. The cool night air seemed to carry their conversation away into the darkness, the rhythmic thud of their footsteps echoing like a team of synchronised steeds. With the cityscape merely a distant glow, Djoser halted, a familiar sensation enveloping him. The trail stirred a forgotten memory of a younger self, clutching his father's hand while engaged in jovial conversation with his mother and brother. A smile broke across Djoser's face, the bitter pang of nostalgia swiftly replaced by the warmth of the present moment - his own son and two companions at his side. Upon reaching the plateau, they found groups of stargazers sprawled in lounge chairs, their gazes directed towards the majestic constellation of Leo.

In the prevailing hush of the moment, Djoser, his

voice an echo of the ancient world, draws their attention back, "What, indeed, is the energy of emotion? Unseen, many would dismiss it as a mere fancy. Yet, in every fleeting facial shift, a tale unfolds, a memory is etched, driven by the ebb and flow of joy and sorrow, the yin and yang of our sentient existence, a dance of understanding, a journey towards taming the wild stallions of our internal cosmos."

In the heart of the innovative discourse, ideas pulse and bubble forth. Like divine scribes, the scholars orchestrate a symphony of intellectual exploration, their hands dancing over tools of their craft: the equal space divider, the triangle, the parallel ruler, and the protractor. Each instrument a testament to their proficiency, a subtle articulation of their prodigious talents.

Akin to the ancient hieroglyphic scribes meticulously transcribing tales of pharaohs and gods onto sacred walls, they faithfully record angular measures between celestial bodies, etching the mathematical truths into fine parchment. In each line of ink, the parchment whispers the echoes of their discoveries, resonating with the time-honored wisdom of the ancients, yet devoid of references to the solar deity, for this narrative is a nocturnal hymn.

Though the nightscape now refrains from the brilliant allure of the sun, it unfolds a grand tapestry that elicits awe in its simplicity, mimicking the austere grandeur of the Great Pyramid. The stellar mysteries become a riddle, much like the Sphinx, its solution lying hidden within the cosmic labyrinth. To the uninitiated, the mathematical revelations remain obscured, cloaked in the regal mystique of ancient Egyptian cryptics. But to the learned scholars, the secrets of the cosmos unfurl like papyrus scrolls, every new revelation an invitation to delve deeper into the celestial abyss.

In their pursuit of knowledge, they embody the spirit of ancient Egypt: its intellectual curiosity, its reverence for the mystical, and its ceaseless quest to decode the universe, establishing a powerful harmony between antiquity and the present, resonating in their rhythm of discovery and comprehension.

Basking in the thrills of the evening, Djoser enthused, his voice laden with fervor. "Tonight was a spectacle! May the positive vigor we unearthed remain a constant in our quotidian lives." His proclamation was met with light laughter and appreciative nods as they shared their discoveries with the curator, their minds brimming with the evening's events.

Hepu, invigorated by the nocturnal escapade, unveiled his revelations to his companions. "Tonight," he announced with a profound twinkle in his eyes, "has given birth to new muses within me."

As they descended the trail, their feet barely grazing the earth beneath them, Mitry, like a gazelle, dashed towards the awaiting Nile, inciting a friendly challenge. "The last to join me shall be likened to a turtle!" His words hung in the air as they raced after him, their laughter rippling through the night, their playfulness echoing off the riverbanks. One by one, they plunged into the cool embrace of the Nile, their bodies slicing through the moon-kissed waters.

Hypnotized by the cosmic dance of the moon's

reflection on the undulating waves, Djoser marveled at the joyful chaos. Hepu was the heartbeat of the group, inciting jests and initiating friendly tussles. Djoser, immersed in the spectacle, took a mental photograph of the moment, appreciating the simple euphoria that life offered him.

"The Nile cradles us with an ethereal warmth tonight," Djoser murmured, his gaze never leaving the liquid silver before him. "A fitting conclusion to an unparalleled day."

Their camaraderie, strengthened by their shared exploits, led them to deep conversations, personal anecdotes, and laughter that seemed to rival the star-studded sky. The evening's magical charm, however, was gradually giving way to the advancing night. "Time draws her veil upon us," Hepu reminded them gently, "we mustn't keep our homes waiting."

As they trudged back into the city, exhaustion etched into their demeanor, Khamet parted with a final thought. "This euphoria, let's invite it again soon. Until then, fare thee well, friends," he wished, as he vanished into the labyrinth of the city.

Mitry bid his adieu, choosing a divergent path towards his homestead. "Until we meet again," he echoed Khamet's sentiment. The remaining two, Hepu and Djoser, spoke in unison, "Night," their voices soft with the echoes of the adventure that had woven itself into the tapestry of their lives.

"Allow us a deviation, Father," entreats Hepu, a playful challenge glinting in his young eyes. Amid the ever-enveloping shroud of twilight, father and son tread a hurried path, their destination a mere stone's

154

throw from the city's brimming periphery. The faint murmur of distant activity stirs Hepu's curiosity, his keen eyes drawn to an unfamiliar spectacle just ahead.

Cloaked figures, alien in their mien, bustle about, their activities illuminated by the soft glow of the moon, its light touched on food-loaded carts drawn by sturdy horses. The tableau evokes Hepu's questioning spirit, "Father, the commotion there, who are these strangers?" In response, Djoser, his voice rippling with experience, imparts, "These are the Natufians, dwellers of a few valleys yonder. Our city's surplus sustenance finds its way to them."

Out of the shifting obscurity, Djoser gestures towards an imposing figure by the wagon. A man, his hair a wild cascade, his attire a mosaic of animal hides, marked by a fulsome beard speckled with grime and bisected by a bold scar over his right eye. "Observe him, that is Bolus, the chieftain of those distant valleys. Their perceptions of existence are not akin to ours," Djoser explains, his voice laced with a strange mix of curiosity and regret.

"But why?" Hepu retorts, his innocent belief in unity resilient, "Why won't they join us?"

"Son, not all hearts can harmonize with ours. We, the torchbearers of civilization, evoke fear in those who stumble in the shadows of comprehension," Djoser explains, his gaze locked onto the distant Natufians. "Fear of our wisdom... of our way of seeing, of our grand ambitions. They take refuge in a place that cocoons their comfort, yet it is a haven fraught with drawbacks – the perennial scare of depleting sustenance being one."

Hepu finds himself lost in his father's words, his young mind grappling with the stark realization. He casts a last lingering look at the distant figures, their world a contrast to his own. It's a lesson learned, one that he would not forget as he traversed the maze of human existence.

In the nebulous cloak of night, the incandescence of firelight wove ethereal patterns, casting dynamic shadows upon the broad face of Bolus. His heart pounded with an instinctive premonition, the instinct of a predator noticing another lurking in the fringes of his territory. Slowly, he turned, meeting the steady gaze of Djoser, his ire kindled in the glowing embers of recognition.

A sudden shift in the aura captured Hepu's attention, the silent currents between the two men did not escape his discerning eye. In an effort to demystify the tension, Hepu voiced his curiosity, a whisper lost among the desert winds, "Why do your eyes strike lightning across the night, at the sight of Bolus?" The two men disappeared from his sight, swallowed by the vast Egyptian darkness, leaving Hepu to contemplate the echoes of silence.

Djoser responded, his voice a rich baritone that resonated with the authority of ancient pharaohs, "Bolus is a man who wields his power with the unyielding strength of an iron scepter. He relishes the taste of dominance, the thrill of instilling fear in the hearts of those weaker than him. Our paths crossed once, and I made my displeasure of his rule known."

His words, delivered with serene gravity, floated like a feather on the river of night, "Power in the wrong hands distorts the balance of life, Hepu. A lion, as a king of beasts, knows this well. When it snarls and snaps at its own young, it instills fear, creating weak, timid creatures, robbed of their rightful strength. Yet, a lion who allows his cubs to play, to bite and claw at him without retaliation, encourages their budding confidence. This lion raises heirs, kings and queens of their own realms."

He paused, his gaze lost in the shifting sands, "The line separating healthy resistance from overt oppression is as delicate as papyrus. Everyone bears their burden differently, their resilience unique as the patterns on a scarab's shell. Thus, the wisdom of the ages, the voice of our ancestors guide us. Experience and time become our greatest teachers in mastering this art." The air around them vibrated with Djoser's wisdom, infused with suspense, a story from the annals of time yet to unfold.

In the quiet stillness that followed their shared revelries, Djoser and Hepu concluded their warm embrace, their paths veering toward separate destinies. Hepu discovered Alara patiently awaiting his return, her eyes brimming with eager anticipation.

"Dearest Hepu," she initiated, the subtle hues of her voice resembling the soothing tones of night breeze, "I trust your day was filled with joy? Your laughter echoed from the hilltops, it warmed my heart. Adeem and I, too, were blessed with a splendid day. We found companionship in my cherished friend Renni, and her charming little daughter Kiya. A truly flawless day unfurled before us, filled with prosperity and fulfillment as we tended to our duties."

However, an obelisk of silence loomed ominously between them, a profound disquiet perceptible in Hepu's gaze. Noticing his troubled demeanor, Alara ventured, "What has perturbed you, my love?"

"I glimpsed them today," Hepu confessed, his voice strained with concern, "the ones who dwell beyond our city walls. They bear a countenance far removed from our mirth. It troubles me, Alara. How can our realities be so starkly different? My encounter was with but a handful, yet I shudder at the thought of their urban plight."

Alara considered his words, her voice acquiring a softer, more consoling quality, "We are indeed gifted, my love, in our existence and our worldview. Perhaps time will bring them the enlightenment we've found. Do not burden your heart, Hepu. All will be well in due course." Her words resonated in the still air, an optimistic promise to soothe Hepu's troubled mind.

CHAPTER 5 - ADEEM

Tucked amidst the stone threshold, a young canine of earthy brown hue with a distinctive white marking adorning his chest peeks at the warm, bustling interior of Hepu's and Alara's abode. Alara's voice, like nectar infused with cinnamon, wafts through the air, "Do come hither, sweet soul." A quiver of apprehension courses through the dog as he gradually edges into the hearth, a visitor in the intimate scene where Hepu and Alara dote over little Adeem who is ambitiously attempting to navigate his first few steps.

Alara's hands, gracefully skilled, prepare an assortment of ripened fruits, while the dog continues his cautious approach. An inner conflict is palpable within him, torn between the warmth of the dwelling and the freedom of the outdoors. Just as he contemplates retreat, a band of children bursts into raucous play in the street, sending him scuttling under the shelter of the kitchen table, nestled between Hepu's sturdy feet.

With a soothing tone, Hepu murmurs, "What ails you, little companion? You seem lost." His breath rises and falls in rapid waves, a telltale sign of thirst. Overcome by the delicate charm of their unexpected guest, Alara muses, "She's a beautiful creature, isn't she?" Hepu's brow furrows with curiosity, wondering aloud, "Whose hearth has she strayed from, I wonder." He rises with intent, stepping outside to inquire about their newfound friend.

Meanwhile, within the comforting realm of the home, the dog begins to familiarize herself with her surroundings, sniffing at the lingering scents of the inhabitants. Adeem, with the tender innocence of a yearling, teeters around the room, a charming spectacle under the watchful eyes of his doting grandparents. A pause in his shaky journey is prompted by the sight of the dog. A cherubic grin breaks out on his face as the dog ambles towards him, finally surrendering onto her back. A cascade of sweet, youthful laughter fills the room, as Adeem delights in the pleasant company of the canine.

"Do you find favor in the hound, Adeem?" Alara's words are a playful lilt as she rubs the belly of the intriguing creature, her fingers sinking into the soft fur. A dulcet chuckle escapes her lips as she sets down an earthen bowl brimming with cool, life-giving water.

Meanwhile, as Hepu strides through the labyrinthine neighborhood, his voice echoes off the sun-baked stones, reaching from one dwelling to another, seeking anyone who could shed light on the dog's story. The community responds with shrugged shoulders and heads shaken in bemusement. No whisper of recognition or claim on the four-legged visitor. With a sigh, Hepu resigns himself to the mystery and returns to the comforting familiarity of his abode.

His return finds Alara and Adeem embraced in the tranquil realm of repose, the peculiar dog nestled snugly by their side. Hepu's report fills the air, his voice a low thrum, sharing his failed search and the promise he made to watch over the four-legged wanderer until a rightful claimant should surface. Alara, ever the radiant queen of their little kingdom, greets him with an understanding smile, leading him to the peaceful tableau of their slumbering child and their unexpected guest. "See, beloved, how the creature takes to our young prince."

The dog's form is a graceful curve in the dim light, a testament to the comforting bond that has swiftly grown between the two. The image, though transient, births a hopeful thought within Alara's heart. "Could it be that this creature sought us out with intent? It's almost as if she's become an addition to our family."

Her words, dipped in a sugar of wishful thinking, make Hepu pause. His voice is gentle, a reminder of reality's unpredictable whims, "Remember, my dear, not to bind your heart to her too tightly. Her rightful guardian may appear at any moment, and we must prepare for such a parting."

Alara, steeled against this potential heartache, retaliates softly. Her words resonate with an undeniable sweetness, "In this grand city, sometimes strays wander into lives unexpectedly, hoping to find a new family, a new home. Let us hope that is the case here." In her words, there's a silent prayer that their son's first encounter with such profound affection won't be cruelly ripped away.

In the soft cocoon of morning, Adeem fluttered into consciousness, lured from slumber by the tantalizing aroma of his preferred breakfast. His faithful canine companion, a lovable creature of glossy chestnut hues, danced at his bedside, her tail wagging in joyous rhythms of affection. Simultaneously, his mother Alara, radiant with an unusual glow, prepared herself for the demands of the day, a thrill of anticipation twinkling in her eyes.

The source of her jubilation was her impending partnership with Renni, her companion in labor. There was an uncanny chemistry between the two, a synchrony that had the texture of a well-conducted orchestra, lending their work an ambiance of comfort and conviviality.

With punctual precision, Alara and Renni converged at their place of work, their gaze settling on the formidable mound of soiled garments. A soft sigh escaped their lips as they integrated their offspring with the eclectic group of children from their fellow laborers. Wise elders, statuesque pillars of knowledge and discernment, oversaw the young brood, disseminating wisdom, keeping an eagle eye for any abnormalities, and preserving harmony in this vibrant tribe of future leaders.

The garments, were plucked and sorted. Large carts, hauled by dedicated teams, conveyed the laundry to the washing sanctuary, from where they were folded with care and prepared for the nocturnal shift. As the day matured, rivulets of sweat traced a path down their faces, but the women remained undeterred, their spirit of duty unwavering.

A welcome intermission came in the form of lunchtime, where they made their way to the communal tables, welcoming a moment of rest and camaraderie. Renni, amidst the sea of familiar faces, spotted a garment she recognized - a shirt marked by a small tear, one she remembered tending to a few days ago.

"Behold! That garment on yonder man was cared for by these hands," Renni announced, her voice ringing with a sense of accomplishment. "Our tasks may appear trivial to some, but when I see our toil woven into the tapestry of our people's daily lives, it brings a warmth to my heart."

Alara, smiling sweetly, agreed wholeheartedly, adding her own sentiment. "Indeed, it feels as though we are part of something grander, an intricate mosaic of existence. What we do crafts the societal framework, offering a taste of profound satisfaction." The conversation imbued their labor with an added sweetness, the knowledge that their work had purpose, contributing to the rhythm of their community. It was a day like any other, yet unique in its small joys, a testament to the endurance and spirit of the hardworking women of their time.

In the atmospheric embrace of a bustling gathering, Alara and her friend, resplendent in their fine garments, delicately settle down with their progeny. Amidst the lively chatter echoing around them, they partake in a feast, savouring both the taste of delectable cuisine and the stimulating camaraderie that flavors their surroundings. Adorned with the beauty of youth, the children, mirror reflections of their mothers' grace, laugh and babble, creating a symphony of joy around them.

An age-weathered matron, her eyes gleaming with a blend of nostalgia and admiration, observes this scene with benevolent delight. " Your offspring are truly captivating, like young pups playing under the watchful eyes of goddess Bastet," she speaks, her voice gentle yet firmly rooted in wisdom.

The corners of Alara's lips turn upward, offering a sweet smile that adds a pinch of warmth to the ambience. "Indeed, we behold them as our most cherished treasures," she warmly accepts the kind words, her eyes sparkling with maternal pride, void of any sunbeam yet filled with a light of their own.

In the nocturnal tranquility, Hepu stepped across the threshold, trailed by an older man. His hair, a tangled sea of silver-gray strands, reflected the weary tales of his life. An aura of unkempt disarray hovered about his slightly dirt-streaked visage, and his clothes bore the obvious signs of harsh wear, a testimony to his travels. On catching sight of the stranger, Alara's gaze traced the distinct silhouette etched against the twilight filtering through the window. A ripple of disquiet surged through her.

"Meet Ongara, a sojourner from the city of the Natufians," Hepu introduced in a melancholy tone. "He's on a quest to find his lost canine companion."

"In slumber she lies, nestling beside Adeem," Alara responded, her voice scarcely above a whisper. Hepu initiated the journey towards Adeem's quarters, with

Ongara shadowing his steps. As they treaded the familiar path, Ongara began, his voice a mixture of desperation and hope, "I've been tirelessly scouring for her; she's mine."

As they entered the sanctuary where the dog and Adeem rested peacefully together, a torrent of tears broke free from Alara's eyes. Hepu shot her a compassionate glance, saying, "The attachment I warned you about..." He paused, gathering his thoughts before continuing, "That's why we kept her past a mystery, for her journey began leagues away before destiny guided her to us."

Ongara stood still, transfixed by the tender sight of the canine and Adeem in their shared serenity. The room, absent of sunlight, bathed in the soft, ethereal glow of dancing candle flames casting their wavering shadows upon the walls. Silence reigned supreme, leaving Hepu and Alara in suspense of Ongara's concealed thoughts.

Eventually, Ongara broke the stillness, his voice barely audible yet laden with raw emotion, "A son... a desire unfulfilled, as no woman chose to share her life with me... Your city, it's unlike ours... How I wish..."

A tear escaped his weathered face, plunging to the floor in a quiet surrender. The sight of the healthy, loved dog, her coat reflecting the flickering candlelight, caught his tear-blurred vision. A tumult of emotions swirled within the room as Ongara silently acknowledged the wellbeing of his lost companion in her newfound home.

Hepu, the figure of quiet wisdom, and Alara, embodiment of compassionate warmth, bore witness to the visible struggle consuming Ongara, their hearts strung taut with shared sorrow.

A canine form, subtly stirring from slumber, lifted her head at the sound of Ongara's voice, her curious gaze marking him. After a brief moment, the hound sighed, nuzzling her head back into the comfort of Adeem's embrace, allowing the embrace of sleep to reclaim her.

Ongara's voice, rich in anguish, echoed in the sparsely furnished abode, "I yearn to belong, to exist within the intricacies of your culture, but Bolus' refusal echoes louder than my desires. His heart doesn't resonate with yours."

Alara's response was swift, the generosity in her voice melting the silence, "Our home, our hearts, will always welcome your presence. Do not fear about fitting in…"

But her words were interrupted by Ongara's sudden movement. He pivoted on his heel, his countenance shrouded with a veil of sorrow, tears carving rivulets down his cheeks, "She will find greater happiness here… It is unjust to separate her from your son. My heart… it struggles…"

Alara, her voice tender yet firm, countered, "Heed your heart's whispers, Ongara, for they seldom lead astray."

His query, almost whispered in the tense silence, caught them off guard, "May I… may I see her occasionally?"

Alara's response was cut off mid-sentence as Ongara, with a palpable sense of urgency, bolted from the house. His silhouette faded into the twilight, leaving behind the comforting boundaries of their shared dwelling, the trail of his tears merging with the mystical obscurity of the Nile Valley.

Hepu and Alara remained, guardians of the now peaceful Adeem and the canine companion curled beside him. Alara's voice, reflective and tinged with melancholy, filled the still air, "Initially, I lamented our circumstances, but now my heart aches for Ongara. How I wish for a world untouched by imperfections... but alas, life is an ever-changing canvas, transforming slowly, subtly, and unavoidably under the steady gaze of the cosmos." The suggestion of an unspoken hope rested on her lips as they bore the weight of their friend's sorrow, echoing into the star-lit void of the Egyptian night.

In the bustling play yard, the melody of childhood joy is composed by a symphony of nimble movements. Children's laughter echoes as they navigate through the labyrinthine jungle gyms, seizing turns on swaying ropes, propelled by the sheer force of juvenile energy. The carousal adjacent to the famed Inspiration Portal becomes their whimsical stage, where they pirouette and twirl in a dizzying dance.

Adeem and Kiya, caught in this harmonious cacophony, begin to mingle with the mirthful crowd. Their nascent interactions unfold like the lotus flower, cautiously opening to reveal an innate charm, which is keenly observed by vigilant guardians who stand ready to mediate any arising conflicts and maintain an environment conducive to growth.

Observing this tableau of youthful euphoria, Nebet, her features chiseled with wisdom, expresses a solemn sentiment. "Our progeny's mirth is the seed of our future. Each child, an embodiment of Osiris' gentle spirit, bears unique challenges and gifts. We view their struggles as akin to misaligned chakras, capable of creating emotional turmoil and self-destructive tendencies. An unhappy child, like a crop without the gift of water, will never truly thrive. Our duty is to identify these areas for growth and guide them, forming a curriculum comparable to the steady hand of Thoth. It is in their play that we discern their essence, an insight crucial for our role."

The elders and teachers, guardians of this youthful treasure, stand as stoic sentinels. Their patient watchfulness becomes the ankh, symbol of life and protection, their gaze never wavering as the whirlwind of play gradually evolves into a vortex of innate curiosity. As the transition occurs, a soft bell, reminiscent of the music of the temple, tolls. It signals the children to form an orderly line, ready to make their symbolic journey through the Portal of Knowledge.

Echoing the grandeur of the Great Sphinx gazing upon Giza, the stage unfurls beneath the auspices of the celestial Leo. In a feat of monumental human ambition, earthen piles are painstakingly crafted into a grand circular arena of unmatched precision. Its circular majesty extends 321 meters in diameter, a perfect 360-degree symbol of unity, mirroring the celestial order above.

A narrow gateway beckons amidst the towering ramparts, beyond which lays a cavernous depression within the earth's embrace. Just as the sacred Nile carves its path through the land, so does this doorway invite the young souls into the enchanting world beyond.

With the innocence of youth reflected in their wide, starry eyes, they traverse this portal into an extraordinary realm, their young hearts pulsating with the rhythm of shared fascination. An assembly of nascent minds converges here, their interests as diverse as the cosmos, their curiosities forming constellations of possibilities in their fertile minds. Each career is unveiled to them, an egalitarian display of human endeavor in all its vibrant variety.

The space is alive with the hum of free-flowing inspiration. Random clusters of eager minds form around each booth, their eager questions met by mentor's smile imbued with wisdom and encouragement. Individual interests are carefully noted, crafting a bespoke mosaic of learning tailored to elevate each child towards their unique potential.

As the day dwindles to a close, the children depart in a seemingly random fashion, each carrying an indelible imprint of the exhibit deep within their minds. An aura of enlightenment lingers in their wake, a testament to their journey of self-discovery.

With the sagacity of an ancient pharaoh, the curator addresses the silent arena, "The path you tread today and the one you shall traverse many times henceforth... it will illuminate what you must behold." His words are a beacon of hope, a testament to the beauty and potential that lies within each child, guiding them to the stars.

In the heart of an ancient city stood Alara, a mother to an ebullient five-year-old boy, Adeem, and a newborn, Maya. Her home was a radiant sanctuary of laughter and merriment, a testament to the years spent nurturing and educating her children. A loyal companion, their dog Ona, shadowed Adeem, its fidelity unwavering. At her side, Alara's longtime friend, Renni, cradled her infant daughter, Teo, while her elder daughter, Kiya, stood defiantly close.

"Our offspring embark on their scholastic voyage today," mused Renni, a note of disbelief lacing her voice. Kiya, curiosity twinkling in her eyes, tugged at her mother's sleeve, "Why is it necessary for us to partake in this, mother?" Her innocent query provoked Adeem's laughter, causing Kiya to bristle. "Cease your mockery, Adeem! You aren't the possessor of all wisdom," she retaliated, defending her dignity.

Apologetically, Adeem echoed, "My intention was not to wound you, Kiya." Alara's teachings had instilled a mature empathy in him, which was now evident. Sensing Kiya's discomfort, he cavorted like a jester to distract her from his earlier jest. His antics were rewarded with an accepting smile, a silent pardon from Kiya. In retort, Kiya quipped, "At least I do not claim to discern air!" and both erupted into hearty laughter, their bond seemingly strengthening.

Their uncanny timing of birth and an unwavering camaraderie, often elicited Renni's mirth, "Their rapport is uncanny, considering they share nearly identical birthdates!" Alara, looking on fondly, voiced her hopes, "Witnessing their growth side by side has been a delight. I aspire for this bond to remain unscathed through time."

At the helm of their first scholastic journey stood

Nebet, a slender figure in her prime, draped in the wisdom of her early twenties. Her long, obsidian hair framed her warm, brown eyes that sparkled with an undying fervor for teaching. "The inaugural day is a sight to behold," Nebet began, "Their untouched minds resonate with an insatiable curiosity. I'm Nebet, and it is my privilege to guide your children on this journey of knowledge." She spoke to the attentive mothers, her words echoing the promise of an exciting new chapter in their children's lives.

A palpable twinge of apprehension courses through Alara, her gaze transfixed on the bundles of joy that are her children. She voices her concerns to Nebet, her words ringing with the dulcet tunes of a mother's undying love. Renni, her partner in this grand journey of parenthood, displays her shared apprehension, affirming Alara's sentiments with a silent nod.

Nebet, their trusted guide and teacher, radiates an aura of tranquility, an oasis of reassurance in the desert of their fears. She listens, her eyes the embodiment of understanding, empathy etched in their depths. "Fret not," she consoles them, her words imbued with the experience of a seasoned guardian. "It is only natural to feel this way. The bonds between parents and their offspring are the most sacred. My role, though seemingly daunting, is a source of immense joy to me. And, with my trusted team by my side, we make the transition effortless for these little souls."

Her gaze sweeps over her diligent helpers, devoted individuals who pour their heart into nurturing each tender mind. A silent communication passes between them, their smiles revealing a shared commitment to the cause. Their roles are not merely to impart knowledge but to ensure that every child's individualistic essence is understood and embraced.

"There is a unique beauty that lies in each child," Nebet continues, her words echoing the wisdom of ancient times, "They are not tabula rasa. They bring with them a mosaic of talents, deficiencies, and affections, remnants from past existences. It is our duty, our privilege, to understand these diverse needs, to foster their individual growth, and to prepare them for the sacred journey they are about to undertake."

She concludes her comforting sermon, leaving Alara and Renni with a newfound sense of peace, a testament to the ancient Egyptian wisdom of nurturing the individual soul on its journey through the mysteries of life. After the morning session concludes the children are allowed to play among each other outside of the classroom which is designed to put into practice the teachings they have just encountered. Nebet notices Adeem trying to make friends with one of the other boys in the class that seems to be having trouble understanding the lesson, the boy gets frustrated with Adeem and walks away. Adeem looks puzzled, Nebet walks over, "Some children understand lessons sooner than others. Don't let it bother you.... you did the right thing caring about him." Adeem responds, "I was sitting next to him and noticed that he wasn't interested in the things he was being shown so I tried to become his friend." Nebet smiles at Adeem and gives him a hug. Comforted by his teacher Adeem notices Kiya across the school yard and goes over to her.

A fleeting sense of curiosity enveloped one of

Nebet's diligent aides, observing the unfolding rapport, he sauntered over and inquired, "What just transpired?" Nebet, with a reflective gaze, responded, "In my years of imparting wisdom, rarely have I encountered a soul as receptive as Adeem. He possesses an uncanny ability to comprehend intricate concepts with remarkable swiftness. It's truly delightful."

As the school sessions gradually unfurled under the ancient hieroglyph-etched ceiling, Nebet introduced an unconventional topic; perception training. This was designed to mold the young minds into instruments of positivity, encouraging them to interpret the world and its tribulations through an optimistic lens.

Late in the day, under the watchful eyes of sacred effigies, a disturbance arose. Nebet spotted Kiya, her small frame convulsing with sobs. With the grace of a panther, Nebet rushed to her side, her voice imbued with concern, "What befell you, Kiya? Why are the tears of Isis gracing your cheeks?"

Choked by sobs, Kiya finally managed to point a trembling finger at a boy in the class. "He assaulted me, without any provocation! He simply approached me and struck," her voice was shaky, muddled with tears.

"Oh, my dear Kiya," Nebet's voice soft with empathy, pacified her distress. After a moment of silence, as serene as the tranquil desert night, Nebet continued, "There, there. I assure you, he meant no harm. It's merely that he is still learning to interact with the fairer sex," her soothing words diffused in the air, like the gentle breeze that rustled the palm fronds outside.

Espying from a distance, Nebet observed an aide who had detained a young boy, readying to chastise him. A resolute figure adorned in the flowing linens customary of ancient Egyptian attire, Nebet interjected before the reprimand could commence. "Halt, let us not hasten to condemn," Nebet enjoined, guiding the aide, the two children, and herself towards a sturdy wooden bench nestled adjacent to the vibrant playground.

In an ambiance that was touched with subtle tones of papyrus and hints of sacred lotus, Nebet questioned the boy, her words a symphony of sternness and empathy, "Can you share why you felt the urge to act thusly towards Kiya?"

With a shuffling of feet against the baked earth, the boy confessed, his voice like a haunting echo of guilt, "I experience an odd sensation around her, which propelled me to act...I am unaware of its root, and I acknowledge my misconduct, yet I allowed it to dictate my actions."

Under the diffuse glow of the celestial vault, untouched by the direct rays of the sun, Nebet urged further, "You comprehend the impropriety of inflicting harm upon others, do you not?" The boy nodded, expressing remorse with a plea for forgiveness, "Yes, my sincerest apologies Kiya...your allure befuddles me...can you extend your grace and forgive my indiscretion?"

Kiya, although her heart echoed with lingering confusion, accepted his contrition with a nod. Nebet, the mediator of this unforeseen ordeal, worked patiently to unravel the threads of the incident, helping the children grapple with their feelings before they returned to their companions.

A look of consternation marked the aide's face as he whispered, "I can hardly believe that a boy could strike another without rhyme or reason." Nebet replied, her voice a soothing balm against his disquiet, "Let's not hasten to judgement, for he remains a well-meaning child who erred. Wisdom lies in understanding, not swift condemnation."

"Despite relentless tutelage and rigorous trials, he still stumbles? It's beyond my comprehension! I poured my very essence into his education, steadfast in the belief that my words were not falling on deaf ears," the aide lamented, his emotional storm brewing.

Nebet, a beacon of serenity amid his turmoil, meets his gaze with ancient wisdom gleaming in her eyes, "Let us not forget the sage advice passed down through our revered ancestors... never brand a child as a failure or a fool, for their understanding does not bloom in our dictated time. The mysteries they struggle with today may well be the knowledge they master tomorrow."

As the academic cycle dances its course, each pupil evolves, their hearts and minds enriched by the profound wisdom gifted by Nebet and her dutiful aides. As the sands of the year run low, Nebet infuses the twilight of the term with her ultimate impartations, revealing the purpose behind their inaugural year of enlightenment.

"You are beings of dual nature. One aspect is that which you perceive – the tangible, the intellectual, the immediate. Yet, there exists another facet, unseen, untamed - your subconscious. This enigmatic realm holds the seeds of your creativity, joy and self-definition. It will silently shape your identity, casting your journey through the cycles of existence. The subconscious, hidden yet significant, craves nurturing through mindful thoughts and actions, guided by your conscious self."

Remembering the old wisdom, the aide's agitation subsides, replaced by a renewed dedication. The ancient teachings of Egypt echo throughout the hallowed halls, guiding their youthful charges towards the dawning of their individual destinies.

"Heed your emotions, for they serve as your most authentic compass, elucidating the veracity of your present circumstances. Your heart is an unerring beacon; let its rhythm guide you. Always treasure these teachings, for their significance shall unfurl with time," Nebet, in her sage-like demeanor, imparted her final wisdom to the youthful audience. As she expressed her profound joy and esteemed privilege in having played a pivotal role in their formative journey, a subtle feeling of completion hung in the air. As the young souls, burgeoning with knowledge and wonder, began their departure, each halted momentarily to embrace Nebet and the assistants with heartfelt appreciation. Their goodbyes marked the dawn of summer, a time of freedom and camaraderie, which they embraced with laughter echoing throughout the room.

As the shadows of the night draped over the city, the flicker of a solitary candle undulated across Adeem's room, casting a spectral dance of light and shadow.

Adeem, in his bed, watched the play of luminescence with eyes wide awake. The soft creak of the door opening and the faint sound of footsteps marked the entry of his father, Hepu. With a whisper softer than the desert breeze, Hepu asked, "Are you awake, Adeem?"

"Yes, Father, slumber eludes me tonight," Adeem confessed, his voice laced with boyish innocence.

Hepu replied with a fatherly smile, "It befalls us all sometimes. On the morrow, there will be no class to attend, and I have something special to show you."

Adeem's eyes lit up with an eager spark, "Yes, Father, I would love to see it."

Thus, hand clasped in hand, the father-son duo left their humble abode, journeying towards the majestic silhouette of the Great Pyramid that loomed in the distance, under a sky blanketed by a million twinkling stars, beckoning them towards an unfolding adventure.

In the stillness of a late summer night, as the celestial bodies cast their silvery glow upon the partially risen pyramid, a certain hush descended upon the world. The pyramid, still shrouded in the enigma of incompletion, boasted a central chamber now hidden from sight, its guidance shafts recently sealed. New courses of stone were meticulously aligned, paving the way for the upcoming correction chamber, slightly offset from its predecessor. The luminous kiss of the moonlight traced a perfect geometry on the towering wall nearby, rendering an impromptu canvas to the shadows that lay against it.

From the cavernous innards of the pyramid emerged

the silhouettes of two figures - Hepu and his young son, Adeem. Seated on two solitary stones scheduled to be shifted later in the building process, they appeared to be both part and paradox of the chamber's starkness. Their eyes were drawn to the vault of the night sky, lost in the indigo blanket strewn with the twinkling jewels of constellations.

As they sat there, Hepu unfolded tales of celestial narratives to his wide-eyed son. After a moment of shared silence, his voice cut through the tranquillity, "Do you comprehend why I summoned you to this hallowed place, Adeem?" The boy, still in the tender embrace of youth, shook his head in negation.

"I desired to reveal the uniqueness within you, to share that the destiny of our lineage is intertwined with your future decisions. Despite your tender years, this is where your epoch begins," Hepu voiced solemnly. His eyes, reflecting the soft lunar glow, were set firmly on his son's face. "Understand this, Adeem, your mother and I stand by your side, guiding you through the labyrinth of life."

He paused for a moment, before continuing, "We want you to tread your own path, to seek your own truths. Even though I shall strive to illuminate your path with my wisdom, it won't always be unerring. Your convictions, your decisions, must be your own." The profound silence echoed his sentiments, and the stone chamber bore silent witness to a father's earnest lesson imparted beneath the luminescent blanket of an ancient Egyptian night.

In the silent darkness, Hepu, his sun-kissed skin adorned in a simple linen kilt, his eyes reflecting the celestial wonders above, gestured towards the grandeur of the heavenly mosaic. A glittering tapestry of celestial beings weaved in the firmament, Osiris' constellation shimmered with an ethereal luminance. He turned to his young son, Adeem, his voice echoing in the silence, as though carried by the cool zephyrs sweeping through the grand corridors of the pyramids. "Do you perceive Osiris' girdle, my son?" His question floated on the desert air, filled with ancient wisdom and paternal warmth.

Adeem's youthful eyes, mirrors of a soul filled with avid curiosity and nascent ambition, sparkled in response. "Yes, father," he declared, his voice teeming with the desire to learn. Hepu, heart swelling with pride, pointed to a particular star in the constellation, its brilliance slightly offbeat. "Observe the third star to the left of the divine belt," Hepu instructed, "It shimmers distinctively. This unique star, Adeem, has been my life's purpose, my legacy."

In the silence of the pyramid's zenith, the stars bore silent witness to this father-son ritual. Their surroundings, ancient stones imbued with tales of pharaohs seemed to hold their breath as Adeem responded. His voice, tender with awe, echoed around the structures. "The heavens are exquisite, father. I am indebted to you for sharing this."

The elder, wise in his years and laden with paternal affection, responded, "My dear Adeem, the baton of destiny now passes to you. You are destined for greatness, my son. Harness the strength of your self-belief, let it guide you. Live righteously, and life will unfold as a series of miracles. Life is a divine offering, one that should be embraced with joy and purity."

Staring into his father's eyes, Adeem nodded, his

young voice firm with conviction. "I will strive not to disappoint you or mother, father."

As the hourglass of night shed its last grains, Hepu ended their discussion, guiding Adeem through the maze-like pyramid corridors. Their trusty servant Ona maintained a respectful distance behind them. Upon reaching their abode, Hepu laid his son down to sleep, his voice a lullaby of assurance. "Sleep well, my boy. I envisage grand things for you... I hold a great love for you, Adeem."

Adeem's smile was the last thing Hepu saw as he moved towards Alara, his beloved wife, and their new-born miracle, Maya.

CHAPTER 6 - OSIRIS

The atmosphere in the humble atelier was awash with bustling fervor, as Djoser and his son, Hepu, toiled over an extraordinary undertaking that was edging towards its grand culmination. This unique enterprise entailed the creation of twin parabolic gold discs, each of astonishing proportions, spreading wide to ten feet in diameter, hollowed out in a gentle concave fashion. Like the ancient pectoral pieces of Ra, they bore a perfect polish, their surfaces radiating warmth and blinding brilliance.

These discs, akin to radar units of a time yet to come, were intended to harness, then redirect, the energy of the universe onto a singular, predetermined locus. Hepu had been appointed as the project's guardian, carrying forth the baton from Djoser who had diligently laid down the initial groundwork and architectural framework.

Radiating an aura of contentment, Djoser strolled over to the sphere of his son's industrious actions. "Hepu, my son," Djoser began, his voice filled with a father's pride, "they are beginning to take shape just as I envisioned in my dreams." Intrigued by the possibility of imperfections, he queried, "Has the surface of the golden discs attained the desired smoothness necessary for the energy to focus correctly?"

Hepu's fingers traced a gentle arc over the cool metal, every crevice and bump noted with a craftsman's keen sense, each minute flaw a whisper from the material to its shaper. As his hand came to rest on a cluster of minute indentations, his father's voice echoed in his mind, a mantra passed from generation to generation. "Indeed, there are some irregularities here, father," Hepu declared with resolute determination, "but as you've always said—"

He was interrupted by Djoser, the elder artisan smiling as he completed the adage, "any task worth undertaking is worth doing to perfection." Hepu nodded in silent agreement, the fervor in his eyes reflecting his steadfast resolve. "I'm on it, father. I yearn for these discs to be a testament to our craftsmanship, a gift worthy of the Pharaoh."

On a table nearby, the rest of the crew was engaged in the delicate task of casting a ceremonial headdress from molten gold, a regal ornament intended for an upcoming celestial event at which the Pharaoh was slated to preside.

As the day drew on, Djoser wore a subtle smile, the pride of a grandfather shining bright in his eyes. News had reached him that his first grandson, Adeem, was flourishing in his studies, mastering his seventh year of training with commendable resolve. Though mere children, Adeem and Kiya shared a bond that surpassed their years, their affection for each other conveyed through the simple, yet profound act of holding hands. As the sun set on another day, the air in the atelier was alive with promise, echoing with the whispers of work well done, and filled with the anticipation of the magnificent spectacle that was to come.

As the sun's fiery disc slipped beneath the veil of the horizon, casting its dying embers onto the majestic silhouette of the Great Pyramid, Hepu and Djoser stole away from the hubbub of their bustling shop. They navigated their way through the labyrinth of narrow alleyways and emerged onto an open street that offered an unhindered panorama of the colossal monument.

Their keen eyes drank in the spectacle unfolding before them. "The architectural marvel progresses admirably," Hepu observed, his voice echoing the satisfaction etched on his face. "The recent amendments have lent it a renewed vigor, allowing the tireless builders to continue their sacred duty."

Djoser, with the glow of the setting sun accentuating the lines of wisdom on his face, nodded in agreement. "All of life is but a tapestry of interconnected events, Hepu," he pontificated. "Our sojourn to the mysterious Stonehenge, the inspiration it kindled... it all conspired for the greater good of our people."

In the distance, a stone block was maneuvered into place, fortifying a cornerstone of the pyramid's internal ramp system. The event marked the dawn of a new phase, a stepping-stone toward the completion of the structure. Sharing a warm smile of camaraderie and satisfaction, they retreated back into their sanctuary of craftsmanship, leaving the monument to bask in the twilight.

Meanwhile, in a different corner of the vibrant city, the Pharaoh was stirring from his nocturnal repose. He awoke within the humble confines of a local dwelling, a world away from the opulence typically associated with his station. His current host, a hopeful family grappling with the sorrow of childlessness, had invited him into their hearth and home. Such arrangements were not uncommon, for the Pharaoh, much like the Nile, was a life-giving force, his mere presence alleviating the afflictions of his people.

His aura, brimming with a calming energy, had a soothing effect on those in his proximity. The Pharaoh was a transient monarch, his heart too large to be confined within a palace. Every night brought with it a different hearth, a different family, their unique tales of joy and sorrow. This nomadic lifestyle was fueled by his devotion to his people, a desire to serve that superseded the comfort of a permanent home.

His selfless love, combined with the ever-present need for his benevolent intervention, ensured a new roof over his head every evening. As the Pharaoh awoke to the gentle kiss of dawn, he prepared to pour his spirit into the challenges of another day, living his life as a servant to his people, a beacon of hope in their world.

In the hallowed annals of the ancient Egyptian civilization, the Pharaoh's stature wasn't a birthright or wrested by brute force, rather, it was a mantle earned, bequeathed by the populace who revered them. This symbolic elevation was not an arbitrary decision but rather, the result of a delicate and intricate ballet of introspection, personal evolution, catalyzed by an ongoing assessment of the individual's actions and their subsequent ramifications on the lives they touched.

This developmental journey often spanned multiple lifetimes, a gradual process like the ceaseless flow of the mighty Nile, carving and shaping the landscape of their soul. It was through this iterative dance of existence that regret and remorse served as stern taskmasters, providing invaluable lessons, subtly chiselling the raw, unpolished being into a harmonious embodiment of humanity, refined to its ultimate expression.

Perseverance in this pursuit imbued the Pharaoh with a mystical aura, an empirical energy that resonated with others. An unmistakable signal, much akin to the indomitable sphinx amidst the shifting sands, commanding recognition and reverence. This vibrancy, born of trials and transformations, was not universally equivalent in its progression. Like the lush diversity of life along the Nile's fertile banks, the pace varied, creating a diverse tapestry of evolutional rhythm.

Indeed, the journey was not merely a linear path but rather, an ascending spiral of growth. The metamorphosis was not uniform; some strode with the vigor of a charging ibex while others, like the patient crocodile, waited in the depths, emerging only when the time was ripe. Yet, each contributed to the collective wisdom, fostering an enduring ethos that would echo through the sand-kissed corridors of time, defining the complex narrative of the Pharaoh's mantle, and consequently, the ancient Egyptian civilization.

The ancient civilization was one deeply entwined in the pursuit of intellectual and spiritual ascension, fervently seeking the enlightenment of the psyche. As tightly knit with the fundamental particles of existence as with the verdant soil beneath their feet, these ancients divined from the heart of the Earth itself the knowledge they craved.

This unique understanding was rooted in their communion with an array of stones assembled within a sacred courtyard. Each stone, varied in substance and origin, interacted uniquely with the emotional wavelengths of humanity. In times of penitence and compassion, the rocks resonated, weeping a liquid substance, an empathetic echo of the humans' sorrow. This was a place of profound congregation, an expansive platform capable of supporting hundreds, where layers of these responsive stones were artfully arranged, bearing witness to humanity's collective emotional confession.

In the midst of this sacred architecture, they constructed channels, guiding the tears of the stones to collecting vessels at each end of the platform. This "anointing fluid", a substance slightly denser than water, was recognized as an extraordinary tool. When applied to the faces of monolithic stones, it temporarily transmuted their molecular structure, softening the outermost layer for a few days until the original molecular arrangement returned. This rendered the stone surfaces malleable, as if the very heart of the Earth was yielding to human touch.

In this advanced society, the selection of the Pharaoh was a solemn affair, taking place within these cavernous, gently illuminated sanctuaries. People, young and old, arranged themselves into serried lines, facing different directions, forming intricate patterns of human connection. A single, soft chime of a bell echoed, signalling the beginning of their slow march. As they moved within their lines, they encountered each other, their gaze meeting for the briefest moment - a fleeting communion.

This was the process known as "Pointing", a mechanism driven by an intuitive glance and the perception of the other's soul. It was a simple question asked silently, "Does this person carry a purer spirit than mine?" There was no place for self-righteousness in this exercise, for everyone knew the survival and future of their kind depended on the honesty and purity of this ritual.

The Pointing, this act of discernment, held immense gravity for them, for the selected Pharaoh was tasked with guiding the virtuous into their next existence, leading them to their next planetary home. This was a duty of transcendental importance, a responsibility that served as a beacon for their collective pursuit of spiritual and intellectual ascension. Thus, they continued their journey, intertwined with the earth and the atoms of existence, seeking wisdom and spiritual elevation.

In the silent eternity of those countless hours, a grand design gradually materialized - a pyramidal hierarchy traced out in lines, placing the most esteemed beings on its sublime apex. An invisible hand plucked the topmost threads from hundreds of such gatherings, weaving them into a tapestry spanning eons, even transcending the confines of singular lives. The final weave was a solemn verdict, pointing the way to the ascension of a Pharaoh.

This honor was not bestowed frivolously. Rather, it was an accolade that distinguished the pinnacle of human excellence, chosen after intricate calculations and mysterious deliberations, worthy only to those destined for greatness. The insignia of Pharaoh was an all-consuming beacon of affirmation and reverence, inflaming the incumbent with a fiery passion and a thirst for knowledge, that was unlike anything known to the common man.

This divine consecration served to intensify the Pharaoh's comprehension of the enigma that was existence itself, granting them amplified insight into the often convoluted tapestry of life. Their heightened perception sent ripples throughout the universe. It was charged with an energy so profound that it reshaped their understanding of reality, allowing them to grasp concepts beyond the comprehension of most humans.

Embracing the mighty mantle of the Pharaoh ignited a transformation so significant, it dwarfed the mundane and earthly concerns of mere mortals. The Pharaoh, through their ascension, was allowed an intimate glimpse into the wellspring of universal knowledge, shedding light on aspects of existence far beyond the reach of the average human being. The mystery of life was thus unveiled, allowing them to magnify their faculties of perception, transcend their earthly confines, and soar into realms previously uncharted.

The spectacle of the Pharaoh's ascension was a testament to the intricate weave of destiny and the profound depths of human potential. This was the ultimate purpose of the silent ceremonies - the creation of a beacon of knowledge and power, forever shining in the annals of time.

The morning twinkled like a star in the darkest night as a deep groan and grumble could be heard throughout the city while the construction of the Pharaoh's Pyramid continued at a steady pace. People are gushing with anticipation as each layer of the pyramid was completed. The Pharaoh would be seen admiring the work being accomplished as he made his way to the next family in need. Random people flocked around the pharaoh to experience his energy and then resume working or tending to their family and friends. The completion of the pyramid would be the pinnacle achievement of their human existence.

As the star-strewn night unfurled, celestial spears arched in the heavens, their incandescent trails the very embodiment of cosmic forces, releasing their kinetic vitality into the eyes of the fortunate onlookers. Amid this radiant spectacle, figures of prominence, including the revered Pharaoh himself, descended to the sacred retreat of the Contemplation Natatorium. They converged, eager to draw from the universal energy that painted the firmament above on a night resplendent in crystalline clarity. A sense of conviviality permeated the atmosphere as melodies weaved seamlessly with flowing wine, wrapping the already mirthful assembly in a comforting cloak of mild inebriation.

Amid this jubilant milieu was Hepu, the man of the moment, basking in the company of his beloved kin and compatriots. His joy, however, was soon punctuated by the arrival of a messenger, a harbinger dispatched under the mandate of the Pharaoh himself.

"Is the gentleman Hepu present?" inquired the envoy with utmost courtesy. Hepu, his gaze unbroken, acknowledged his identity. With an inviting sweep of his hand, he graciously offered the newcomer a place among them, "Join us?"

In response, the messenger humbly declined. "Honored sir, I am here on the Pharaoh's bidding. He seeks your audience - privately, if it would not inconvenience you."

The Pharaoh's request was overheard by Alara. Her eyes sparkled with an amalgam of elation and pride, her heart throbbing with anticipation at her spouse's summons. Hepu, acceding to the request, disengaged from the comforting warmth of the lower bath. With measured strides, he followed the messenger, ascending towards the upper precincts where the Pharaoh basked in the silvery glow of the moon.

"Gratitude for your presence, Hepu," the Pharaoh acknowledged his arrival, his voice barely above a whisper. "Will you partake in the blessings of this bath with me?"

In answer, Hepu immersed himself in the grand basin, letting the heated water's soothing caress envelop him as he joined the Pharaoh, their silhouettes etched against the iridescent backdrop of an ancient Egyptian night.

In the gentle embrace of the evening's calm, the Pharaoh, donned in regal grandeur, began to articulate his thoughts. "There is something enchanting about this nocturnal cloak, Hepu," he stated, his eyes reflecting the twinkling constellations, "It's a time when solitude bestows upon me its tranquil charm, allowing my thoughts to journey unguided through the abyss of introspection."

Across the ambience of the spa, Hepu found a comfortable perch, taking to his tasks diligently, refilling the sovereign's goblet and his own with the ruby-hued nectar of the vine. His curiosity, however, was beginning to rival the ambrosial liquid. "Might you be wondering, Hepu, why I've requested your presence in this celestial hush?" posed the Pharaoh, his voice echoing off the stone walls. Hepu's nod in affirmation was discreet, his attention momentarily lost to the divine nectar he swirled in his cup.

"Word has reached me of your commendable resolution of the quandary that previously bound us," the Pharaoh expressed, gratitude weaving its way into his tone. "A tribute to your merit is due."

The sense of pride that blossomed within Hepu was evident in his eyes and the arc of his lips as he replied, "Serving the kingdom with my skills has been an honor unparalleled."

He let his gaze wander, becoming entranced by the dance of moonlight on the water's surface. It was as if a silver-scaled shoal was frolicking just beneath the surface, their scales twinkling with each ripple. "I do hope you won't mind, Your Majesty, if I seek clarification on a matter or two?" Hepu inquired, pausing momentarily before proceeding. "The link between here and yonder..."

However, the Pharaoh, comprehending Hepu's query even before it was fully voiced, began to navigate through the tranquil pool towards its edge. As he leaned over the side, a second pool revealed itself. This one was a mirror to the world, its surface unbroken, a perfectly still body of water lying just beneath their own, a mystifying spectacle under the stars.

Bathed in the ethereal glow of moonlight, the tranquil surface of the pool shimmered like a polished slab of obsidian, immaculate and enigmatic. Poised at the water's edge, the noble Pharaoh spread his arms wide, a measured distance separating his hands. His sovereign demeanor portrayed an unruffled grace as he dipped his index fingers into the still pool, just breaking the serenity of the water's surface. The action initiated gentle disturbances, concentric circles of ripples spreading outwards, a spectacle mirrored on the pool's floor with stark clarity, thanks to the divine illumination of the celestial night.

Drawn towards this sight, Hepu, the Pharaoh's confidant, positioned himself beside the regal figure, his eyes observing the spectacle. The Pharaoh, meanwhile, began a rhythmic dance with his fingers, a meticulous and enchanting back and forth motion over the water surface. The resulting pattern was a symphony of wavelets, a grand ballet of concentric circles radiating from the royal digits, their paths echoing throughout the pool.

Between the Pharaoh's fingers, the waves met,

merging and progressing unabated, as if galvanized by their interaction. They seemed to gain momentum upon crossing, their ripples cascading outwards like messages sent to the universe. "Observe, Hepu," the Pharaoh whispered, his voice a hypnotic lullaby in the stillness. "See how alternating waves unite, fostering a connection between two points?"

His words wove an intricate narrative. "Just imagine the slow turning of time's fabric as our Earth accelerates its rotation, moving in tandem with the other celestial bodies that harbor life. As they twirl and hum in the symphony of electromagnetic energies, they weave the connections between one another, forming a bridge across the cosmos. This is the chariot that shall carry us to a brave new world."

His display of mystic water orchestration continued, the pulsating waves bearing testament to his powerful assertion. Then, as suddenly as it began, the Pharaoh withdrew his fingers, ceasing the rhythmic dance. He retreated back, sinking into his regal seat, his gaze lost in the depths of the star-drenched sky above.

"I could spend an eternity basking in this view," he murmured, his tone one of quiet reverence for the nocturnal beauty that unfurled around them. Hepu echoed his sentiments, nodding in agreement, finding solace in the peaceful night. "Indeed," he murmured, settling into his own seat across from the Pharaoh. "So could I... so could I."

As the echoes of the final Pyramid's construction dissipate, a distinct sonorous hum rises from a distant field, setting in motion a grand spectacle of creation. Emissaries of the Pharaoh, potent and resolute, delineate the skeletal framework for a monumental vantage point, a surveillance platform ordained for the highest power of the land. The framework is not just a motley assembly of wooden beams, but a gigantic circumzenithal arc, a semicircular testament of wood standing tall, an epitome of craftsmanship stretched across a hundred feet, its ends breaching the sky.

Upon nearing completion, a celestial exchange unfolds. From the heart of Djoser's sanctum, twin artifacts of resplendent gold - two magnifying dishes, are summoned. Conceived in the artisan's workshop, these golden discs are meticulously affixed at each towering end of the wooden arc. Suspended thirty feet aloft, they command an unhindered view of the cosmos, ready to harness the cryptic energies of the universe.

Bathing in the effulgent beams cascading downwards, a flattened table rests at the crux of the apparatus, laid out on an innovative track system, poised to receive the concentrated bounty of celestial energy.

In the sanctum's observatory, scholars clad in scholarly vestments labor with an air of intense concentration. Their task? To divine the precise cosmic hour for the grand spectacle. The heavens answer their call. A mere four nights remain until the cosmic ballet unfolds.

In the midst of familial engagements, the Pharaoh is apprised of the progress and the prophecy. Guided to a chamber of meditation, he finds himself encircled by a gathering of Electrolytes, a small but potent cohort.

A paradigm shift is about to occur in the life of the Pharaoh. He bids farewell to the family, promising to return transformed. In the days that will precede the grand spectacle, he consigns himself to the care of the Electrolytes. Together, they plunge into a realm of deep mental ablution, fostering and expanding magnification through the positive harmonic vibrations resonating from humanity, the echoes of their lives from far-flung corners of the world, and even more intensely, from the throbbing heart of the city itself.

As the day of the spectacle draws closer, anticipation crescendos, a prelude to an event that is destined to change everything. The Pharaoh, his gaze fixed on the horizon, prepares for the grand unveiling. As the curtain of evening unfurls, the cosmos meticulously configures itself into a cryptic celestial codex, awaiting decipherment. Embraced by the ebon depth of night, the lunar beacon embarks on its solitary sojourn to the opposite reaches of Gaia, while the constellations shimmer in the firmament like myriad ephemeral fireflies.

The silhouettes of colossal monoliths, amongst which the noble Sphinx holds dominion, emerge as phantasmal sketches, dancing on the canvas of the night. Their spectral reflections flicker in harmony with the myriad lanterns punctuating the cityscape, their light interwoven with the texture of the dark. The joyous cacophony of laughter, jubilant cheers, the clinking of goblets, and the enticing aroma of abundant feasts saturates the air, as a sea of humanity gathers to celebrate the event.

Reclining in his sanctum of preparation, Pharaoh is

the focal point of a hive of activity. Attendants flutter around him like industrious bees around a revered monarch. He is the cynosure of every eye, dressed in the most resplendent of fabrics, his regality further amplified by a magnificent headdress of pure gold.

The headdress, a veritable masterpiece, resembles a perfected diamond apex, bearing intricate channels. It is not mere adornment, but a symbol of profound cosmic connection, a conduit crafted with purpose. It is believed to channel the divine, unifying the Pharaoh with the esoteric dimensions of their own humanity. This direct link with the universe is paramount, a mystical alignment, heralding not just a physical transformation, but a celestial dialogue with the essence of their being.

Immersed in a melodic embrace, the metropolis resonates with the symphony of stringed instruments and ethereal singing, the rhythmic cadences intertwining in a ceremonial prelude to the anticipated augury. Emergent from the shadowy sanctuary, the Pharaoh, in all his royal regalia, makes his appearance. Adorned in a headdress of unique creation, befitting of the occasion, he embodies divine authority.

As his silhouette is unveiled to the public gaze, a solitary cheer ascends, igniting a euphoric eruption of joyous acclaim throughout the vast gathering. A duo of men stand at the helm of each ceremonial dish, their readiness underscored by a solemn aura of purpose.

Once the Pharaoh graces the epicentre of the grand tableau, he reclines in regal resplendence upon the appointed table, his figure echoing an immortal engraving on the tapestry of time. The celestial sphere above glimmers with a chorus of twinkling stars, each a celestial beacon eager to impart its cryptic knowledge to the earthly monarch. The mystery of the cosmos dances on the precipice of revelation, its ancient secrets ready to unfurl in the hallowed court of the Pharaoh.

Beneath the indigo cloak of the night sky, an expectant hush blankets the vast assembly. Hepu, Alara, Adeem, and their infant gem, Miya, stand as a beacon of familial unity in the midst of loved ones, their hearts nurturing the seed of anticipation for the ritual's successful outcome. Like a vessel guided by the invisible hand of the cosmos, the Pharaoh, veiled from the world of sight, is led towards the ceremonial table.

His ascension onto the platform is akin to an ethereal ballet; he reclines delicately, presenting himself to the infinite cosmic expanse above. The platform, a symbol of celestial alignment, glides him into position between the arms of the sacred dishes. Its tracks, honed to a flawless smoothness, silently guide the Pharaoh to the heart of the grand arc, its curve mimicking that of the distant horizon.

At journey's end, a faint chime of metal resonates, signaling the merging of the Pharaoh's headdress with the golden receptor plate of the arc. It's a union of the temporal and the eternal, a tangible mark of the Pharaoh's communion with the cosmos. Poised on the periphery, four scribes stand vigilant, quills at the ready, prepared to transcribe the messages whispered from the lips of the universe into the subconscious of the Pharaoh.

The command is issued, and the sacred discs cast

their gaze skyward. Amplified by the night, their focus descends onto the Pharaoh's countenance, his eyes shut in reverent patience. In this moment, he becomes a conduit, awaiting the cosmic enlightenment that the universe is poised to bestow upon him.

The distinguished Djoser, his son Hepu, and their entourage stand imposingly at the terminus of the sacred arch, their countenances illuminated by the radiance of gleaming gold discs hovering aloft. "Behold the fruits of our labor, Hepu," Djoser proclaims with a reverential upward glance.

Casting their shadows long, the assembled multitude kneel, their hands angled outward, flanking their visages in a reverent plea to draw from the wellspring of cosmic vitality. Hepu, with eyes awash in uncertainty, queries his father, "What pace will he garner the essence?"

"As swift as the discs align with the veiled facets of his gaze... It establishes an immediate pathway into his psyche," Djoser elaborates, his voice threading through the now hushed whispers of the expectant gathering.

Perched at the nexus of anticipation, the Pharaoh holds a quill in each hand, poised as if a conductor of an orchestra unseen. Scrolls of parchment lay eager to etch the wisdom of the ages, their fabric stretched taut, awaiting the rhythm of a scribe's dance.

And then, like silent thunder, energy beams converge upon the Pharaoh. Resembling serpents of lightning, they gently graze his figure, stirring his hands into a slow dance over the parchment. As the connection solidifies, the spectacle unfolds - the Pharaoh's hands transcribing divine knowledge with fervor, then a wild tempest of script.

With parchment cascading through their fingers at an unheard pace, the scribes struggle to keep pace with the inked choreography. Djoser points, his voice resonating with wonder, "See the marvel!" The gasp of the crowd is a collective intake of breath, a whisper of awe threading the air. The transformation of the Pharaoh's eyes into twin vortexes of electric azure is the crowning spectacle - an echo of celestial energy mirrored on the earthly realm, leaving the crowd entranced in the cosmic ballet.

Exhaustion draped itself like a thick shroud around the once radiant Pharaoh. His strength, usurped by the transcendent event, diminished and his once steadfast gaze had lost its lustre. As if driven by the unseen hands of the gods, he was gently ushered from the vortex of attention, no longer the fulcrum of this grand spectacle. His entourage guided him towards the sanctuary of solitude, a serene chamber that offered restorative reprieve. In that space, he was to convalesce, the echoes of the grandeur that was, serving as a tender lullaby.

The ethereal rhapsody had reached its crescendo and now gently faded into the annals of memory. The congregation of awestruck observers began to scatter like the remnants of a potent dream at dawn's first light. Amidst the ebbing crowd, a fellowship of faithful individuals converged upon Hepu, their gratitude cascading in a symphony of praise for his monumental contribution at Stonehenge.

With the passage of a magical night and the retreat of

the merrymakers, the ambient air seemed to embrace the surface of serenity. Hepu found himself ensnared in a tender moment with Alara, their lips meeting in a sweet exchange of shared triumph before she escorted their progeny and kin home. Their voices, a dwindling symphony, carried tales of an unforgettable night.

In the wake of the vanishing festivities, Djoser and Hepu remained, their figures outlined by the ethereal glow of the arc above. As the moon bore silent witness, the echoes of exhilaration retreated, giving way to a hushed tranquility. The night, once alive with emotional fervor, surrendered to a quiet, tranquil zenith, their shared gaze lost in the intricate tapestry of the cosmos above.

In the echo of a long past silence, Djoser finally vocalized his thoughts, "The artisans of words will indeed face a Herculean task." Hepu, his offspring, contemplated the silence before inquiring, "So, our calculations have proven accurate?"

Djoser affirmed, his voice resonating with an air of mystic knowledge, "Indeed, the communion was fruitful, judging by the magnitude of script that now lies before us. They will decipher the enigma of data in the days to follow. Then, with certainty, we will bear the knowledge of our departure timeline."

Father and son shared a moment of silent admiration, absorbing the significance of the celestial marvel they had just witnessed. Djoser, the fountainhead of wisdom, began to enlighten his son once more, "Every life-bearing entity in the cosmos reaches its zenith. Our earth is at its apex of glory, yet its subtle trembling hints at its ephemeral existence.

In every star system, a planet teems with life, nestling at varying stages of existence. It is our duty to seek out such a planet and comprehend its position in the grand cycle of life. Similar to the cosmos, our earth is teeming with a myriad of souls, each unique in their own essence."

He locked eyes with Hepu, his voice softening, "My beloved Hepu, you are not merely a son to me, but an amalgamation of many past existences. I see glimpses of my own mother and your mother within you. Life holds more magic and wonder than the majority ever comprehend, and we are truly fortunate to be among those discerning few who understand its intricacies."

His voice carried the rhythm of the cosmic dance, "The river of time can flow backwards or forwards, much like alternating current. The cosmic law of Karma steers our destiny by harnessing the energy created by our existence. Time is the cosmic scale that ensures balance, as our actions and thoughts shape the life force that guides us to a specific life and era."

A knowing look passed between them, followed by an affectionate smile, their shared understanding cementing their bond. A warm embrace followed, as they turned towards home, their thoughts filled with the loved ones waiting for them.

CHAPTER 7 – FIRST LOVE

Etched into the rich tapestry of existence, an ancient adage reverberated in the eager minds of Adeem and his companions. This resounding wisdom flowed through the amphitheater, carrying the weight of centuries, as they found themselves in the midst of their inaugural lesson of the day. Lifelong comrades, Anen and Kawab, bore witness alongside Adeem to the unveiling of truths transcending temporal bounds; shared trials and triumphs of adolescence under the watchful eyes of the pyramids had forged an unbreakable bond between them.

Their mentor, a figure of compelling distinction, dominated the space at the heart of the room. His towering form was a tribute to his unwavering spirit, defying the toll of time, whilst his silvery mane cascaded over his shoulders like a stream reflecting the moonlight. The contour lines on his face, etched by the endless flow of years, were a testament to his deep-seated wisdom, yet bore the subtle hint of past sorrows. As his twisted smile played upon his lips, he beguiled the students, unveiling the mysteries of the most potent of human forces - love.

"Love," he began with a resonant timbre, "is an energy constantly yearning for manifestation." He allowed his words to linger in the hushed air, drawing the young minds deeper into his woven tale. "It is this ethereal force which constitutes our very humanity. It holds enough power to either amplify or subdue your own life energy, oscillating you between the realms of joy and despair."

With a penetrating gaze, he swept over the sea of youthful faces. "Neglect the teachings of this class, and you will pay the price in the currency of your future happiness."

Transcending time and space, love was not merely a transient feeling but an eternal force passed down through the ages. This was the paradoxical challenge they had to conquer. Their education would serve as the igniting spark, not just for a romantic relationship but for a deeper understanding of human connection, harnessing love's energy in its raw, primal form, shaping their destinies forever.

Enshrouded by the shadows of the lecture hall, Ipy's students exchanged glances, beginning to comprehend the magnitude of the journey that lay ahead. The scribe Ipy, in his twelfth season of enlightening the minds of the forthcoming generation, did so with a joy that resonated in the sacred halls of learning. He, like an old temple wall bearing the wear of time, did not shy away from revealing the mosaic of his emotions, having been honed by life's trials, tempered in the fires of regret.

Ipy, a man molded by the Nile's ebb and flow, was not without his faults. In the twilight of his own folly, he had tread paths he knew to be fraught with peril. Yet, despite his better wisdom, he had plunged headlong into these ill-advised rites of passage, etching into his mind an indelible testimony of their consequence.

With a memory as enduring as the Sphinx, he bore the weight of his past transgressions, understanding how they had reshaped the contours of his life. Surveying the sea of youthful faces before him, a multitude of dreams and aspirations reflected in their eyes, he recognized his profound impact. His words, like a chisel upon a stone tablet, could sculpt their identities, and thus, he chose them with the utmost care, mindful of the powerful legacy his teachings would bestow.

"Without love, existence becomes barren," was the primordial wisdom imparted during the inaugural lesson of Adeem's tutelage. Now twelve, Adeem had blossomed into a vivacious youth, who savored existence and the fellowship of those who shared his world. He navigated through his years of learning, radiating a vitality that was infectious, his spirit always undulating with a sense of positivity.

Adept at harnessing his thoughts, Adeem learned the art of forgiveness, understanding that striving for perfection meant embracing a life journey brimming with as few regrets as possible. His inherent wisdom, betraying an age beyond his years, evoked admiration among his mentors and companions, creating ripples of awe as he traversed his path with an uncanny maturity.

At the room's farthest corner, two tutors' aides conversed in hushed tones, their eyes fixed on the young Adeem. "Behold, there he stands," one murmured to the other, a finger discreetly pointing towards the boy. "It is he, the one touched by the extraordinary gift," she declared in a whisper that barely reached the other's ears. "Undoubtedly, echoes of past life wisdom are resonating within him," the other affirmed, adding an air of mystique to the young prodigy.

In the ambience of an intellectual gathering, Adeem found himself ensconced comfortably, nestled amidst his preferred instructive exploration, under the erudite guidance of Ipy, the cherished mentor. Their initial encounter was serendipitous at the quaint locale of Djoser's establishment, where Adeem's father was a frequent patron. Adeem's presence there, initially incidental, metamorphosed into a profound meeting of minds. Ipy, in the midst of seeking inspiration for his creative endeavors, was drawn to the latent wisdom shimmering within Adeem. A congenial rapport swiftly took shape, founded upon a mutual magnetism and a shared proclivity for positivity, which was the essence of Ipy's demeanor.

Kiya, a harmonious spirit, would often accompany Adeem in these scholastic pursuits, their camaraderie rooted in intellectual discussions and insightful interpretations of their teachings. It was during these shared moments of discovery that Ipy would suddenly pronounce his cryptic yet intriguing philosophies.

"Envision love as an acquired sagacity, the master key to unlock the vault of bliss," Ipy would proclaim to the eager young minds in his purview. His words, mysterious and seemingly disconnected, served to stimulate their attentiveness, fostering a classroom dynamic of anticipation and curiosity.

"This is Ipy, standing before you, bearing the privilege of illuminating your understanding of the elusive energy of love. As we navigate its course, the repercussions are vast and transformative. Love, a potent force, engenders life yet can metamorphose it into the harshest reality conceivable. Imbued with the knowledge that the equilibrium of life's forces is crucial for our journey, it becomes vividly apparent that this balance can easily falter if the engaged individuals lack the consciousness or appreciation of their shared circumstance. The quest at hand revolves around the amplification of our vital life force, an ethereal potency within which one can actualize monumental feats aligned with life's vibrant objectives.

This is the reason for your presence here, an earnest desire to gain wisdom, and to set a course towards the most pivotal epoch of your existence. I stand before you, assigned to serve as your guide on this heroic odyssey upon which you are on the precipice of embarking. You have already encountered diverse shades of love. The familial bond shared with your parents, siblings, and even the affection bestowed upon your cherished pets. Friendships too offer a variant of love, establishing connections that transcend the bonds of kinship. These variations of love, though significant, are not the ones that will accompany you entirely. The love destined to transform your existence, an eternal companion, is the love of your life.

This significant other is the one with whom your fate will remain inextricably entwined, traversing the infinite continuum of time. This is why you find yourself within this scholarly setting, for it is intended to pave the pathway towards your ultimate contentment. Drawing upon ancient wisdom and timeless truths, we venture forth into this journey of love and life, leaving behind the familiar, embarking on the uncharted. The echo of our past guides us, as we strive to remain mindful of its lessons, but our eyes remain fixed on the future, excited by the possibilities it holds.

Yet, ere we embark on this journey, let us gaze upon the tapestry of existence in its entirety. For indeed, the resonance of the affection you will come to know is undeniably nourished by the grandeur of our milieu. If the world were steeped in the bitter brew of intolerance and bigotry, gleaning a substantial measure of love's pure energy would prove arduous, for the reservoir to draw from is meager. Love, while kindled by two, finds fortification in the collective. This truth, etched in our consciousness, reverberates even now as we perceive our existence requiring refinement, fully cognizant of our flaws.

Yet in the age to come, we may be recognized not for what we are but for something fundamentally different. The cyclical rhythm of Gaia's dance upon the cosmic stage intimates that we are nearing the zenith of cerebral alignment with our universe. As this ephemeral moment fades into the annals of time and we make our exodus from this world, a new iteration of humanity shall inherit the earth. These successors, burdened by diminished computational capacities, may find themselves ill-equipped to make judicious decisions, thus catalyzing an avalanche of emotional devastation. Emotions, though volatile, operate within a defined schema. Upon realizing this, we gain the wisdom to harness them judiciously, mitigating the specter of remorse. This transformative understanding paints the path forward, a journey brimming with potential for enlightened love, unshackled by the ghosts of regret."

Amidst a gathering of eager eyes, Ipy found his seat of wisdom, carrying the gravity of an orator. He reached out to a modest chalice, delicately etched with ancient symbols. Tenderly, he took a sip of the life-giving liquid, its coolness whispering a story of existence that had traversed the veins of his land. Placing it back, he began to share the rivulets of his memory.

"In my youth, much like yourselves, I too sat among knowledge seekers, learning from a mentor, an echo of my current self. She forewarned me about the unpredictable flames of love, the consuming fire that could be tamed but never truly controlled."

His eyes wandered into the distant past, exploring a tale of a maiden, "A gentle soul bore affections for me, yet my heart did not echo her sentiments. I was a willful pupil, challenging conventions." A ghost of a smile crossed his lips, reflecting a tinge of regret.

"Tuya... her name was a song in the wind. Her allure was undeniable. And yet," Ipy's voice wavered, "her heart belonged to another."

He rested a moment, savoring the bitter sweet draught from his cup. "It is said that women possess a keen intuition in selecting their mate. My foolish heart would not heed. I danced the fool's dance, laying bare my feelings for her. I let the embers of other possibilities die out... extinguishing potential love."

His gaze, intense and sincere, swept over his audience, "Can you fathom? Love, the most exquisite gift, was within my grasp, and yet I let it pass me by. In time, Tuya found solace in the arms of her beloved. And I, I found myself alone."

"No room for envy or jealousy, we respected each other's sentiments. Then came Menna, a sweet soul who loved me fiercely. At times, I reciprocated, yet failed to truly appreciate her unwavering affection, resulting in an undercurrent of dissatisfaction."

His words stirred the air, "We shared a lifetime, an emotional dance at a fundamental level. Every time we aspired to ascend to the higher realms of love, our disparities pulled us back, the euphoria dimming into a low hum."

"The energy of love," he mused, "is a complex tapestry that lures us, prompting our every action. What you weave in this existence will shape the next, just as the threads of your past lives have interwoven into the fabric of your present."

His tale completed, Ipy receded into silence, his audience captivated by the undulating rhythms of his life story, etched in the timeless sands of the heartland.

As the final bell tolls, Adeem and his companions, Anen and Kawab, make a swift departure from the austere confines of the school. They weave their way to the vibrant heart of the harbor, where the skeletal forms of countless vessels are nestled under the attentive gazes of their artisans. Amidst the bustle and the brine-soaked air, a team of laborers turn their focus to a craft that has been marred by a recent tempest, their hands dancing in unison across the scarred hull. They carefully carve fresh timber and forge the thick wedges which serve as the sinews of the sea-bound behemoths.

At the boatyard's farthest reach stands a lengthy jig, cradling a soon-to-be mast submerged in a concoction known only to the skilled shipwrights. "Behold," Adeem muses to his friends, their eyes wide at the spectacle, "this is not quite the same as our regular school day." Their shared laughter echoes amidst the cacophony of the work site, drawing the attention of a seasoned worker.

"You lads appear enamored with our craft, why not come and lend a hand?" He beckons with a grin as warm as the breeze. Without a moment's hesitation, the trio rushes to the heart of the boatyard, their youthful energy a stark contrast to the weathered hands of the workers.

"If your hearts desire to learn our trade, we welcome you after your duties at home and school," he continues, his voice seasoned with a lifetime on the docks. Their response is unanimous and quick, their young voices harmonizing in their eagerness, "Yes, please. We would like that very much."

Their beaming faces, reflecting the joy of their newfound opportunity, bring a reminiscent smile to the worker's face. Their youthful enthusiasm, bright as a crescent moon on a midsummer's night, is a familiar mirror of his own deep-seated love for the boatyard, reminding him of his early days in this bustling maritime sanctuary.

In the golden epoch of a forgotten time, the ebullient initiation of youthful aspirations was not merely tolerated but championed by the venerable masters of their craft. These elder artisans perceived the dreams of the younger generation as the lifeblood of their sacred wisdom, an unbroken cord weaving the past into the future. In a harmonious world suffused with a transcendent positivity, humanity had evolved to accommodate longer craniums, vessels for the enigmatic abilities of telepathy and telekinesis. The dissemination of ancient wisdom from one generation to the next was tantamount to the symbolic rebirth of these esoteric abilities, each era uncovering innovative ways to amplify their inherent talents.

A currency of passion replaced tangible means of exchange, eradicating commerce altogether. In this societal paradigm, individuals dedicated themselves to the disciplines they adored, rendering services out of love, rather than obligation. The concept of individual success was rendered obsolete in this collective society—no single inhabitant could claim victory unless the triumph belonged to all.

Beneath the tutelage of these practiced artisans, the youth initiated their sacred dance with their chosen crafts, their nascent talent shimmering like stars against the inky expanse of the unknown. Among them, Adeem, a promising novice, was carefully observing the rhythm of his labor. His cheeks were adorned by a sheen of perspiration, as his grin bore the testament of his contentment. A silver droplet, having escaped from his brow, hovered precariously in mid-air, evoking a captivating, yet transient, moment of serenity.

Meanwhile, Kiya, a young maiden radiating a celestial charm, was gracefully approaching Adeem, her arm outstretched with a plate of sustenance—an age-old symbolic gesture marking her choice of a lifelong companion. As their hands clasped, a profound energy ignited between them. The palpable oscillation of positive and negative energies marked the inception of their shared journey, echoing the cosmic dance of unity that was at the heart of their civilization. The silent pact was thus made, a testament to their commitment in a world where every being and action held a grander significance, transcending the mundane into the extraordinary.

Amid the hallowed sands of time, the tale of Adeem and Kiya echoes, their mutual affection creating a harmony seldom found. Their connection, etched in their hearts, was as captivating as it was profound. They embraced, letting their love manifest as an ethereal halo of radiant gold light. This spectacle, raw and genuine, sparked a spark in the spectators at the boat yard.

The energy emanating from them was so potent that it was tangible. The onlookers, both young and seasoned, beheld the spectacle, caught in the wave of their love. Their applause and rhythmic shouts reached a crescendo, then gradually dwindled into a poignant silence.

Meanwhile, the Pharaoh was alerted about the spectacular scene unfolding. Upon his arrival, the expanse of silence served as a canvas for the vivid illustration of their love. The couple, Adeem and Kiya, were soon in his presence, their love story becoming a shared narrative.

As the moonlight danced over the trio, they basked in their silence. Their emotions were as grand as the obelisks that lined the royal path, a silent affirmation of their deep connection. A multitude had gathered, drawn by the echo of their love. Everyone sought to catch a fleeting glimpse of the beautiful spectacle, a beacon of pure energy amid the tranquil night. Theirs was not a mere love story; it was an unforgettable chronicle of affection etched in the annals of time.

In an unhurried, revered motion, the Pharaoh lifted his arms, his palms ceremonially touching in a skyward gesture. In the ethereal vicinity of his hands, Kiya and Adeem felt a profound stir within their souls, akin to an inner magnetism drawing upon their vital forces. Amidst this uncanny sensation, they beheld a diminutive orb of luminescence burgeoning just above the Pharaoh's hands.

Gradually, this orb of light evolved into a holographic spectacle - a dove, resplendent in its brilliant whiteness, hovered in stationary flight. The wind's gentle kiss played upon its wings, emblematic of the ebbing flow of time. The extraordinary tableau illuminated the visages of the spellbound observers, reflecting the wonder of the moment.

Kiya and Adeem, touched by the symbolic bird, found their souls in a tacit communion as the Pharaoh's soft utterances wafted around them. "This is your love, untouched, pristine," his voice resonated, entrancing them into a profound connection of their life energies.

In the city's distant quarter, the news of this budding romance reached the ears of their elders, Dosjer and Hepu. Discarding their protective attire, they burst into jubilant laughter, the infectious sound marking the beautiful commencement of their progeny's journey. The boatyard beckoned them, their hearts swelling with joy at the Pharaoh's divine intervention.

The Pharaoh continued, his voice filling the air, "This dove symbolizes your love. It shall soar on the winds of understanding, flying true only when you both comprehend the sacred journey that lies before you. Through the epochs, you'll learn from each other, instill wisdom in each other, building the bedrock upon which your family shall thrive. There will be tribulations and missteps, but be prepared to surrender your individual selves, for each other... else, you are not yet ready to embrace love."

An enchanting symphony had been set in motion, its melody seeping into every crevice of the jubilant gathering. The esteemed Pharaoh's wisdom unfurled like a sacred papyrus, unfaltering and poignant. "The genesis of any journey holds the keys to its eventual glory. In the realm of love, too, one must strive for a heart unburdened by remorse. For it is regret that clips the wings of the dove of affection, sending it spiraling towards doom."

In the midst of this, Hepu, his gaze as sharp as an obelisk, discerned Dedu, Kiya's sire, observing his progeny and Adeem from the crowd's periphery. With the grace of a warm breeze, he approached the elder, confiding in hushed undertones. "A premonition tugged at my intuition regarding those two, their bond seems almost ethereal. It's as if they've been sculpted from the same stone, destined for a grand tapestry woven by the divine loom."

Their eyes met and locked, watching the tender spectacle of their offspring dancing on the precipice of a blossoming romance. Emotion surged like the flooding of the sacred river, unbidden tears mirroring the profundity of the moment. They embraced, their hearts beating the rhythm of shared sentiment. "Our path lies in shepherding them through this journey, Hepu. Your lineage's confluence with ours brings me a pride as vast as the earth itself," Dedu proclaimed.

In the gentle stillness, Alara's gaze finds Adeem's calloused palms, a testament to his recent endeavors. "Such hands are now born of the boat yard, I see," she notes, her words weaving through the air with maternal concern. His face softens, the corners of his lips reluctantly unfurling into a smile of undisguised joy, rivaling the lustrous crescent of the moon above. "Mother, I discovered something else today. An emotion, profound and uncharted," he confesses, hesitating to catch his breath.

"Love. It's Kiya, mother. Our souls sing in harmony and I have never known such happiness. I yearn for your blessings, and father's too. I wish to spend my life adoring her," Adeem reveals, his voice imbued with sincerity. Alara falls silent, retreating into the sanctuary of her thoughts, her heart heavy with the poignancy of her son's transformation. She had once cradled a loving infant; now, she witnessed the evolution of his being through the prism of love.

A tear, the crystalline mirror of her emotions, escapes her eye, drawing Adeem closer. He instinctively enfolds her in his arms, offering solace. She whispers amidst sobs, "These are not tears of sorrow, but joy, my child. The radiant bloom of your happiness and love... it's every mother's dream."

Adeem, confounded by his mother's tears of happiness, holds her closer, their shared comfort nurturing their bond, their intertwined emotions quieted. "I had seen it, Adeem. When you both were just children, I sensed a connection so unique, so extraordinary," Alara admits, the soft murmur of her words fading into the evening air.

With their hearts swathed in contentment, they ready themselves for the impending merriment. Laughter and song punctuate the night as the celebrations unfold, an aura of euphoria enveloping them. Food and drink abound, the communal harmony persisting under the canopy of the star-studded night, painting a timeless tableau of shared joy and revelry.

In the throbbing heart of antiquity, young Adeem found himself ensnared by the merciless claws of tardiness, an untamed beast spurred by restless sleep. It was a drowsy morning, weighed down by the intoxicating aftertaste of yesterday's exhilaration. As he sped towards his academic sanctuary, his comrades Anen and Kawab found solace in shared mirth, their chuckles dancing in the quietude of the scholarly ambiance.

"Ah, Adeem, a refreshing sight indeed!" exclaimed Ipy, his voice a resonating echo of ancient wisdom, "It is a joy to witness such youthful vibrancy bear fruit in our midst."

Immersed in this cradle of civilisation, the denizens of ancient Egypt revered the transformative potency of love. For them, it was not merely a fleeting sentiment, but an intricate tapestry woven into the very fabric of their existence. They held this compelling energy in sacred esteem, recognizing it as the celestial chariot that set life in motion.

Ipy, the seasoned pedagogue, proceeded to elucidate the multifaceted dimensions of love. He extolled the love of kith and kin, of feathered companions, of confidants and sweethearts, and the innate, profound affection for all that Mother Earth cradled in her bosom. Each manifestation of love, he taught, had a unique role in the theatre of life, shifting and evolving under the steady march of temporal waves.

The Egyptians dedicated their intellectual prowess to demystifying the enigma of love, setting their sights on understanding the genesis and evolution of relationships. Despite love's elusive nature, they embarked on a systematic quest to kindle sparks of affinity. They carefully charted the contours of individual characteristics, introducing a plethora of potential companions until, at last, the magical elixir of love was concocted, stirring the depths of hearts and souls.

In the heart of the ancient Egyptian realm, maidens, pure and unblemished, were placed under the watchful eyes of venerated elders. Their role, as significant as it was intricate, involved the scrutiny of character and the examination of prospective pairings based on harmonious energies. Some unions shimmered with an innate resonance, a dance of souls creating a transcendent experience of unity. However, other combinations required the commitment to endure the challenges and discomforts that came with achieving balance.

The magnetism of natural desire served as the foundation stone, the prelude to the orchestration of love's potent energy. For once the initial flame of love was ignited, it birthed an undying spark, a luminous testament to the union's divinity. Subservient to the omnipotent force of love, they embarked on a lifelong quest to master the delicate artistry of love's craft.

The wise Ipy, in the midst of his enlightening discourse, caught the undivided attention of his captivated audience. His question, laden with deep implications, echoed in the silence: "What depth does your love reach? What quality, what integrity?" His words stirred the unsuspecting crowd, many of whom had envisioned love as a simple endeavor.

"Love is more than a mere feeling," Ipy imparted, his voice carrying the weight of ages. "It is a craft to be honed, a talent cultivated over numerous lifetimes. Every action you undertake sends ripples through time, influencing those around you, permeating the reality we collectively shape. It is a symphony of energies, each note propelling us higher, as love is shared, fortified, and multiplied."

Pausing for a moment to catch his breath, Ipy

scanned the crowd. Their eager eyes mirrored the wisdom of his words. Raising an eyebrow, he resumed his discourse with renewed vigor. "If you must fear anything, let it be a life devoid of love." In the wisdom of the ancients, love was the cornerstone of existence, a beacon guiding one's journey through the labyrinth of life.

A tradition deeply entwined with the fabric of ancient Egyptian society, this profession meticulously maintained detailed chronicles reflecting individual responses towards the symbolic trinity of the feline, the bovine, and the avian. Quantitative analysis was performed on this carefully curated information, forming the groundwork for matchmaking - an intricate dance designed to harmonize two souls. Each prospective pair was presented with a spectrum of potential challenges, encouraging introspection before embarking on the path of courtship. Devised as a safeguard, this system was predicated on the fruitful blossoming of love, thereby ensuring the serene continuity of familial bonds on either side. It mirrored the undisturbed flow of life akin to the serene Egyptian landscapes, unfettered by the disruptions of the shifting sands.

Immersed in his emotions, Ipy bore the burden of his past with a graceful melancholy, the pang of his lost love self-inflicted, an errant architect of his own demise. He found himself besieged by torrents of grief, his eyes betraying the poignant secrets of his soul during the day's lessons. His heart, having weathered the storm of personal anguish, developed a yearning for ameliorating the travails of his disciples, to instill within them the roadmap to success and spare them the torment of life's trials.

The impediment of annoyance, though often regarded as a nuisance, was paradoxically the most yearned-for once it had been eradicated. Much like the end of a difficult journey, the absence of such a hurdle leaves a void, echoing with the bittersweet memories of the challenges overcome.

Love, in its intricate labyrinth, often mirrored the confinement of a prison when misconstrued; a battlefield of perceptions, requiring endurance to weather the storm and retrospectively acknowledge its higher purpose. Its complexity mimicked that of an electrical motor interacting with opposite poles. The more energy fed into it, the stronger its desire to repel, thereby inciting the armature's rotation – a delicate dance of forces and counterforces, akin to a sorcerer's spell.

The rhythmic ebb and flow of emotions serve as a crucial component in the individual calculus of life, their oscillations either magnifying or mitigating situations based on the dual aspects of compassion and tolerance. However, it is the intrusion of falsehoods, the corruption of sincerity, that destabilizes this equilibrium. Love's energy, when fostered in a heightened subconscious realm, ascends to unprecedented magnitudes, forging a deeper, more profound connection between two souls.

As life's grand tapestry continues to unravel, couples of diverse vibrational frequencies engage in a cosmic dance, their distinct energies merging and clashing in an extraordinary spectacle of love and emotion. As such, the dance of life persists, oscillating between the vast spectrums of human experience.

In the realm where perfection is an elusive mirage, existence becomes a dance with varying shades of imperfection, akin to an assemblage of intricate hieroglyphs that narrate tales of growth and resilience. This dance requires a relentless pursuit of equilibrium, a delicate symbiosis nurtured through a rigorous journey of enlightenment.

Upon the silent consent of two souls intertwining, a novel phase of elevated tutelage commences. As if echoing the harmonious cadence of an ancient Egyptian hymn, their kin are interwoven into the fabric of this newfound bond promptly, strengthening the twine of affinity. It is this very communion, an echo of the earliest throes of love, that seeds the fusion of hearts and minds, much like the symbolic unification of Upper and Lower Egypt.

Their perception is honed, transforming ostensibly adverse circumstances into valuable reservoirs of wisdom. Much like the omnipresent cycle of Ra's journey across the Duat, casting away shadows and renewing existence, their experiences help wash away remnants of past follies, thereby liberating them for the journey ahead.

The pedagogy extends to a sublime craft, that of enduring vexations with grace, as mastering this art bestows upon the adept the weightlessness of a feather, as found in Ma'at's balance, soaring to hitherto unexplored realms of self-realization. The dance continues as they compare their own narratives, whether they resonate with humility or companionship, each cognizant that their fate is sculpted by their deeds and contemplations. The echo of their journey lingers, a testament to their transformative voyage through the realms of love and understanding.

As the lunar crescent's dwindling illumination painted a spectral shadow over the cityscape, Hepu found himself pensively gazing from his chamber window. Visions of his youthful offspring stirred in his consciousness, an unwelcome contrast to his habitual refusal to let such preconceived notions influence his interpretation of their filial bonds. Yet, such contemplation proved irresistible.

Hepu's heartstrings were tugged by recollections of the sweet melodies Alara would lull their son, Adeem, with. As nightfall cast its veil over the city, young Adeem would lie tucked into his cradle, the erratic dance of candle flames reflecting upon his innocent countenance.

The acceptance of familial progression gnawed at Hepu's heart, as the poignant yearning for bygone eras began to consume him. The past seemed a halcyon chapter that resonated with vibrant euphoria, he coveted those moments, an era he considered the zenith of his existence.

Such was Hepu's internal strife, a man wrestling with the unalterable march of time, the inevitable evolution of his lineage, and the ephemeral nature of life itself. The woven tapestry of family ties and passing generations, illuminated under the dim glow of a waning moon, was a testament to the ancient rhythm that flowed just as the lifeblood through his veins.

At long last, Hepu discerns the familiar echo of Adeem's footfalls ricocheting down the avenues, a chorus of homecoming reverberating toward their shared abode. "That rhythm is unmistakable," Hepu muses, a warmth kindling within him as Adeem breaches the threshold to an awaiting embrace. "A serene evening it is. And how fares Kiya? Your shared vigils under the starlit canopy echo the tender memories of your mother and myself in our youth."

"A strange sight, is it not? Me traversing the path you once trod?" Adeem's voice wove into the tapestry of the quiet evening. "Perhaps," Hepu concedes, his eyes a wellspring of wisdom, "yet it's the cycle of existence. After living a chapter, the next unwritten page beckons, and we yearn for our beloved to savor the same flavours of life."

Pausing for a breath in the ebb and flow of their discourse, Hepu turns to Adeem, his right hand, a symbol of guidance and support, gently resting on his son's shoulder. "Cherish her, Adeem, as I am confident you will."

As the cradle of the night begins to rock, Adeem pivots towards his resting place, his feet following the weary path of habit. Hepu, voice soft as a lullaby, whispers, "Your mother sends her blessings from the stars, slumber peacefully my child. My pride in you knows no bounds." Leaving Adeem to the sanctity of sleep, Hepu retreats to his chamber where Alara, his pillar of solace, awaits to soothe the edges of a long day.

Adeem, with a serene gaze reflecting the maturity of his spirit, perched himself in disciplined repose on this particular morn, enraptured by the class he favored: "Chi and Kundalini Energy". This esoteric field of knowledge gifted him the metaphorical ankh, the key of life, to transcend challenges strewn along the path of existence, whilst fortifying his mental and physical resilience.

The teachings embodied the philosophy of harmony, of striking a balance within oneself and one's surroundings by the meticulous process of self-introspection. It was like unveiling the hidden glyphs of one's spirit, harkening to the sotto voce whispers of the inner self through meditative pursuits. These moments of quiet contemplation unmasked frailties, rendering them into stepping stones towards the elevation of one's vital energy.

Chakras, akin to the segmented chambers of an ancient Egyptian pyramid, were employed to mark progress in distinct facets, a method that imbued discipline, akin to the austere training of a temple acolyte. Along with it, it brought a not unwelcome discomfort, a stinging reminder of the growing pains associated with the path of learning, not unlike the sculptor chiseling a raw block of stone into a magnificent statue of spiritual evolution.

In the intricacies of the mind, dual existences dwell as one - the conscious and the subconscious. The right hemisphere perceives all that the aware mind experiences, maintaining a unique, separate existence while still entwined with its counterpart. Each realm of thought is tasked with specific talents, forming a balance within our cerebral world.

Bridging the chasm between conscious and subconscious is not a matter of force, but rather, it comes with grace. The bridge manifests subtly, in instances of profound joy or situations steeped in desire. Melodies, like hieroglyphs etched on the walls of ancient Egyptian temples, serve as the translating medium, the right brain interpreting these auditory codes into palpable pleasure.

Social engagement, such as the vibrant energy of a festive gathering, can also ignite the conversation between the conscious and subconscious, stirring an internal dialogue. The conscious mind leans on the right hemisphere for gifts of joy, a testament to their symbiotic existence. The right hemisphere, in its mysterious ways, comprehends the conscious in its entirety.

Yet, the power of this hidden awareness unfolds itself in mysterious ways - it could either bring about an upheaval or an evolution. Our subconscious guides our physical form, cell by cell, the essence of our unconscious mind molding our existence, much like the unseen hand of an ancient Egyptian deity, subtly shaping the world of the mortal realm.

Steeped in the mystique of ancient Egypt, yet devoid of overt symbols such as the revered Nile or the omnipresent Sun, a novel method to commune with the unseen universe within us unfolds. Gazing into the multifaceted mirrors of an animal's eyes, one can discern an inherent connection to the realm beneath conscious cognition. Their brains, attuned to the harmonics of living energy, gauge and perceive levels of vitality with nuanced acuity, presenting a model of primal understanding.

In every human eye, a small area known as the punctum caecum, or 'blind spot', exists, acting as a gateway to our subconscious mind. This seemingly obscure region is shrouded in darkness for the conscious mind, precisely due to its engagement with the subconscious realm, revealing a complex interplay between the seen and unseen in our perceptual reality.

In the heart of this world removed from time and space, the seekers would journey inward. Seated solitarily amidst the obsidian expanse of an unlit chamber, they were accompanied only by the inconsistent dance of a solitary flame. A mirror, an extension of the seeker's right hand, held out at shoulder height, mirrored the unseen behind the right shoulder.

Looking forward into the emptiness, with softened gaze but unwavering focus, they allowed the ambient mirror to enter their peripheral view. As the conscious mind began to register the reflected eyes in the mirror, a transformation commenced. The mirror became a portal, offering the vigilant conscious mind a fleeting, yet profound encounter with its introspective counterpart. The observer and the observed converged in an otherworldly dialogue, a unique glimpse of the subconscious mind gazing back, heralding the start of an extraordinary inward voyage.

"Ipy, dear friend, is that you disturbing my tranquility?" Adeem's voice echoes within his sanctuary of solace, abruptly interrupted from his profound mental voyage. "Indeed, it is a journey of the mind where the profoundest of mysteries unfurl... a charm I am quite enamored with," he adds, his voice a whispering rhapsody. Adeem, ever the intense and devoted mystic, often extended his meditative sessions far beyond the rest, a peculiarity that Ipy had grown accustomed to over time.

Meanwhile, beyond the boundaries of the tranquil enclave, Kiya, her spirit aglow with anticipation, awaited Adeem's emergence. Upon his arrival, she greeted him, her voice carrying the resonance of a heartfelt melody, "Greetings, beloved Adeem, your absence today was profoundly felt, for thoughts of you were my constant companion." Love, that ancient alchemy, was blending their energy in a powerful embrace, a testament to their enduring bond.

Their love was radiant, reminiscent of the inaugural flares of creation, its brilliance mirrored in their shared knowledge of what their intertwined destinies held. The essence of their companionship was a rare gift of youth, and with the wisdom of their extensive training, they navigated the terrain of expectations and aspirations, shaping their own unique understanding of love and partnership.

Bathed in the tender glow of the celestial satellite, the young enamoured pair, Adeem and Kiya, sought tranquillity by the river's edge during the stillness of midnight. With the bustle of daylight subdued, they found solace in the rhythmic dance of the moonlit waves, resisting the primal pulse of their burgeoning desires.

Adeem, having outgrown his father in stature and girth, bore the physical hallmarks of his labour at the shipyard, his physique sculpted by the burden of hefty cargo. Meanwhile, Kiya, on the cusp of womanhood, was blossoming into an enchanting silhouette, a tribute to the divine femininity of their times. "Tonight, your beauty is ethereal," Adeem professed, awestruck by the moon's soft illumination adorning her youthful countenance. "And you too, Adeem," returned Kiya, her voice suffused with affection.

Their conversation, an orchestration of love, soared

and plummeted, dancing from serene interludes to turbulent crescendos. The wisdom of Pharaoh, the royal sovereign, served as their guiding beacon; their love, despite its painful trials, was the most valuable treasure they possessed. The necessity of heartache only fortified the potency of their love's energy.

Intervals of silence marked their dance of dialogue, a testament to their deep, unspoken understanding. To escape the strife of their more contentious exchanges, they retreated into innocent chatter, deferring the resolution of their disagreements for a more reflective time. Nostalgia for their lineage and past intertwined with the solemn joy of their burgeoning family, as they navigated their disparities and sought a shared platform of mutual delight. Together, they were building a harmonious symphony of their lives, a complex rhythm of joy and sorrow, forever interlaced in the dance of their love.

The distinguished scholar of Ancient Egypt was profoundly dedicated to fostering the evolution of his people, using each lifespan as a stepping stone toward an expansive, transpersonal evolution. It was their deeply entrenched belief that life was an interplay of love, energy, and the cultivation of interpersonal bonds, honing talents over a myriad of lifetimes, gradually eradicating individual imperfections.

Their conception of the afterlife was a mirror to the subsequent life, nestled not in a river of time's ceaseless current, but in an immutable space unmarred by the dance of daylight and darkness.

From the poignant lament of lost love to the exuberant joy of rediscovery, the visage of an erstwhile beloved would reemerge in the birth of a new child, a fleeting echo of a prior existence hastily sculpting into a novel form. While the child was invariably a blend of its progenitors, the quintessence of the soul persisted.

Reentering the temporal spectrum, consciousness dimmed, cushioning the turbulence of birth and the abrupt immersion into existence anew. In the case of a first-born son, he would bear the influence of his mother's lineage more prominently, while a first-born daughter would reflect her father's lineage. This predilection waned with the arrival of subsequent offspring, the intensity of ancestral echoes fading into an harmonious equilibrium.

In harmony with cosmic patterns and age-old rhythms, men and women of maturity ritually enact transformations, signifying their readiness to embrace the essence of the opposite sex in the life to come, having fulfilled the obligations of their current gender. The males, adorned with feminine headdresses, denote their willingness to embody feminine energy, while the females engage in a corresponding ritual.

This birth and rebirth across generations, embracing a gender not of their physical form, cultivates an exquisite symmetry in the psyche, a profound harmonious balance manifesting as mental perfection. Yet, the untimely demise of an individual, claimed by unforeseen disaster, disrupts this rhythmic dance of souls. Such a premature end to life's journey shakes the harmonious rhythm, causing ripples in the cosmic waveform.

In the quiet cadence of consciousness, one's intellect finds itself tethered to the grand tapestry of the cosmos. Each destiny, like an intricate hieroglyph etched upon the unfathomable scrolls of time, emerges from daily discourse intertwined with the cosmic mechanism. Witnessing these vibrations of existence enables one to accrue wisdom and, in time, exert control, scripting each sunrise and sunset with deliberate intention.

Responses to life's myriad trials could be reframed, transformed into seeds of optimism. Through tireless vigilance of one's thoughts, a sense of honor would serve as the catalyst, propelling one's mind to ascend to unprecedented planes of cognition.

Though the shadow of negativity is an ever-looming presence, one learns to acknowledge it yet promptly let it pass, like a fleeting zephyr. Rare is the moment when life unveils its underlying truths, but it is in such instances, understanding instills solace, illuminating the resilience born from our struggles.

Change, the master sculptor of human existence, is often met with aversion. Many opt for stagnation, an easy comfort in the known. Yet, echoing the wisdom of our ancient predecessors, one discovers that embracing the unpredictable fosters growth, kindles a ceaseless flame of ambition. Although cloaked in discomfort, such uncertainties are merely catalysts in the grand design of our becoming.

The conundrum was not centered on the method of the occurrence, but rather its underlying rationale. Humanity persists as a solitary harmonic wave, each ripple influencing the next in a cosmic melody that either synergizes into serenity or descends into discord. Achieving a harmonious relationship with the omnipresent energies in our environment requires an equilibrium, often referred to as Kundalini—a powerful union of all energies.

This balance not only heightens the sensation of joy but also fuels creativity, allowing further exploration of previously uncharted planes of consciousness. Like the sinewy strength of a well-conditioned muscle, the cortex adapts, expanding in concert with the burgeoning mental activity to support this voyage of self-discovery, providing a malleable course and an enhanced ability to modulate frequencies.

Ascension, in its manifold facets, can be intensified by harnessing the latent power of the subconscious through the adroit use of certain chemical catalysts. Organic compounds, such as ayahuasca, and other mind-expanding concoctions serve as gateways, opening the doors to a mental state capable of feats far beyond those achievable in ordinary cerebral operations. Through this prism, shrouded in the mystery of ancient Egyptian wisdom, the human experience transcends the commonplace, reflecting the interplay between our internal energy and the universe around us.

Adeem and Kiya

Amid the crisp breath of dawn, the season's whispers were beginning to weave their shift. Djoser and Hepu, stationed near the apex of the Pyramids, watched as the pristine white limestone, cut with astonishing precision at a 51.85° angle - the culmination of intricate mathematical revelations - was hauled into place by bustling teams of men.

A symphony of labour and intellectual prowess resounded throughout the area. Like clockwork, each hewn slab was arranged with an uncanny precision that imprinted itself onto the third and final pyramid, aligned with the celestial robe of Osiris himself. The almost finished structure stood as a testament to human ingenuity, its looming presence graced by the divine sparkle of the stars themselves.

The blinding reflection cast by the monolith's colossal face was a spectacle, its mirror-like visage bouncing the dawn's light with unassailable dominance. An army of workers danced beneath its glow, their steps choreographed in their individual assignments - a sight that echoed wonder in its beholders.

Djoser and Hepu drank in the staggering vista, their senses awash with a humbling realization of what was unfolding before them. Draped in the shadow of the pyramid, they turned to return to their workshop. A hive of activity buzzed around them, echoing the same rhythm of work that was at play at the pyramid's base.

The city was pulsing with a tangible expectancy. The promise of the imminent culmination was an irresistible force, uplifting every corner and crevice of the place. Laughter echoed off the stone walls, intermingling with the cries of emotional upheaval, an ebb and flow of human sentiment towards the inevitability that lay before them. The magnitude of their collective accomplishment and the uncertainty of the future evoked profound responses that danced across the spectrum of human emotion.

As sunlight dances upon the water, its intricate ballet

paints an ethereal pattern upon Adeem and Kiya, seated together at the serene water's edge, a welcome reprieve from the lively hum of the shipyard and harbor. Kiya embraces her beloved, the intimate promise of eternity etched in her voice. "It's incredible to think we are bound to share our lives forever," she murmurs.

A flicker of contemplation crosses Adeem's face, prompting Kiya to probe the depth of his thoughts. He shares his disquiet, the words of his mother weighing on his mind, questioning the fundamental essence of free will and destiny. His voice, a mix of confusion and resolve, lingers in the air. "How can it be that we lack control over our destiny, if we are free to ponder and deliberate our decisions?"

Kiya replies, her wisdom borrowed from generations past. "My great grandfather used to say, we can't truly determine right or wrong in the moment. Only with the wisdom of hindsight can we learn from our choices." She pauses, allowing the potency of her words to sink into Adeem's consciousness. The tension on his face begins to dissipate.

She presses on, "Every occurrence has its purpose. Life, in its simplest form, is joyous and carefree, follow your heart, it never lies." A playful spark ignites in Adeem's eyes, a prelude to his amorous jests, coaxing an infectious laugh from Kiya.

As their mirth settles, Adeem leans in, his voice hushed yet resonant. "This... this connection, it's why we belong together. From our youth, I felt your gaze on me, and I've always felt at peace in your presence." His features soften, as if unburdened from a hidden weight, as his thoughts, once entangled, now flow freely.

Their relationship, resilient and malleable, pivots into uncharted territory, the duo complementing each other's strengths. Together, they manage to diminish the bewilderment of life's puzzles, their diverse talents weaving a tapestry of mutual support and love.

Adeem, scion of a highly esteemed mathematician and visionary, was a testament to an inheritance of paternal brilliance. His character, however, was painted with the soft hues of his mother's side, radiating an empathetic immediacy that rendered him both understanding and forthright. Adeem, in a moment of candid revelation, concedes, "Those that hold our hearts in their hands wield the greatest power to wound us." In a gentle breath, Kiya, his love, responds, "My gratitude for you will eternally persist."

As an initiation into the realities of existence and as an examination of their romantic dedication, they are offered a sanctuary in the solitude of the wilderness, far from the comforts of civilization. This serves as their new dwelling, if only for a temporal sojourn. Adeem and Kiya, in this reclusive abode, are tasked with implementing the wisdom of their mentors, engaging in the primeval craft of subsistence.

It is within the confines of this sanctuary that they will begin to weave the first threads of their shared life, forming the foundational fabric of their love story. They will wrestle with the everyday, discovering each other anew in the face of adversity and triumph, armed with their mutual affection and teachings from those who guided their path thus far.

These experiences serve as the crucible of their relationship, testing, refining, and ultimately solidifying their bond. The echoes of ancient Egyptian values of perseverance, communal reliance, and balance permeate their lives, an undercurrent in their narrative that ties them irrevocably to the world that surrounds them.

For a fleeting instant, the relentless march of time yields, gifting Hepu a respite of introspection. He kindles memories of Adeem, his evolution from infancy into a being of independent spirit, both poignant and unsettling. His heart pulses with a symphony of emotion, resonating with the resonant thrum of a distant past and the tense anticipation of an unchartered future.

Nefret and Alara, vested in hope and tinged with apprehension, stand as silent witnesses, their hearts echoing with the same thrum. Their offspring, on the precipice of a survival quest, are mere silhouettes against the vast expanse of the impending unknown. Their existence intertwined with a bond as resilient as the lotus, blooming amidst the chaos of life.

Adeem and Kiya, on the brink of the visible horizon, cast a lingering look back. The air vibrates with cheers and applause from their tribe, punctuated with an occasional piercing whistle, a testament to the communal spirit. A shared smile, an unspoken pact, and they embark, stepping forward into the waiting arms of destiny.

Their individual existences dissolve, merging into a symbiotic unity. They are reflections of one another, echoing each other's strengths and flaws. The journey ahead will test the strength of their devotion, a testament to their unwavering commitment. Now is the moment where promises are weighed against actions, where love transcends into reality. Each stands on the brink of proving their worth, not merely in their eyes, but in the mirror of the other's soul.

Once the taxing day's journey was accomplished, they came upon the predetermined stone cluster. They bore minimal sustenance, sourced from the earth's bounty, nurturing an ethereal connection of their spirits. "It's a favourable location, certainly feasible for habitation," Adeem speculated, scrutinizing their newly claimed shelter, whilst setting his pack upon an interior precipice.

Kiya's laughter rippled through the air, interrupted when her gaze was drawn to an inconspicuous fissure in the stony canopy above them. Through this fracture, the celestial sky revealed itself, the distinctive third star of Orion's belt smiling back at her. She pivoted toward Adeem, the joy causing her to twine her arms about him with giddy excitement.

Adeem, although seasoned by solitude, perceived the dew of Kiya's teardrops as she surrendered to the overwhelming tide of her transforming existence. The heaviness of this evolution was a shared sentiment, though Adeem held steadfast, portraying an edifice of unyielding strength. As he consoled Kiya, her lean toward him was a declaration of faith, a trust forged in their shared journey. She sought refuge and reassurance in Adeem, firm in her belief that she had discovered not only what her soul yearned for, but also a haven for the nascent life within her.

In the quiet sanctum of their private sanctuary, a

solitary flame wavered, casting ephemeral shadows on the stone wall. The gentle candlelight served as the only source of illumination within the room, the fluctuating radiance illuminating the figures of Adeem and Kiya. As they settled into the soft embrace of freshly woven linens, the intimate warmth of their bare forms next to one another was the only testament of the events to come.

Their journey until this moment had been punctuated with an array of emotions, as pure and straightforward as the cotton sheets that cushioned their bodies. They have seen love and heartache, passion, and a silent longing that mirrored the quiet hum of the universe. A myriad of sentiments that were now reduced to a delicate precipice of anticipation, simmering beneath their skin, ready to surge forth in the most primal of instincts.

The electricity between them was tangible, a mystic force that coalesced their energies, binding them in an intimate dance as old as time itself. The unspoken promise of togetherness, an eternal whisper in the wind that fluttered from the heart of Adeem to the core of Kiya, echoed in the silence of the room.

Adeem's eyes, those deep pools of midnight blue, looked upon Kiya with a reverence reserved only for her. Each trace of his fingers on her skin was like a lover's sonnet written across the canvas of her body, each touch a verse in their unending love story. His hands moved like an artist, appreciating every curve, every plane of her form, a silent prayer that sought her pleasure before his own.

Kiya, in response, found herself lost in the cosmos of their shared desire. Every flicker of the candlelight, every whisper of his breath against her neck, all led her on an odyssey of the senses. She reveled in the delicious tremors that coursed through her under his gentle ministrations, her body responding in kind to his affections. Her heart beat in tandem with his, two drums in the orchestra of love that played only for them.

Their dance continued, an intimate ballet choreographed by the cosmos itself. The rhythm of their hearts, the melody of their sighs, harmonized in a symphony of their shared desire. Their forms intertwined in an intricate dance, each push and pull echoing with the poetry of unspoken emotions. And when the crescendo of their desires peaked, the sound of their shared climax reverberated within the stone walls, echoing into the still night, a testament to their shared passion.

As the echoes of their pleasure slowly faded into the canvas of the night, Adeem and Kiya lay entwined, spent yet complete. The dance of their shared energy, once a fiery maelstrom, now quieted to the gentle ebb of satisfaction. The night air, once thick with anticipation, now sang with the melody of their love, resonating with their shared contentment. The lone candle continued its flicker, casting a warm glow over their joined forms, a silent sentinel to their newfound unity.

In the nascent veil of the second twilight, the twosome braved a relentless tempest that violently reshaped their surroundings. The heavens unleashed an elemental fury, rain descending in cold torrents, hammering relentlessly on the earthen terrain around them. They nestled together, hunkering low near the muted glow of a modest flame, a paltry bulwark against the unyielding chill.

Amid the storm's cacophony, the scent of dried sustenance permeated the humid air, a testament to Kiya's resilience and foresight. As the wind howled, whispering echoes of unseen phantoms, she offered their meager repast, a beacon of hope against the elements' insistence.

A solemn promise, a covenant, emerged from Adeem amidst the clamor. "We shall remain, entwined in our fates, till the end of days," he vowed, his voice steadfast over the discordant symphony of the tempest. Their bodies melded into an intimate silhouette, a sculpture shaped by life's chisel in the face of adversity.

Their heads rested against each other, forming a shared pillar of strength, their breaths intermingling, creating a rhythm that resonated against the backdrop of the unquiet storm. Their spoken affirmations carved a path into the heart of each other, unearthing truths born of passion and hardship.

In the cocoon of their shared warmth, their vows reverberated into the stormy abyss, a pledge of souls, their hearts resonating in silent harmony. And so they cast their promises into the winds of time, fortifying their bond under the harsh scrutiny of the storm. The silent witness of the night listened to their timeless dance of words, an ode to an enduring love, a saga penned under the trials of a relentless storm.

Splayed across the banquet tables were blooms of orange, pink, and white, their fragrant tendrils winding through the array of sustenance and libation, all laid out to commemorate the triumphant return of the newly bonded pair. As the luminary of the day began to concede to the velvet canvas of night, the atmosphere pulsated with jubilant applause that surged like a vibrant tide in anticipation of the weary couple's arrival.

This celebration marked not an end, but a thrilling genesis of the duo's shared voyage into maturity. The gathered assembly cheered fervently, their voices intertwining to form a symphony of goodwill, a chorus of hope serenading the promise of enduring love. The spectacle was a riotous sea of color as petals of every hue showered down upon Adeem and Kiya, creating a blushing carpet underfoot as they crossed their proverbial finish line, their faces alight with smiles broad as the horizon and brimming with joyous anticipation.

Then, the pair were treated to the age-old cleansing ritual, bathed in waters laden with fragrant oils as the onlookers held their breath in respectful silence. The feast that followed was a delight to the senses, the couple fed with choicest morsels, while the revelry around them built to a crescendo. Music reverberated through the night air, harmonious melodies woven into the tapestry of starlight, and laughter echoed as tales were spun, imbued with wit and vivacity. The night unfolded, a beautiful spectacle etched in the annals of time, celebrating the vibrant beginnings of two souls bound in unity.

CHAPTER 8 – GATE OF THE SUN

On the cusp of evening, an intuitive assembly of both tender and seasoned ages found their convergence upon the elevated terrain known as Observation Hill. Amidst them, the freshly betrothed duo of Kiya and Adeem, their bond now an acknowledged chapter of community lore. The luminary of their gathering was Raia, a regal matron radiating an equilibrium of wisdom and tranquility.

Her beauty resonated not solely from the facial symmetry etched delicately in the silver tracery of her years but emanated from an internal brilliance honed by life's intricate tapestry. Draped in a sheath of alabaster linen, a silent testament to her well-trodden journey, she held the attention of her audience as a queen would her court.

With an almost ethereal grace, Raia declared, "Behold my beauty, yet know that it extends beyond my countenance. It is the fruit of the life I have led, and the insights I gathered in the dawn of my existence."

As her gaze ascended toward the cosmic tapestry overhead, the stars, like a celestial choir, held their brilliant notes in a sky freed from the moon's modest veil. A sweeping expanse, it formed a spectacular backdrop to her silhouette, a sculpted monument under the watchful eyes of the cosmos. The earth beneath their feet shimmered with the elusive luminescence of starlight, casting a dreamlike aura around the forms that dotted the landscape. Thus, under the celestial theatre, the stage was set, and anticipation hung thickly in the air like unseen threads weaving tales yet untold.

"Within the grand tapestry of existence, there exists a delicate equilibrium, a balance between presence and absence, a harmony of being and unbeing. This delicate interplay pulsates with life, underpinning the architecture of time and space and their antitheses. Such elemental principles converge in an intricate dance, a vibrant friction that brews matter itself.

Nestled within the cosmos, our radiant orb is enveloped by an embrace of potent magnetic energy. Here, amidst this celestial ballet, non-sequential fusion takes birth. Our world, spinning within this maelstrom of magnetic energy, portrays an air of unassuming innocence.

Our lunar satellite, a testament to silent observation, orbits our planet at 29Hz. It beams a pulsating signal towards the distant constellations, an interstellar envoy in our corner of the cosmos. Across the reaches of space, solar systems decipher this cosmic communique, transmitting back an encoded binary echo. An echo that resonates within the hearts of every living being across the multitude of planets. Mother Earth, in her wisdom, listens and in response, tilts on her axis, a gentle swaying of 30 degrees every 13,000 years.

Our thoughts, our actions, resonate with this cosmic code, influencing the master blueprint that the cosmos faithfully records. The universe is not merely a repository of knowledge, but a grand orchestration wherein all events are coaxed into fruition. Each unique phase of the moon ushers in a distinct potential for tapping into a kaleidoscope of energy seldom offered.

As the lunar siren mathematically aligns with the planets in our cosmos, it engenders an unparalleled potency hailing from the depths of the universe. This potent force imbues the mind with an accelerated pace, facilitating the absorption of knowledge.

The lunar cycle, that grand symphony of the moon, is the cornerstone formula, the key that unlocks the enigmas of the constellations." Raia, in the midst of this revelation, gracefully descends into the lotus position, her spirit retreating into the quietude of her inner cosmos. Her audience, entranced by the revelation, follows suit, their hearts beating in tune with the cosmic rhythm.

" In the sprawling, infinite cosmos resides all wisdom. It is the universe's orchestration that directs all things," Raia imparts her concluding wisdom before surrendering herself to her private cosmos. Her cognition manipulated by elixirs of mystical properties, she embraces her role as the conduit, an intermediary capable of harnessing the transcendental energies of the universe.

She is part of an elaborate ritual, a tableau of seekers poised in silent reverence, their bodies meticulously arranged to mirror the vast belt of the Milky Way. Like a celestial compass, they align with the dance of contrasting forces swirling in the galactic vortex.

Across the ebony expanse of the heavens, constellations flow in an eternal celestial ballet. Amid this dynamic tapestry of starry luminescence, one constant beacon stands out, the unwavering focus of the sky's wheeling panorama - Alpha Ursae Minoris, known commonly as Polaris or the North Star.

This stellar entity is Earth's immutable point of reference, the mathematical anchor that sets the cosmic gears into motion. Amid the ceaseless flux of the universe, it remains the fixed truth, the unwavering lodestar that charts the course of celestial movements. It is akin to an astral symphony, an elegant composition of wisdom and emotion, whose magnetic resonances civilizations across the globe fall subject to.

Its divine cadence echoes in their hearts and minds, silently directing their stories and cultures. Much like the celestial bodies in their orbits, they too are caught in the magnetic pull of Polaris, guided by the knowledge and wisdom resonating from its steadfast glow. The ancient Egyptians might have called it the Eye of Horus watching over them, ever constant, ever guiding, even as everything else in the universe is in a state of unending flux.

"Ah, such an exquisite feeling radiates within me following our spiritual gatherings," Kiya voices to Adeem, her words draping over him like a fine linen shroud as he clumsily navigates the rocky terrain adjacent to their congregation spot. She waits, the torchlight dancing in her kohl-rimmed eyes as she takes in his disarray with a fondness that transcends the bounds of mortality.

"Look, Adeem," she breathes out, the pitch of her voice gently rippling in the quietude. "A small token, birthed from our intertwined spirits. An emblem of our unity that rivals even the potency of the lotus and the papyrus."

Unveiling her masterpiece, her delicate fingers present an intricate figurine, skillfully chiseled from granite and seamlessly interwoven with teak, spiraling in a manner defying comprehension, reminiscent of their own interwoven souls. "This... is us," her eyes shimmer with raw affection as she gifts Adeem a tender gaze, "An emblem of our love, as unyielding as stone and as versatile as wood."

"Amor meus Adeem," she whispers, her declaration of love settling on his ears like the tender kiss of an evening breeze. The boundaries separating their forms vanish in a comforting embrace, a moment of silent adoration under a sky studded with a thousand astral bodies.

A crisp night chill whispers through the silence, prompting Adeem to glance towards their homeward path. "The evening cloaks itself in coolness, we should commence our journey back," he suggests, his tone tinged with regret at parting from their tranquil retreat.

"Tonight has been painted with hues of joy," Kiya smiles warmly, her statement echoing in the starlight, acknowledging the beautiful mosaic of emotions their shared experience had woven.

With the serenity of the ancient city humming around them, the duo traced their path back into the inviting arms of their dwelling place, where familial love was simmering in the cauldron of an upcoming feast. The labor of love was bestowed upon Djoser, Hepu, Dedu, Henite, Alara, and Nefret - a band of kin, carefully chosen for this divine culinary artistry.

Hepu found himself momentarily ensnared by a meditative trance, ears attuned to the symphony of jovial voices exchanging tales and jests. An otherworldly energy wafted through the air, swirling around them, as if painted by an unseen artist in hues of camaraderie and kinship. The intoxicating allure of this bond drew bystanders into the orbit of their conviviality, pulling them into the vortex of warmth and shared tales.

This tangible atmosphere of unity radiated a certain electricity, creating an aura of magnetism that captured the essence of each newcomer. The evening's aura transitioned into an ethereal azure, reflecting off the culinary delights taking shape in the hearth's fire. This magnetic congregation manifested fluctuating luminescence, their radiance rooted deep within their shared familial spirit.

Suddenly, a ripple of excitement washed over the crowd. A cascade of delight spilled into the room as Adeem and Kiya, the newly betrothed pair, made their grand entrance. Their arrival was met with an eruption of joyous applause, their presence revered and adored as if they were celestial beings descending upon the mortals. An air of veneration enveloped the duo, their burgeoning love held in the highest regard, a spectacle that brought delight to all those who bore witness.

As they stepped onto the metaphorical stage of their new journey, they found themselves under the spotlight of the collective gaze. They stood as the epitome of harmony, their resilient love admired and celebrated - a testament to their enchanting bond that whispered tales of their unwavering dedication and mesmerizing aura. Indeed, it was a love that mirrored the timelessness and enduring allure of their ancient homeland.

Under the silver splendor of the lunar presence, the majestic Great Pyramid, nearly at its completion, dominated the skyline. Soft illumination emanated from the sprawling metropolis, casting a dreamy glow on the grandeur of this man-made marvel. Each facet of its sturdy walls, bedecked in pure white limestone, shone with a unique sheen, an earthly reflection of the cosmos above. It was as if the pyramid itself was a cosmic beacon, an architect's dream wrought real upon the fertile soil of Egypt.

Every city dweller fixated their awe-struck gaze upon this marvel of their own making. It was more than just a symbol of their power and prowess, it was a

testament to their shared vision, a beacon of unity
and resilience in the face of adversity.

A peculiar, almost mystical feature of this awe-
inspiring monument was the inexplicable radiance it
emitted. This was no mere luminous spectacle. The
pyramid, it seemed, had become a life-giver, its
radiant glow producing an uncanny shield around the
city. This unexpected, yet welcome side effect,
shielded the dwellers from maladies of every kind.
Like a beneficent guardian, it watched over its
creators, ensuring their well-being.

But this healing glow was but an incidental boon.
The Pyramid, in its colossal glory, was designed with a
purpose far beyond this. A purpose veiled in the
enigma of the universe itself, cloaked in the profound
wisdom of its builders, and etched into the enduring
stones of this testament to human ambition.

On the far reaches of the metropolis, a haunting
lament ensnares the frosty grip of the ebony night.
Life essence seeps into a vast, hollow vessel, its
surface vibrating in harmony with the silent echoes of
regret. A stately platform, meticulously hewn from
the heart of an ancient oak, cradles a form tailored to
its contours.

A decapitated human form, still radiating the residual
warmth of existence, lies in poignant stillness, while
those who shared its journey weep, their grief a
torrent in the silent night. The severed head, a
macabre testament to the fateful choice, rests beside
its body, a veil of purest white bestowing a measure
of dignity upon the chilling scene.

In the face of life's relentless cycle, one soul had

elected the release of oblivion, severing the ties that bound it to the fabric of its existence. Tortured by the crushing weight of deceit he had inflicted upon unsuspecting souls, his actions took an irrevocable course.

Though cherished by many, he had chosen to surrender his life force to the cosmic abyss, a testament to his desperate yearning for transformation. His energy, once vibrant and teeming with life, would reemerge elsewhere within the vast weave of the universe, released from the tormented husk of its previous incarnation.

The family—an ensemble of souls, a pulsating river of shared essence—ebbs and flows through the cosmic rhythm of existence, its vibrancy augmented or diminished by the deeds of its constituents. For him, it was but a fleeting illumination in the void, the herald of his inaugural breath, yet for those who harbored affection for him, it painted a vastly different tableau. To the ancient Egyptians, this schism was likened to the celestial mysteries, a constellation-linkage while affection patiently lingers in the cosmos.

This cosmic dance was artistically encapsulated in the pictorial narratives of the Narmer Palette and other hieroglyphic chronicles, etched into eternity by the wisdom-imbued hands of the ancients. It was a ballet, slow and melancholic, performed upon a stage where teardrops mingled with the motes of dust suspended in air, and figures sought solace in the warmth of shared sorrow.

This raw, poignant surge of collective emotion is the celestial currency, the requisite cosmic capital, required to weave the essence of a departed loved one back into the tapestry of existence, through the portal of birth, and into the spatial-temporal fabric. Absent this energy, a soul risks being entrapped in an aimless cycle, re-emerging in a kinship bereft of love, a cosmic pariah.

Commiseration might stretch into weeks, a lengthy nocturne that is eventually broken by the gradual dawn of hope, rising to dispel the pervasive melancholy. The comprehension of life's cyclical nature, this transmigration from existence to existence, holds the power to dispel the specter of the enigma that is the afterlife. With understanding comes a release from the shackles of fear, a liberation from dread of the uncharted, opening the heart to the boundless beauty of the cosmic dance.

Awash in the purifying streams of regret, the human spirit finds itself reborn, ennobled by the alchemical transformation. These very echoes of the heart, which ripple outward and tie the destinies of individuals together, hold within them a powerful connection, akin to the unseen threads that bind the stars in the firmament.

Casting away the shadows of the past, the conscious mind releases its hold on the dimly lit archives of memory. In tandem, the subconscious takes the lead, orchestrating a regeneration much like the silent, gentle unfurling of the lotus at dawn. This cyclical resurrection, akin to the mythical phoenix rising from its ashes, echoes the transitory yet timeless nature of existence.

In the grand tapestry of life, every birth becomes a beacon, a poignant marker of returning souls, reincarnating at their unique tempos. The grand play of life and death continues unabated, with the arrivals of fresh souls sometimes occurring beyond the visibility of a single human lifetime.

Each departure from life is carefully noted and revered, with a record of individual passions, aptitudes, and affections preserved like cherished hieroglyphs on a papyrus scroll. These vibrant notes of existence, recognized and nourished early in each new life, serve to fuel eternal progression. This ever-evolving pattern of spiritual growth underpins the structure of an enduring and harmonious family nexus.

Imbued with the wisdom of the ancients, yet moving with the rhythm of the present, this age-old practice transcends the mere tangible. It mirrors a balance - a concept as timeless as the eternal dance of the cosmos, evoking a sense of harmony that mirrors the stability of the celestial order.

The harmonious symphony commences, inviting kith and dear ones to imbue the proceedings with their own rhythms, their heartbeats playing an exquisite, final ode that the departed had penned in the script of their existence. This rite deepens the engraving of the experience into the fabric of collective memory. When an entity has not journeyed to the full expanse of its allotted existence, an echo of unsettled harmony reverberates, perceived as a youthful impetuousness born of limited experiences in its antecedent life.

The more challenging emotional echoes become resonant, trailing behind the soul's brighter facets. They serve as poignant reminders, a stark contrast to the luminous vibrancy the spirit once embodied.

Even in the hallowed land of the Pharaohs, where the shadows of the pyramids stretch towards the stars, it remains a universal truth: where light shines brightest, the shadows are deepest. The echoes of unprocessed emotions in the music are akin to these shadows, a silent testament to the incomplete journey of the soul.

In the vast expanse of the ocean, life thrives unseen by human eyes. The mystery and beauty of its depths create a stage for a myriad of inhabitants. In this silent domain, myriad species of fish navigate the currents as if bound by an unseen thread of collective existence. Their vibrant energy, though manifesting in varied temporal frames, resonates harmoniously, bearing the markings of lives born of different instances, yet connected in the seamless flow of the aquatic ballet.

Every corner of our world echoes this profound concept. Be it the nimble herd of mountain goats traversing the rocky crevices, or the rhythmic dance of a bird squadron slicing the azure sky, these creatures respond to an instinctive feeling that transcends mere thought. It is a dance guided not by cognitive processes bound by time, but by an inherent force intertwined with existence itself.

Infused within every facet of life, this phenomenon resounds. It speaks to us in the coiling vine of a lush rainforest, in the stoic endurance of a cactus in arid lands, in the silent procession of the night sky's glimmering gems. This unity, this synchronicity, it is the rhythm of life. This unseen conductor orchestrates existence, creating an elegy for all life forms, each verse echoing through time, transcending the constraints of human comprehension.

The chorus of the natural world sings in perfect harmony, each species performing its part with precision, guided by an ethereal baton. This symphony exists outside the dominion of our consciousness, embodying an instinctive rhythm that stretches across the breadth of existence. It's as if a celestial scribe, untouched by the temporal spectrum, chronicles the unfathomable tale of life, etching every pulsating heartbeat, every fleeting breath into the fabric of reality itself.

Like a hieroglyph, this truth is etched in the marrow of existence: life, in its myriad forms and rhythms, is an exquisitely orchestrated symphony, playing to the beat of the unseen drum of time. Despite the difference in birth instances, a shared life energy binds all beings, a testament to the tapestry of existence woven in perfect synchronicity, transcending the linear constraints of time. Thus, the earth is not merely a vessel for life, but the silent storyteller of the ages, singing an ancient lullaby that echoes the harmony of existence.

Framed by the vast expanse of celestial ebony, the nearly consummated Great Pyramid monument splinters the lunar luminescence into fragmented shards, its grandeur ascending heavenward. At its majestic foot, silhouettes punctuate the ethereal glow, etching a triad of familial unity - Dosjer, Hepu, and Adeem. In the hushed murmur of night, their shadows sketch an indelible image of three men bound by the shared essence of ancestry, their vitality merged in the singular purpose of preservation.

These moments are when universal wisdom is bestowed upon the collective consciousness, a subtle osmosis of intermingling essences - the communion of akin energies, facilitating the interplay of ideas, and nourishing the seed of familial perpetuity. A likeness mirrored not only in thought but also in their physical aspects, these men serve as individual embodiments of a singular essence, unique portals into the undulating continuum of existence.

This cosmos we inhabit is a cauldron of constantly metamorphosing energies, undergoing a rhythmic lifecycle of birth, crescendo, maturity, and rebirth. It hums like an electric symphony in harmonic resonance, embodying a cosmic dance of opposition and alignment, the unseen hand that shapes all creation. Each pulse, each ebb, and flow is a testament to the cyclical narrative of existence, echoed in the moonlit silhouette of the three men against the backdrop of the monument, symbols of their own cycle within the grand design of the universe.

CHAPTER 9 - THE NATUFIANS

Precious droplets of water seize the breath of air as they are the first to be expelled from the impending descent of the ocean's crest. As the world at large reaps the advantages of our celestial position, we commence an unwilling regression towards a nocturnal era, inciting portions of society to covet possessions and alliances. The proliferation of positive energy necessitates the efforts of multitudes across centuries, yet, lamentably, the deterioration of intellectual capacity is a malady swiftly caught.

When these societal clusters succumb, it is akin to an insidious plague corrupting an erstwhile pristine being. Our progeny bear the initial brunt, their resonant laughter begins to dim and their radiant joy withers, causing the beautiful mosaic of enduring affection, built over successive eras, to shatter into lesser fragments of its majestic past.

In this narrative, imbued with Ancient Egyptian undertones, the Nile could serve as a metaphor for life-giving energy, gradually being drained due to the backslide into ignorance. The imagery of a once vibrant society gradually crumbling into darkness is reminiscent of the fall of the Old Kingdom, leading to the first intermediate period of Egyptian history. This period is known for its decline in centralized power, an increase in provincial power, and an overall lack of resources, which caused significant social and political changes. This context adds depth to the text, providing a more vivid understanding of the societal decay depicted.

Positioned amidst the bustle of the food depot, Adeem, Djoser, and Hepu engage in the painstaking labor of provisioning a caravan destined for the remote Natufian villages. As they maneuver the laden carts tethered to sturdy oxen under the desert's dusky veil, the air fills with a poignant blend of duty and expectation.

Beneath the weight of sacks brimming with sustenance, Adeem finds the words that echo his thoughts, "Compassion, this is the trait that truly shapes us as people." His voice rises above the steady drone of their activity, directed towards his companions. The sentiment paints an unspoken picture of unity and shared responsibility in their minds.

Djoser, his physique echoing the strength of the limestone monoliths nearby, replies with a certain bitterness clinging to his words. "Perfection is our pursuit, they were once an element of us." His remark bears the weight of a historical divide that lingers between their city and the remote villages. A history only they remember, a memory only they carry.

The conversation hangs suspended in the desert twilight, only to be concluded by Adeem, a sense of resolution in his voice, "Yet, we are compelled to bolster their survival." His statement, a testament to their moral code, pierces through the veil of dusk.

Hepu, a man known for his gleaming smile as much as for his work ethic, lifts another basket of food with a startling ease. His contentment is the embodiment of their shared belief - an act of service is an act of joy. With a quick maneuver, he loads the basket onto the cart, which soon disappears into the obsidian cloak of the night, headed towards the anticipation of empty bellies.

These are the unseen inhabitants at the edge of the civilization, the fringe population that will eventually shape the legacy of the Natufians in the annals of Ancient Rome. And yet, for now, they remain an unnoticed note in the symphony of history, their future importance hidden beneath the shroud of time.

With a note of distress subtly coloring his voice, Adeem shares, "I find myself unsettled at the sight of our nourishment arriving." He hesitates, a shadow of foreboding crossing his features, "I suspect it will be a challenge for quite some time to come." Djoser, the wisdom of years etched into his countenance, perceives the inner turmoil roiling within Adeem, a mirror to the chaos that had unfolded before his very eyes. The pain of watching others succumb to their own desperation in the face of protecting someone dear is a torment no soul should bear.

Djoser, the sage mentor, gently advises, "The celestial rotations bring transformation. We are denizens of its dominion, our purpose is to discern its signs and adapt to its ebbs and flows." A certain warmth would bloom in his chest each time he imparted a sliver of his knowledge onto Adeem, witnessing the epiphany alight within the young man's eyes.

Offering a soft smile, Djoser confesses, "The privilege of guiding you, as both my progeny and grandchild, has graced me with an existence richer than I could have ever fathomed. You have given me lessons in abundance." The three of them then became entwined in an embrace, basking in the rarity of this shared silence, etching the moment into their collective memory.

A few more lunar cycles, and the Great Pyramid would stand completed, marking the skyline of their city. The air was already humming with the collective anticipation of the citizens, the very atmosphere quivering with the thrill of their imminent accomplishment.

Bearing many commendable qualities, the discordant civilizations bore an intriguing resemblance. The disparities only emerged once one ventured into their core, and truly observed the nuances of their inhabitants' expressions. The omnipresent rodents and insects were keen perceivers of the human's dwindling vitality, audaciously asserting themselves as unwelcome cohabitants.

Local fauna, challenged by their inability to adapt, met with the tragic fate of multiple stillbirths. Meanwhile, the early Natufians were confronted with disturbances seeping into their own health and vitality. In response to these unsettling events, the art of entertainment flourished, acting as a balm to soothe the spirits and briefly replenish the diminishing reservoirs of joy.

Storytelling ascended to the pinnacle of this newfound distraction, with the allure of song and dance ensnaring the populace. This strange blend of antagonistic tension and soothing consolation birthed an irregular symphony, setting the stage for a new era.

Meanwhile, the confidence of children waned, adversely affected by the unconventional methods used to guide them towards rudimentary learning, and eventually coerced professions. This imposed pathway bred a form of destructive behavior - a psychic shield against the mounting feelings of frustration and inferiority. This was their subconscious retaliation, a desperate attempt to ward off the encroaching despair.

In the realm of the Natufians, the complexity of mortality was a maelstrom that agitated the collective conscience. The gradual distortion of this understanding became the hunting ground for certain opportunistic factions, who, recognizing the fertile plains of human vulnerability, seized upon it to wield their dominance. They offered an anchorage of solace during turbulent times of bereavement, cunningly hoisting themselves as the custodians of life's enigmatic cycle.

The realm of the mind was esteemed, as tales unfolded, entwining the grotesque and the glorious in a dance both captivating and repelling. Intricate narratives spun from their loom, some fading away into the ether, others contesting for permanence, until one emerged, bearing the mantle of spiritual balm. This tale, this panacea, delivered the absolution that eased the sting of introspective condemnation.

Despite their environment, slowly eroding under the unyielding march of time, the Natufians fostered a grand illusion, an image that echoed the notes of ascendency. They clung to the shimmering mirage of supremacy, an ironic contrast to their subtly diminishing world, the veil of self-delusion serving as their defiant shield against the encroaching reality.

Incapable of grasping the venerable knowledge of Botany and Phytotherapy, the Natufians bore the brunt of lethal viral onslaughts. All too often, they pointed an accusatory finger at the Egyptians, insisting they held responsibility through mystical curses, said to be bestowed by their serpentine deity who had bitten their populace. Outrage intensified as countless individuals bore witness to the ebb of vitality and affection, slipping through their fingers like water. In their pursuit of understanding, they clung to their own deductions, providing alternative interpretations that only served to increase their growing vexation. Searing frustrations simmered under the surface, threatening to erupt into a torrent of despair.

As an irksome sliver that slowly grows from a prickle to an unbearable thorn, disapproval for the Egyptians subtly mushrooms within the community, akin to an undercurrent growing in force before it becomes a rushing torrent. Inspiration finds a home in the minds of the populace, gathering resonance like a struck gong, and even the hesitant among them are gradually swayed to join the rising tide. United in their thoughts and indictments, the collective resentment burgeons into a powerful surge of planned retribution.

Weapons and strategies are not far behind, taking form as the tangible manifestations of their shared animosity. This discontent and the urgent need for counteraction weave an intricate tapestry that lays the groundwork for a strategic offensive against the perceived aggressors. The Egyptians, once companions in peaceful coexistence, are now the target of this rapidly amassing storm. The communal force escalates, preparing to unveil their crafted arsenal and carefully designed tactics against the newfound adversary.

Subtle tremors, registered in the hushed whispers of Egypt's seasoned sages, triggered the mobilization of watchful guardians who roamed the landscapes in search of the Natufians. Diplomats, vested in tranquility, were dispatched to negotiate peace with the tribe leaders, hoping to quell the turbulence simmering between the two civilizations. Yet the Natufians, ensnared in the conundrum of their destiny, found no solace in reasoning. They rebuffed every olive branch extended by the Egyptians, casting aside each proposal with a vehement disdain. The scent of despair hung heavy in the air, a gloomy harbinger of conflict, escalating from the simmering cauldron of discontent.

"Incredulity pervades the air; I can scarcely fathom the proximity of our grand endeavor's culmination," Adeem exclaims, his voice slicing through the spectral silence that has ensnared our usually bustling workshop. We stand, transfixed by the hush that cloaks the room, as if time itself holds its breath. The hum of life outside contrasts with the eerie stillness inside.

In the midst of us all, Djoser rises, his towering figure casting an imposing silhouette over the sea of loyal subjects. His presence is palpable, a beacon, drawing our rapt attention and guiding the overflowing curiosity of those who had spilled into the streets.

"The hour has drawn near," he begins, his words ringing clear, a tolling bell echoing through the gathered crowd. "The hour when every man must rise, when he must cast aside hesitation and valiantly defend his convictions, his cherished existence. He must stand tall or bear witness to its cruel usurpation."

His voice, firm yet compassionate, washes over us. "We've been told a neighboring tribe has conceived hostile intentions towards us. This new revelation casts a somber shadow on our faces; readiness must now be our steadfast companion in these uncertain times." With a deliberate motion, Djoser gestures towards an imposing table, its surface laden with recently crafted weaponry, the fruits of our labor glinting ominously in the muted light.

"Reflect upon the bonds that bind your hearts, the cherished relationships you aim to safeguard," he enjoins us, "Reflect on our mission, the journey we are bound to complete." His words stir a deep resonance within the men, their eyes meeting in a newfound understanding, an understanding now steeped in the stark reality of survival and the defense of their beloved families.

With steadfast resolve, Djoser declares, "Select your weapons immediately!" His words resonate with an imposing weight. The room, once enveloped in quiet, is now immersed in an even deeper hush. Every gaze shifts to the impressive collection of arms—once mere dormant tools, they now represent our hope for survival.

The silence shatters as the first hand reaches out, grasping a massive sword. The ensuing wave of movement breaks the tension, a surge of bodies flooding towards the tables, leaving them bereft of metal. The sight is stark and chilling in its implication.

Now divided into factions, the men of Egypt embark on their transformation, from craftsmen to warriors, individuals to a unified force. They are now destined to become formidable defenders, the guardians of our world. Vigilant bands take turns patrolling the city borders, their spirits fueled by the grim prospect of turmoil threatening their tranquil realm.

The city lights, once a symbol of life and activity, now cast an illuminating glow on stoic faces hardened by the looming threat. Their shadows dance on the ancient stone walls, like silent specters whispering of the trials to come. These are men who stand prepared to stake everything for their homeland's security, men ready to etch their valor into the annals of Egypt's illustrious history.

Armed with primitive implements of war, Bolus commanded the rapt attention of his fellow warriors. His voice, raw and resonant, echoed across the expanse of gathered men. "They once dwelled among us!... Yet, they have elected to curse us with their insidious enchantments!" he thundered, his words heavy with the weight of their shared history. "We stood idle, mere spectators to their malevolent schemes!...That ends now!"

His proclamation, tapping into primal instincts, spurred a communal chant among the men. A rhythmic "Hoot, hoot, hoot", followed by another resonating trio of echoes, "hoot, hoot, hoot". This pulsating mantra surged through their veins like potent nectar, fanning the flames of pack consciousness, bonding them with invisible yet indomitable threads of unity. They were no longer just an assembly, but an army of three hundred souls, steeled to lay down their lives for the sake of a profound conviction.

In the surrounding hills, distanced from the heart of this fervor yet irrevocably connected, Adeem, Kawab, and Anen swiftly climbed atop their steeds. A silent, quicksilver decision propelled them into the unforgiving arms of the inky night. In response to the unmistakable tremors of disruption vibrating through the earth beneath them, they disappeared, making their way homeward with a dire urgency borne of the palpable unrest. They were driven by the knowledge that their tranquil existence had been irreversibly marred by the fires of rebellion.

Under the icy veil of an obsidian night, a hum of profound depth reverberates through the air, as if the very core of the earth were murmuring its secrets. Bolus, along with his stalwart warriors, establish their presence on the edge of the Egyptian encampment, a silent threat lurking in the gloom.

The resonating alarm pierces through the heart of the settlement, a cacophony of fear and uncertainty. As if bound by an unseen force, the inhabitants - women and offspring, their faces shadows of worry, huddle within the confines of their abodes. They tremble, huddling closer, their hearts pounding in sync with the alarm, terrified of the unknown, the impending doom that threatens to shatter the serenity of their existence. The palpable fear in their eyes reflects an

ancient dread, a horror reminiscent of tales told by
ancients, hauntingly resurfacing under the starless sky.

A cataclysmic fervor grips the Natufians as they
launch themselves towards the Egyptians, their wrath
a tempest breaking upon a formidable wall of
opposition. The intoxicating pulse of exhilaration
supplants all conscious thought, drowned in the sea
of primal instinct, a spontaneous reflex to the
pandemonium that now unfolds. The dissonant
chorus of metal against metal fills the air, punctuated
by the raw, guttural bellows of combatants locked in a
deadly dance.

With chilling swiftness, the picturesque battlefield
morphs into a ghastly canvas of indiscriminate
bloodshed. The wails of pure terror echo through the
landscape, a chilling aria to the macabre spectacle of
men stumbling, grievously wounded and dying. Their
lifeblood seeps into the earth beneath the ethereal
glow of the night sky, stained an unsettling shade of
pale plum, a spectral canvas for this nocturnal tableau.

Across the ravine, the resonating lament of loss and
annihilation serves as a haunting refrain, a poignant
testament to the human toll of such brutal
confrontations. Meanwhile, an uncontrollable fire
assumes its roaring crescendo, gnashing and crackling
with voracious intensity. The expulsion of burning
embers dances in the night, their erratic pirouettes
birthing eerie silhouettes that flicker against the
darkness. Each distorted image, a grotesque
pantomime, mirrors the horrifying spectacle of this

ceaseless clash, the grim theatre of war played out beneath the ancient Egyptian night.

In the tumultuous melee, Bolus spots Djoser grappled fiercely with one of his own warriors, his struggle a futile attempt to maintain an advantage. With a swift, decisive motion, Bolus unsheathes his blade, its lethal edge gleaming ominously in the half-light. The struggle between Djoser and the assailant intensifies until, like a fallen pillar of a once-great temple, Djoser succumbs to the weight of his opponent, his form crushed into the yielding earth.

Seeing this, Bolus charges across the battlefield, a lion drawn to its prey. He sinks to his knees beside the aged warrior, his voice a guttural whisper under the cacophony of battle, "Remember me?"

With the grit of the soil seeping into his mouth and pressed against his time-worn visage, Djoser gazes upward, taking in the sight of Bolus looming over him like a foreboding obelisk. His arm, twisted unnaturally and bleeding profusely from multiple lacerations, is wrenched painfully above his head. Yet his spirit remains unbroken, a pharaoh in the face of his inevitable demise, calm and steadfast.

Feeling a surge of adrenaline, akin to the raging waters of the annual flood, Bolus grips his weapon tighter, ready to deliver the fatal blow to Djoser's exposed neck. However, from the engulfing shroud of night, a figure emerges, an avenger from the shadows - Hepu.

With a quicksilver motion, Hepu lunges forward, his blade becoming a deadly lightning bolt. It skewers Bolus with fatal precision, his life extinguished as swiftly as a candle in the night wind. The looming figure of Bolus topples, the triumph in his eyes replaced with the wide-eyed shock of betrayal. Djoser remains, a survivor amidst the carnage, his fate yet uncertain under the watchful eyes of ancient spirits.

The concluding echo of their fury was as potent as its incipience, leaving the battlefield cloaked in the quietude of aftermath. It was a ghastly tableau that bore the signatures of battle—a symphony of victory and defeat—carved on the earth with blood.

Survivors emerged from this chaos, their spirits sculpted by the violence they had both wrought and witnessed. These warriors bore their scars with honor, transformed into living ramparts against the threat that menaced their loved ones. No longer mere mortals, they had been reborn in the crucible of conflict, seared by the flame of endurance and survival. They stood as valiant guardians, the embodiment of resilience, their duty engraved deep within their souls, as profound as the mysteries of the ancient pyramids.

Yet they were condemned to replay the battle's tumultuous symphony in their minds, each note of violence a testament to their sacrifice. Their dreams would become filled with these memories, a relentless echo of what had transpired. Amidst the tranquility of peace, the echoes of war would forever linger, a haunting melody that was now an inseparable part of their existence.

In the chaotic aftermath, Hepu observes Ongara prioritizing the injured Egyptians over his own kind. An apology drips from Ongara's lips, heavy with remorse, his voice trembling with the violent emotions that had rained down upon them, "This...was not our wish, not all of us..." The pain is palpable, overwhelming; he can barely string together the words that form his contrition.

Drawn towards Hepu, Ongara's arms envelope him in a desperate embrace, seeking solace in the face of despair. Through the haze of the ordeal, his mind turns to the innocence of new life as a shield against the grim reality. Voice barely a whisper, he questions, "Has Ona birthed any pups?" his mind in defense mode, a poignant reminder of life's continued cycle, amidst a scene that echoes the relentless trials of their existence.

In expansive chambers, set aside for those ravaged by suffering, lay Djoser, swathed in bandages, a near-ghostly vision of his former vigor. Administered are the ancient therapeutic concoctions, designed to stimulate the life-force within his veins, yet he remains on the precipice of life and death. His breaths are whispers in the silence, a frail testament to his struggle. Djoser is not alone in his struggle; he is encircled by a halo of kith and companions. His wife, Henite, lies in a similar state, her vitality fading rapidly from the weight of despair.

Tears reflecting their adoration, their family unites the two beds. Djoser, a mortal testament to unyielding devotion, extends his hand towards Henite. Overpowered by her plight, she musters a smile for Djoser, her strength insufficient to reciprocate his gesture. He moves closer, managing to clasp her hand - a final union in the face of imminent parting. The twilight of their shared love has dawned; a solemn silence fills the air, punctuated only by the soft sighs of the dying.

Henite is the first to surrender to the inevitable, her eyes closing one final time, followed by Djoser. The finality of their departure sparks a fountain of tears, and thus commences the heart-rending journey of grief. Embraces are exchanged among the bereaved, solace sought in shared sorrow. Their loved ones stand as just one unit among many forced to navigate such a lamentable catastrophe.

Bearing the weight of an ethereal power unleashed, Pharaoh appears desolate, as though submerged in a sea of tribulation. The unsettling shift in the prosperity of his people leaves him crouched in physical torment, unable to rise to the light of day. His duty, however, remains unyielding. Ensuring his people's needs are met, he then commands nourishment and healing provisions be laden onto a trinity of supply caravans, their course set towards the distant Natufians.

"My grandfather falls to their blade, and now we play courier for them? This is... absurd!" Adeem's voice crackles with fury as his hands morph into clenched fists. "They acted out of necessity," Hepu counters in a hushed tone. "Necessity? You jest surely!" Adeem retorts, his voice strained with the weight of his concealed emotions. With a surge of pent-up frustration, he leaps from the rolling cart, darting into the undulating hills, his heart brimming with resentment towards those he was ironically destined to assist.

"Shall we retrieve him?" murmurs one amongst them. A surge of reassurance fills Hepu's tone as he confidently assures, "He shall endure..." Their gazes linger on the receding silhouette of Adeem, melding into the distant hills. Struggling to comprehend his father's words, Adeem's mind swirls with notions of reconciliation; he grapples with myriad possibilities, incessantly churning over his internal state of affairs. The emotional whirlwind persists until the point of cerebral weariness, even as he unwaveringly pursues the course towards the city of the Natufians. Each stride births new reckonings, like the intricate workings of an ancient lock, soothing the fiery turbulence that threatens to extinguish his essence.

The procession of carts, once a lively orchestra, now drones a dirge, their dissonant rhythm weaving a tale of exhaustion. Against the backdrop of plaintive cries, Hepu maintains an unyielding gaze, his resolve unwavering in the face of impending tribulation. As the gates of the Natufian city loom ahead, they march in, each step heavier than the last, grappling with the uncertainty that gnaws at their hearts. Skepticism meets them, doubt infests them, yet onwards they tread, tethered to their fateful path by unseen chains of destiny.

The aftermath of strife lays bare its teeth, anguish permeating every corner, seeping swiftly into homes and hearts. Soldiers, once proud and upright, now retreat into sheltered corners, their hands cradling their burdens of remedies and sustenance. The echo of an eerie war cry pulls Hepu towards its origin, a magnet to an unseen iron.

There, a glimmer of joy flickers in the gloom. Adeem is found, steadfast and gentle, cradling a grievously injured warrior. The fallen hero wheezes under the glow of sky's tear, which lies affectionately on his brow. A circle of love encloses him, his wife and offspring forming a protective, comforting huddle. The dread of battle is momentarily forgotten, replaced by the tender scene, a testament to resilience in the shadow of despair.

Frozen in the grip of fear, each second was a monolith that seemed unmovable. It was as if the world had forgotten how to spin, the hands of time paralyzed, holding him in this moment of unbearable anguish. In the tremulous quiet, Adeem cradled the youth, whose life was slipping away like the last grains in the hourglass, each heartbeat a stuttering echo of a vibrant existence fading.

Around him, the chorus of mourners echoed his own torment, each face a mirror reflecting shards of his personal heartbreak. An eerie, insistent thought clawed at the edges of his consciousness - a harsh truth, a disquieting revelation. It was always thus - the pure and innocent made to bear the brunt of actions born of ignorance. The sacrificial lambs offered up in the theater of the unenlightened.

Plagued with an onerous burden, clans and companions found themselves mired in the dreary undertaking of etching final resting places, bestowing their dearly departed beneath the embrace of the earth. Each painful plunge of the spade brought not only sorrow, but also a discordant fracture in the familial symphony, echoes of which reverberated through successive generations.

Once teetering on the precarious precipice of subsistence, the delicate equilibrium of life amongst the Natufians now tipped into turmoil. Gaunt faces mirrored the scarcity of sustenance that haunted their hearths, while the instability within their ranks cracked the unity of their metropolis. Their once harmonious cityscape, an embodiment of unity, now lay fragmented into disjoint divisions, a stark testament to their societal disarray. Ancient whispers of Egyptian motifs, subtly reflected in their culture, murmured faintly amidst the chaos, a shadowy reminder of the splendour they once embodied.

Perversion begins to weave its intoxicating spell within the realm, birthing twisted ceremonies involving unseasoned youth, both maidens and warriors alike, all in the pursuit of a distorted equilibrium for the pleasure of their rapt audience. Unforeseen violence, random yet relentless, throbs within the heartbeat of the metropolis, each shriek of

fear an echo of an ever-oscillating existence, born
from intellectual disarray wrought by the inevitable
celestial dance of equinoxes.

 Splintered and fragmented, the Natufian tribes
dispersed along divergent paths, sowing the seeds of
the emergent Greek and Roman civilizations. Each
bore the festering wounds of conflict, their pain
metamorphosing into a potent catalyst for their
evolution. The relentless accumulation of warfare
technology, innovations designed with a chilling
intent to annihilate, were hailed and revered as heralds
of a novel chapter in the annals of mankind. Not a
mere shift, but a colossal metamorphosis, as the
tapestry of human history unravelled, presenting a
new epoch, crafted not by the hand of a divine entity,
but by the mortal aspiration and adversity of
humanity.

 As the dawn of creation etched its mark, remarkable
beings, shaped in awe-inspiring human form, were
imbued with otherworldly prowess, resonating with
the collective psyche of the masses. This mystifying
force, deftly wielded by the high priests, retained
dominion over the populace, enshrouding them in a
mysterious veil of awe and reverence.

 The enigma of the Egyptians' cosmic fate remained
elusive, wrapped in riddles that time seemed
disinclined to resolve. Entranced by this intricate
tapestry of existence, the Natufians were stirred into a
grand voyage. As they wandered, they breathed life
into their unique perception of the world, a fresh and
vibrant iteration that began to unfold in harmony

with their journey, expanding and flourishing with every step they took into the unknown.

CHAPTER 10 – THE EVENT

In the profound quiet, veiled by a total solar
blackout, an ethereal tranquility severs the usual
hustle and bustle of a vibrant metropolis now bathed
in the solar eclipse. The celestial spectacle imposes
chaos on the land, instigating an abrupt disruption in
the rhythmic cadence of day and night, marking the
inception of the transmutation sequences. United in
contemplative peace, the citizens of the ancient land,
their hearts throbbing in their chests, cast reverent
gazes upon the completed machine, an intricate
testament to their shared toil and relentless pursuit of
knowledge. Their figures, still as statues, stand in the
vast expanse, bathed in an otherworldly glow, their
whispers of awe carried away by the mystic wind. The
vast, silent multitude is a tableau of unity, a mirror of
the time-worn ethos that flows like the lifeblood of
their homeland, echoing a reverence that transcends
the annals of time.

As the shroud of obscurity lifts, the magnificent
pyramid transforms into an iridescent beacon of
gleaming alabaster, akin to a hidden power being
awakened. Resounding jubilations reverberate across
the verdant expanse, lauding the monumental
achievement. A frenetic energy animates the
craftsmen's nimble hands, fueling their fervor to
conclude their final tasks.

Beneath the incandescent glow, gold electrodes
smoulder in an ardent dance as they're birthed from
the furnace's mouth, eventually cooling to a solid state
within their moulds. In this pulsating heart of
creation, Hepu, Khamet and Mitry stand united, their
skillful hands in rhythmic harmony, perfecting the
molten miracle, and carefully detaching the
connector. As the golden relic attains its final form, it
is swathed delicately in a protective shroud, preparing
it for its journey beyond the shop's confines.

The rhythmic symphony of their craft is punctuated
by Hepu's voice, a timbre resonating with the rich
wisdom of years. "What a privilege it is to stand here
in this pivotal moment, my friends," he declares, his
voice swimming over the mechanical symphony of
their trade. Khamet and Mitry reflect his sentiment,
their faces graced with understanding smiles. "A
challenging path indeed, but oh, how rewarding."

The clanging hammers continue their ceaseless
symphony, the rhythm of their lives. "I recall the
joyous occasions when our offspring came into this
world, our companionship and the joy brought by our
families... truly, life holds no greater treasure." And

so, amid the thrum of creation, their camaraderie is woven into the very fabric of time, a testament to the richness of their shared journey.

Beneath the shadow of the looming pyramid, Hepu discerns a shroud of uncertainty veiling Mitry's countenance. "The future is cloaked in mystery, is it not?" Mitry's voice wavers, apprehensive words spilling forth like the uncontrollable currents of the mighty river. "What if our actions magnify the turmoil instead of alleviating it?" The air between them thrums with an unspoken tension, the weight of the responsibility they shoulder rendering their silence heavy.

Their eyes meet, and in Mitry's gaze, Hepu reads the echoes of unvoiced fears. "There is no certainty in our task," Hepu admits, allowing a measure of his own trepidation to surface. "But we can place our trust in the principles of the universe, in the exactitude of the numbers. They do not deceive."

Gesturing towards the grand structure - a testament to their ancestors' mastery of these principles - he continues, "Time presses us. We must trust the ancient wisdom, the truths woven into the fabric of our land."

Embracing in the quietude of the moment, they understand the magnitude of their endeavor - their actions will carve a new path for humanity, irrevocably altering the course of destiny. They find solace in their shared mission, strength in their unity, and courage in the face of the unknown.

As an ethereal melody echoes through the artisanal foundries, molten gold is meticulously transformed into fine gilded filaments, then elegantly collected onto grand spindles. Hepu, amid this spectacle, finds himself cast back to that fateful, chilling evening at Stone Hedge, a moment in time marked by an all-consuming loss. It was then that the destiny of humanity was shifted, ignited by a fleeting but profound insight in the depths of his psyche. Yet, he had to wrestle his own thoughts to prevent himself from diving deeper into the enigma. This haunting memory is steeped in ancient Egyptian undertones, eschewing references to specific knowledge, epochs, or any sacred elements, but capturing the timeless aura and mystique of that ancient civilization.

In a location securely removed from bustling city life, an artisan's workspace thrives where they craft the delicate balance of sulfur, carbon, and potassium nitrate. Unlike the clamor of ironworks, this refuge of creation blooms in tranquility, deploying a series of ample pads to mitigate the risk of an inadvertent combustion of the carefully fashioned yield. It is a place where silence whispers tales of caution and precision.

Clouds of particles pirouette in the air as the weight of the horse-drawn carriages imprint their existence on the ancient ground, their journey coming to a restful halt. Sharing a ride with the equine conveyance, Hepu steals a momentary observation of a familiar silhouette. A figure that mirrors the resonance of a past chapter, he who was once touched by Adeem's affections and released his dog

Ona onto him. This spectral apparition appears to be none other than Ongara, a man carrying the residue of a love that once blossomed in his heart.

Bathed in a celestial radiance, the pristine white limestone exteriors of the grand pyramid glimmer enticingly, evoking awe and reverence. Unobtrusive stairways, embedded on its northern and southern flanks, provide the only hint of mankind's audacious endeavors. These stairways ascend in an intricate pattern, connecting to lofty platforms, strategically situated at precise alignment shafts.

An orchestra of movement unfolds as horse-drawn carts approach these staircases in a choreographed rhythm, carrying with them volatile freight of paramount significance. With meticulous care, men of unwavering resolve transfer the cargo onto the platforms in a fluid, synchronized motion.

The inventory is a complex array of technology, an odd juxtaposition to the ancient edifice. Spools of wire, electrodes, and tripods rest in organized chaos, interspersed with layered reaction chambers of gold and lithium, capable of harnessing the power of an electrical storm. Dedicated teams of craftsmen commence the assembly of propulsion devices and rigging, setting the stage for the trajectory of a vision beyond the limits of the horizon.

A maelstrom of life force reaches its zenith as the shroud of night falls, unveiling an awe-inspiring spectacle awash with spectral hues painting the pristine white pyramid. "What an extraordinary evening!" Alara exclaims joyously, directing her voice towards Bunefer and Renni. They blend seamlessly into the festive throng where young ones intermingle with elders, their laughter and linked hands embodying a palpable sense of shared affection.

Within the circular hubbub of the amphitheater, spectators vie for the ideal vantage point before gradually succumbing to a respectful hush. The whispers gradually crescendo as the stage is bathed in a cautious spotlight, revealing the Pharaoh at the heart of it all. He sits at the epicenter, statuesque and restrained, head bowed in contemplation.

Eyes tightly shut, the Pharaoh begins to raise his head in a measured cadence and abruptly rises to full height, radiating a potent sense of unyielding resolve. Clad in shimmering white linen that cascades from his limbs and torso, the material catches the sporadic flashes of light, generating a symphony of changing contrasts.

A hush descends upon the amphitheater as darkness engulfs all but the mesmerizing gaze of The Pharaoh, caught within a singular spotlight. His eyes, windows to a world unseen, widen gradually to unveil a profound linkage to our shared collective psyche.

"Experiencing existence in this fleeting moment is the pivot upon which our shared reality turns," he proclaims, his voice filling the still air, rich with an old-world resonance.

"Through the lens of love, we amplify our wisdom and hammer out the path of our future. Our vision serves as a living chronicle, as the mind navigates the vast sea of awareness. We are not exempt from the ceaseless cycle of transformation and rebirth that pervades the cosmos.

We observe this ever-moving wheel from a moderated vantage point, a unique opportunity to scrutinize our inspiration whilst fashioning the apparatus of creation. The Pharaoh's words echo, spreading their resonance into the darkened void, a beacon of timeless wisdom in the ever-changing theatre of life.

Shrouded in shadows, the pyramidal edifice monument awakens, pirouetting in a symphony of chromatic wonder. The populace reverberates with a collective gasp, seemingly levitating the Pharaoh above his dais. He pronounces, "This triumph of ours guarantees that the legacy of mankind extends beyond our terrestrial sphere and into the ethereal cosmos. In a realm of conformities, we represent the extraordinary, gifted with the capability to transition between different life energies, an inadvertent gift from the cosmos." His voice carries the richness of millennia, an ancient echo from the heart of a forgotten Egypt. His words, a spectacle in themselves, paint an image of both hope and promise in the minds of his awestruck subjects. The ambiance imbued with a sense of silent reverence, the pharaoh's words seemed to hang in the air, like an enduring spell woven in the very fabric of the universe.

Fashioned as colossal energy transformers, these towering edifices draw vigor from the Earth's veins, amassing a potent life essence that induces a luminescent spectacle, enveloping the vast coliseum. This radiant display sets the stage for a global broadcast, its signal amplified by the majestic pyramid network. Mind-altering rituals serve to intensify the global connection, while geometrically precise monuments and illustrious frescoes channel this connection to the extraordinary occurrence.

From every direction, luminary shafts coalesce, spotlighting the Pharaoh as he utters the final, soft-spoken utterances of his earthly existence: "The control of our fate lies in life energy, and time is the equalizing element that brings forth balance." The crowd erupts in unified exultation, unlocking an elusive magnetism that unveils the human spirit in its youthful, untouched purity. This vision of the collective soul forms the crux of a grand spectacle that resonates within the essence of human existence.

The grandeur of the Great Pyramid, meticulously perfected, emerges beneath the lunar radiance. It reigns supreme, a colossal monument imbued with a sublime mystique of yesteryears. Bathed in the pale silver glow, it offers an awe-inspiring spectacle - a sight that transcends mere architectural prowess, bordering on the divine. Suggestive whispers of an ancient Egyptian saga echo from its timeless stones, while an ethereal aura that mirrors its glory. The silent nocturnal breeze weaves through the surrounding landscape, enhancing the tranquil ambiance, turning the scene into a breathtaking tableau of antiquity.

Ensnared in the intense whirlwind of their feelings,
Hepu and Adeem find themselves oscillating between
laughter and tears, a mirthless jocularity intertwined
with sorrowful sobs. A poignant recognition dawns
upon their hearts, the grandeur of the impending
event making itself known in its profound and
weighty truth. The atmosphere thrums with the
vibrancy of anticipation and apprehension,
magnifying the spectacle of their shared experience.

As the dusk of the ancient day yields to an inky
Egyptian twilight, the thriving metropolis springs into
a lively dance of vitality and urgency. In every corner,
echoes of an ancient civilization are at work,
meticulously preparing for the eternal journey of the
departed. Resources are deftly employed, the city's
supplies meticulously gathered, a testament to a grand
tradition that has transcended centuries. Architectural
spaces are not mere structures now but a tableau
vivant, each stone and arch reborn and imbued with
the solemn purpose of the impending rite of passage.
These lively scenes depict the grandiose of an age-old
ritual, the mummification, a spectacle of devotion and
respect to those transitioning into the ever after.

With an ambience reminiscent of the illustrious
courts of ancient Egyptian pharaohs, the grandiose
machine stands ready for its maiden voyage.
Attendants, poised at each alignment shaft platform,
bear the weight of their responsibilities with the quiet
confidence of seasoned artisans. They carefully
retrieve gilded spheres, slightly larger than the heart of
a palm, from the well-stocked repository. Each
spherical marvel, etched with intricate hieroglyphs, is

tethered with a slender strand of gold and endowed with a petite eyelet. This spectacle exudes an aura of an age-old ritual, breathing life into the innovative apparatus for the very first time.

Carved into existence on the opposite flank of the monumental pyramid's gateway, a structure of practicality hums with the rhythm of precision, orchestrating the interaction intervals between laborers and participants. Enshrouded in the ancient echoes of Egyptian heritage, this building offers an embodiment of silent authority, meticulously weaving the dance of collaboration and effort. Each transition, a spectacle of human ingenuity, manifests a rhythm as old as the Nile herself, underpinning a cosmic symphony of harmony and ambition.

As a proclamation resonates, the initiation of the primary pathway is decreed. High above, the spherical forms are uplifted, precisely aimed towards the gaping maw of the abyss. With a resonant sound, not unlike a coin seeking the depths of an ancient well, strands of golden thread unspool, spiraling down into the darkness. Their swift descent dwindles, finally succumbing to the immutable laws of inertia as they meet the granite floor of the King's chamber.

Workers begin the meticulous process of interweaving the gilded threads, meticulously crafting an unbroken bond. Their nimble hands dance in harmony, honoring the time-honored craft of their forebears. Bathed in the eerie luminescence of hidden torches, their task takes on an air of mystique, as if they are not merely laborers, but architects of a magnificent and hallowed purpose.

The aura of ancient Egypt permeates the chamber, reflected in the silent shadows and undulating light. As the work nears completion, it's as if the entirety of the cavern holds its breath, awaiting the unfolding spectacle that promises to bridge past and present, mortal and divine. The scene is set, and the timeless dance of human ambition and cosmic mystery continues unabated.

Amidst the bustling city's heart, where time seems to dance at its own pace, the auditorium subtly metamorphoses. The space breathes anew, a subtle alchemy turning the air into a canvas of emotions and contemplations. This change happens silently, yet it reverberates through every soul present, evoking an invisible harmony. A soft rhythm, not unlike the heartbeat of the city, begins to permeate, emanating from every nook and cranny. It weaves a magical symphony, a delicate ballet of sound, filling the environment with an almost palpable musicality. This spectacle, rich in its subtlety, elicits an ambience that is reminiscent of the serene grace of the Nile and the enigmatic aura of an age-old civilization.

As the obsidian tapestry of night unfurled above, the brilliance of Orion's Belt and Polaris punctuated the darkness, their radiance reflected within the gaze of Hepu. This flickering spectacle, a silent testament of ancient cosmic harmony, echoed in the depths of his eyes. An atmosphere of mysterious grandeur permeated the surroundings, a subtle homage to a civilization deeply rooted in cosmic understanding. All was draped in a magnificence that, once observed, whispered tales of an age long past and evoked the enigmatic charm of Ancient Egypt. Flashes of light appear as thunderous grumbling alert the presents of a storm rolling into the valley.

As the Pharaoh navigates through the harmonic energy sphere enveloping him, he disrupts its nebulous tranquility. His departure from the polished obsidian dais sets in motion ethereal phantasms of bygone affections, each arrayed in resplendent white luminescence. These luminous specters, striking in their contrast, dance and shimmer against the backdrop of oncoming storm clouds, their darkness looming with promises of a torrent yet to come. An exquisite spectacle is born from this collision of time and emotion, a dazzling display seeped in the mysteries of antiquity yet touched by the brush of advanced technology, breathing life into a scene from an era yet to come.

With twinkling orbs of starlight vanishing behind the voluminous and vibrant plumes of skybound vapor, the Pharaoh makes his descent onto the expanse of the plateau, where the monolithic grandeur of the pyramid stands resolute. Surrounding him, two men and two women, adorned in garments of unrivaled finery and magnificent headdresses, assert their presence. In their wake, an imposing formation of over a hundred individuals cast long, sinuous shadows upon the stone floor.

The air is electric with the vocalizations of the assembled masses; their songs and incantations adding to the symphony of anticipation. Witnessing the spectacle, they look upon these five beings, destined to initiate the layers of cosmic passage, starting with the immaculate one. Their procession is slow, embodying an air of dignity that refrains from boasting, a silent decree of their unique stature. Each step they take is a verse in the hymn of an ancient ritual, written not in papyrus but in the universal language of reverence and awe.

As droplets, petite and luminescent, start to descend from the heavens, they adorn the path ahead with their diamond-like brilliance. Journeying on elevated pathways carved from solid granite, the travelers move, their existence creating an increasingly expansive imprint upon the earth beneath them. Cloaked in a subtle ambiance of mystery reminiscent of ancient Egyptian mystique, their every step unfolds a spectacle, a grand narrative untold. All the while, the soft patter of the rain provides a rhythmic backdrop, orchestrating a harmonious ballet of nature and humankind, engaged in a timeless dance across this vast and magnificent terrain.

In the hushed whispers before transmission, diminutive magnetic pulsations dance and twirl, their duty being to examine the range of unseen waves. Inside the subterranean crypts, hewn from the heart of the awe-inspiring edifices of Great and Khafre Pyramids, the harmony of technology and antiquity unfolds. Specialized contrivances, the culmination of meticulous innovation, are affixed to enhance the resonance of the space. Arrayed in a parallel manner, their symmetrical positioning holds court within the curated mounds of energy. Their purpose, to fine-tune the internal symphony of frequencies, the invisible orchestra that fills these ancient vaults with an invisible energy, a specter of the profound culture that once flourished under the shadows of these colossal structures. All the while, the whispers of history sing a silent chorus, a ballad inaudible to human ears, but resonating deep within the marrow of the pyramids themselves.

Bathed in the obsidian night, flashes of celestial fire flicker, illuminating the glossy facades of the monumental pyramids. Shadowy figures, shrouded in ample cloaks, traverse the expansive stone platforms, their forms obscured in an attempt to fend off relentless exposure. Precious auric electrodes are meticulously disentangled while slender filaments of golden wire are deftly woven through minute perforations. Sparks, akin to a meteor shower, erupt from a compromised junction, a dazzling spectacle signifying the preparedness of the electrical current. An air of anticipation permeates the scene, as the ancient land of the Pharaohs whispers tales of age-old mysteries, yet devoid of any mention of the grand river or the radiant celestial body.

Bound by the celestial dance, the terrestrial sphere finds itself beholden to its cosmic placement, coming full circle in a grand epoch of twenty six millennia. The pivot point of this grand oscillation induces a cosmic rearrangement amongst its celestial brethren, unveiling the latent potency of our planet. In an exquisite performance, the rhythm of the universe is tuned to the movements of the Earth, imbued with the mystique of ancient Egyptian wisdom.

Seismic calibrators ensure the target's orientation, as tempestuous detonative elements nestle within the foundation of the propelling crypts, trained on the nascent cosmos recently reaped. Vibrations murmur a promising future, while an orchestra of preparation unfolds within this interstellar theater. Shadows weave an ambiance of focused intensity, and the air, a specter of awe and reverence, whispers tales of cosmic conquests to be.

A throng of onlookers clusters around the threshold, their eyes shining with anticipation of the impending existence that awaits them. A symphony of rhythms weaves through the air, its harmonious tune guiding their thought patterns into a mutual melody of hope and excitement. The atmosphere tingles with electricity, each breath laced with the fervor of what's to come, while an ostentatious display of anticipation unfolds, painting an exquisite scene of communal expectation.

In the isolation of his royal detachment, the Pharaoh advances towards the timeless pyramid, halting suddenly. A fleeting perception identifies the chosen duo from the fringe of his gaze. Embodying the allure of Cleopatra in their gaze, Adeem and Kiya move with a sense of purpose towards their leader. In the quietude of their reverence, they submit to their knees. The Pharaoh, with a tender slow motion, cradles his palms, the luminous dove, a love, pure and untouched, shimmers brightly like a beacon of hope.

Amidst the bustle and effervescent laughter, there emerges a joy that glimmers brighter than any spectacle under the sky. Serenity transforms their faces into canvases of pure bliss as they are gently swept aside, moments away from their meticulously planned ceremonial preparation. The shift in the atmosphere is palpable when Hepu and Alara reveal themselves, their sudden entrance igniting a surge of sentimentality. Emotions surge like a flood, raw and undiluted, as Renni and Dedu surrender to their tears. A beautiful tapestry of love begins to weave itself together, as family, friends, and even strangers reach out to each other in a heartfelt embrace, connecting in a shared moment of profound happiness.

In the heart of Egypt, the Pharaoh stands with poise before his assembled multitude, presenting his final spectacle. The mass of spectators sway rhythmically, a dynamic representation of alternating currents. His countenance, highlighted by erratic flashes of luminescent illumination, is accentuated by the rumbles of overhead lightning. The scene is reminiscent of an artist, presenting his magnum opus after a demanding recital. Enthusiastic applause and cheers wash over him like a tsunami of admiration. This is the pinnacle of human consciousness, a flood of emotions cascading in this monumental moment.

Slowly, with a majesty befitting his status, the Pharaoh rotates to face the iconic Pyramid. His gait steady, one foot cautiously venturing forward before the other. As he steps forward, the dazzling brightness of the passage starts to consume his silhouette. He seems to be moving into a different realm, his destiny awaiting him within the enigmatic heart of the pyramid. His figure gradually diminishes, gradually subsumed by the blinding brilliance of the pyramid's interior. This is his journey, the Pharaoh stepping into his fate.

 Divested of worldly treasures and raiment, the Pharaoh, with sublime serenity, reclines in the confines of the capsule. His compatriots - each holding their breath - tenderly position the cover, permitting a fleeting, final view of their monarch before his confinement. Bereft of outward sentiment, their faces hidden behind a mask of stoicism, they retreat from the sanctum, advancing through the majestic corridor. With each step, the luminescent orbs that line their path extinguish in a harmonized sequence, enveloping the erstwhile vibrant hall in an inexorable cloak of darkness.

 Spectators maintain a respectful distance, drawn into the mesmerizing spectacle wherein only the existence of the Pharaoh dwells, ensnared within the throbbing energy nexus. The celestial vault maps an immaculate synchronization, mirroring the intricate dance of humanity's former days and forthcoming destiny. Animated by cosmic capriciousness, the tempest intermittently liberates shafts of energy, insinuating its consent to engage in the extraordinary act. Engulfed in the womb of darkness, The Pharaoh's pulse is quickened by an underlying sense of mortality, yet he holds steadfast in his assurance, a paragon of audacious confidence amidst the unfolding marvel.

Lustrous coils of metallic thread ascend to align with the towering launch cylinders. Delicate apparatus are gingerly pressed into the heart of the combustion chambers, preparing for the impending spectacle. This meticulous arrangement soon culminates with the careful placement of electrodes, each entrusted with the power to ignite a marvel of human invention.

The whispering dialogue between the two operating hubs and the control nexus validates the operational progression. Shrouded in the hushed ambiance of diligent minds at work, the scene unfolds as a spectacle of human ingenuity. Figures move with precise choreography, their character echoing a shared sense of dedication and focus.

Primed and prepared, the decisive moment has arrived. Gazes lift toward the heavens as a miniature golden firework, dispatched from the control nexus, blossoms overhead, casting its incandescent bloom above the pyramid. In prompt response, the deck engineers kindle the propulsive payload, catapulting the conductive terminals skyward. Battling the elements, they ascend, diverging towards the brooding storm clouds where terrestrial energy is harnessed and tethered back to terra firma, establishing the conduit of power.

As though reaching for life-sustaining hydration, the electric surge is enticed into each conduit, obediently coursing down the wire into the heart of the pyramid

- the sanctum where The Pharaoh anticipates. Bathed in an atmosphere thick with expectancy, the ceremonial scene unveils a spectacle of profound magnitude. The low murmur of machinery and the crackle of energy fuse into a symphony of power, its intensity reverberating throughout the ancient structure. The atmosphere is thick with drama and suspense, in a majestic symphony of human achievement and nature's brute force.

Underneath this grand performance, the Pharaoh stands in the epicenter, the eye of the storm, waiting for the culmination of this extraordinary phenomenon. The buzzing energy within the chamber hums a testament to mankind's audacity and the relentless quest for knowledge, bringing a hush over the onlookers as the spectacle unfolds, their breaths held in awe and anticipation.

Deep within the grandeur of the pyramid, a pulsating surge magnifies, initiating an earthly tether as it navigates through the geometrically precise conduits. High above, where the ethereal sea of clouds reside, a lightning spear makes its ascent, its twin extremities reaching out - one directed toward a celestial terminus, the other toward a perpetual constant - vanishing seamlessly into the realm of the unseen.

Space-time condenses, crafting a path for the signal, its strength fueled by the planet's spin and the lunar patterns. Aided by the vast emptiness of cosmos, a more potent link is birthed. At the inception of this cosmic communion, resonating sound waves permeate each junction, employing a dance of alternating electromagnetic forces, hence paving the way for limitless voyage.

Perched on an adjacent undulating terrain, the Natufians are riveted by the breathtaking spectacle unfolding before their very eyes - myriad bolts of electrical energy crisscrossing the stratosphere, tethering themselves to the cryptic device in a vibrant spectacle of radiant symmetry. As the final vestiges of energy dissipate, the connection fractures, showering the ether with tiny glittering embers of golden brilliance.

An assembly of men, swathed in the determined rhythm of their shared mission, ascend with calculated haste into the sublime architecture of the gallery's heart. Their paths waver amidst the ethereal veils of elusive smoke, painting a spectral dance upon their journey. The seal to the cryptic capsule is gently broken, the motion reveals the corporeal form of the erstwhile Pharaoh, still and serene in his eternal slumber.

This noble figure, an embodiment of departed grandeur, is delicately liberated from his resting place. With the respect befitting of his rank, he is transported through the majestic expanse of the gallery, and beyond the pyramid's stoic walls.

A hive of medical experts awaits, converging on his arrival at the embalming station. There is a symphony of coordinated motion as they each engage in their duties, weaving a complex tapestry of rituals and responsibilities around the royal figure. The air shivers with their collective dedication, casting a solemn reverence over the unfolding spectacle of their ancient artistry.

Amid the quartet, she stands as the premiere, her delicate wave dispersing through the multitude, resplendent in her unstained linen attire - an exquisite equilibrium of intellect and physique. The imminent future waits for her acceptance, as anticipation mingles with optimism in the parting utterances shared amongst loved ones. They partake in the bittersweet ritual of farewell, their smiles touched by the dew of emotional departure. As the queue dwindles to a mere trickle, an ocean of expectant gazes observes the looming industrial apparatus, while a scent, metallic yet fresh - the quintessence of ionization - signals the inception of the long-awaited event.

Inevitably, the teams who manned the complex platform were obliged to rotate duties, an unavoidable necessity born from the pervasive, relentless heat that the myriad of intertwining connections produced. The surging energy, hot and unyielding, traced its fiery course towards its predetermined endpoint, creating a spectacle of raw power and intricate coordination. The atmosphere was alive, pulsing with both the tangible intensity of the work at hand and the abstract sense of purpose that fueled each team member. The entire scene was a display of technological prowess against a backdrop of ceaseless industry, an elegant ballet of human endeavor amidst an orchestra of sparking conduits.

Caught within the brink of timelessness, one existence prepares to be etched into the realm of eternity, while the universe itself vibrates with resonant synchronicity. Across the globe, devoted souls establish their monuments of intention, embodying the tranquility akin to a radio in reception; each triumphant accomplishment punctuated by a unique symphony.

Bathed in the cool allure of the nocturnal ether, Kiya shimmered like an ethereal beacon. Overwhelmed with a profound sense of fortune, Adeem silently mulled over his circumstances. To have been gifted this moment, to exist within the sphere of her enchanting presence, was a blessing he held dear. To experience the intoxicating elixir of love that led him, willingly, towards the inevitable dance with mortality. Such was his luck, such was his destiny. It was to not merely live, but to perish in love.

As Adeem murmurs, "Refrain from envisioning it," they find themselves entwined in a parting embrace. The gradual severance of their contact is akin to forcing apart two magnets; it drives Adeem down to his knees. His body convulses until it is wholly subdued, consumed by a profound sense of loss. Left solitary at the gateway, his breaths shallow and irregular, Adeem surrenders to the warmth of the rain which feels akin to a soothing balm.

His mind surges like a wild tempest, fueled by the agonizing throes of grief. Amidst the rain's rhythmic patter, phantom imageries from the annals of time and glimpses of an uncertain future invade his thoughts, making fleeting instants feel like boundless stretches. As if trapped in an everlasting reverie, the raw intensity of his emotions paints a grand spectacle of his solitude and longing. Every droplet that lands on his curled form magnifies the scene's atmospheric resonance, stirring up an almost palpable sense of his heartrending solitude.

Awakened by a sudden gleam, quickly followed by a piercing crackle of a thunderclap, Adeem gracefully ascends to a standing position, his demeanor reflective of a stance destined for time's annals, his countenance noble and resolute, eyes raised heavenwards. He steals an instant from the unstoppable current of time, absorbing the sensory orchestra around him - the colors and fragrances painting a vibrant palette of life. The memories of his beloved, his familial ties, his companions, and the multitudes who have influenced his existence – they linger as his final sensory feast before they too fade into the ether. Stepping forth into the hallowed geometry of the pyramid, he disappears from view, his form consumed by an ancient mystery, leaving behind an aura of indelible memory.

The waning hours of the night find the stage set, poised on the precipice of change as the latest cadre ascends, the former crew stepping back into the shadows, their duty fulfilled. A pair of potent energies find their place within the vessel, a sizzling dance of sparks casting a fragile, thrilling reassurance in the thickening air. It is a choreographed symphony of imminent release, a fire-lit dance that whips anticipation into a frenzied ballet. Figures in the tableau of shadows, silhouettes against the engulfing darkness, stand resolute, a testament to readiness and resolve, as they prepare for the imminent spectacle of elemental fury.

With an air of purpose, Adeem darts toward the repast module, keenly observing the strewn shards of stone lining the way to the rectangular construct that sparks a surreal familiarity within him. He gently slips into the confinement of the module, maintaining a tranquil facade. His heart throbs with intense anticipation as he surveys the vanishing illumination, while the upper section methodically assembles over him. It resembles a complex puzzle disassembled into fragments, its once resolute form now bearing the scars of relentless wear and tear. The formerly seamless, elegant monument to craftsmanship, now teeters on the edge of decay, yet Adeem finds a quiet beauty in its imperfections.

As the orchestra's final reverberation hovers, electrodes ingeniously synchronized make contact with the heavens. A beast of energy pulses through the infrastructure, held at bay yet undeniably potent, tearing a corner from the ejection pod. Within this vortex of volatile power, the existence of Adeem is siphoned away. His breathless silence contrasts with the wild roars of unleashed electricity, an irony that might have amused him under different circumstances. There's an unsettling beauty to this scene: a brilliant maelstrom of light and energy juxtaposed with the stark stillness of a life departed. It feels as if time itself is holding its breath, the world seemingly trapped in a paradoxical moment of vivid

destruction and peaceful serenity. The grandeur of the
scene, undeniably theatrical, feels eerily familiar, like a
memory of a nightmare brought to life. The harsh
metallic taste of fear, the heart-wrenching sorrow of
loss, and the cruel spectacle of a life-force evaporated,
all swirl together in a cyclone of emotion that is as
overwhelming as it is poignant.

Caught in the mesmerizing dance of transition,
clusters of people, bound by shared joy, raise their
voices in jubilant laughter and spirited cheers, their
jubilation resonating with every represented stratum.
As if on cue, the spent tempest retreats, revealing a
sky untouched and pristine, its transformation
infusing a novel resonance to the atmosphere.
Through our unshielded gaze, we are granted the
privilege to discern the most striking luminaries, their
relevance marked not by their radiance alone, but by
the shift in ambiance they instigate - an intangible
shift, yet as captivating as the spectacle of the night
sky itself. Their shimmering visage stirs within, a
sense of familiarity and wonder, a tantalizing cocktail
of emotions that adds color to the canvas of the
night.

Overwhelmed by desolation, spectators are swept
away in a sea of melancholy as the immobile form of
the Pharaoh surrenders to the stillness of eternal rest
on an embalming altar. A cohort of meticulous
artisans work with precision, methodically evacuating
the vestiges of life from within him. Each organ is
carefully extracted, examined, and recorded, setting
the bar for future comparisons. Soft, careful hands
tenderly initiate the enveloping, with linen swathes

diminishing as they are meticulously wrapped around each limb, adhered securely to his regal form.

Desolation gradually loosens its grip, leaving a hollow sensation as the solemn ceremony of mummification reaches its end. The once-vibrant Pharaoh is respectfully returned to his grieving family, as if in quiet slumber. Affection and longing intermingle as written words of love and aspiration are tucked alongside him, serving as cathartic tokens that aid in severing their earthly bonds. Amidst the soft glow of ceremonial lights and the whisper of sacred hymns, the Pharaoh's final journey commences, a spectacle laden with emotion and intricate ritual, forever etched in the hearts of his people.

From miniature apertures, infinitesimal grains of sediment slip, precipitating a balanced dance of forces that command the regal weight of the chamber's portcullis doors to descend. With a lethargic inevitability, the ancient barrier seals the heart of the realm, veiling the central majesty from the outside world. A symphony of stone and granule, each particle playing its part in this grand performance, animates a spectacle of slow-moving majesty, stirring emotions of profound reverence. The ambience within the chamber morphs, shrouded in an intimate silence that ripples throughout its confines, as if the very stones are whispering tales of times forgotten yet never truly lost. The spectacle, poignant and entrancing, encapsulates the ethereal dance of time, sealing the grandeur within.

Exquisitely shaped and embellished, the funerary mask becomes the final touch as the Pharaoh is carefully enclosed within his sarcophagus. The seal is secured with a solemn whisper, a lasting tribute to the ruler of the land. Gold, with its peerless lustre, mirrors the vibrancy and warmth of life itself, as if its polished sheen encapsulates the essence of the Pharaoh's reign. It stands as a vivid testament, a regal symbol of a timeless ruler who once guided his people with wisdom and courage. His vibrant heart and timeless legacy resonate within the gleaming mask, now a beacon in the silence of his eternal rest.

Beneath the placid terra firma, a complex network of conservation vaults awaits, defying the earth's horizon. On the ceremonial podium, the mighty Pharaoh, our beloved sovereign, is prepared for his eternal rest. He is ensconced amidst cherished keepsakes, tokens of affection bestowed upon him throughout his reign, ranging from grand to minuscule. As the closure of his tomb nears, these artifacts, down to the tiniest trinkets, are respectfully bestowed within, imbuing the space with a sense of eternal regality. Witness to this grand spectacle are silent catacombs, imbued with a solemnity that echoes the profound respect of a civilization bidding adieu to its monarch.

Interlinked in harmonious patterns, resting repositories stretch miles apart in deliberate arrangements, a testament to their concluding function. Meticulously, every location receives a backfill treatment, subtly merging with the unspoiled environment, becoming part of the existing tableau.

With an understated elegance, the transformation leaves no hint of intrusion, rather a respectful integration, enhancing the panorama with a silent, poignant spectacle. Their purpose fulfilled, they whisper stories of life and departure, imprinting themselves onto the canvas of the world in a ballet of silent tribute.

With a symphony of industrious fervor resuming in the air, the majestic pyramid, a feat of human ingenuity, undergoes a transformative operation. Diligent workers begin to meticulously strip away the intricately crafted facing stones, thus cloaking the once visible magnificence of the exterior architecture. Veiled in mystery, this monumental edifice, whose very structure is a spectacle to behold, now stands as an enigma, its original aesthetic splendor now hidden from curious eyes.

Plunged into the shadowed recesses, the protective stone layer is haphazardly obscured. With astute artistry, an assortment of internal filler stones is masterfully arranged to seal the aperture of the ageless pyramid, forever cloaking the entryway. The ambiance is one of mystery and grandeur, a sight that humbles the onlooker. Spectacularly, the enormous stone structure stands as a testament to the ingenuity of an ancient civilization, its secrets lost to the hands of time. The scene, bathed in the moonlight's ethereal glow, silently whispers tales of a forgotten era.

Basking in global harmony, a symphony of voices reverberates, honoring the momentous occasion with awe-inspiring acts of human ingenuity. They sculpt

masterpieces and erect towering tributes, a testament
to their collective spirit. These are not just physical
tokens; they're living tapestries, breathing life into
stone and steel, forever capturing the brilliance of
their creators. These artistic triumphs serve as an
enduring legacy, a priceless inheritance seamlessly
passed from one era to the next, encapsulating the
essence of humanity's indomitable spirit and unending
quest for beauty. The world, like a stage set for an
extraordinary spectacle, mirrors the captivating
radiance of this celebration, silently bearing witness to
the artistry of its inhabitants. Never old just in the
prime of their life the Dendera light symbolizes
energy reaching out to the next world over the void
of time.

A solitary sentinel, the sphinx, presides over the
resting place of her treasured ancients, her gaze a
beacon to the seekers of mysteries. Engraved in her
countenance is a millennia-old tale, each line on her
stony face a testament to history's passage. She rests
in majesty, bathed in the lunar glow, a spectacle
standing tall against the heavens. The gentle whisper
of the breeze, the silhouettes of timeless architecture
against the celestial blanket, and her captivating aura,
create an ambiance that leaves the onlookers intrigued
yet reverent. Bathed in the silver light of the moon,
she holds their rapt attention, as she silently narrates a
tale from a world long past, to all who dare to listen.

In the tranquil hush of creation, a new planet is
ascended upon, kissed by fresh human beginnings, its
fertility summoned forth by the presence of two
hundred and twelve innovative life entities. Their

arrival, both intriguing and unprecedented, intervenes
in the sequence of procreation, reshaping the
fundamental blueprint of existence. The captivating
dance of life and evolution thus commences, draped
in the exquisite mystique of silence, unfettered by the
constraints of yesteryears, weaving an ever-changing
spectacle of life's grand theatre. The ambiance is
ethereal, as if stepping into a realm both foreign and
eerily familiar, undulating waves of tranquility
cascading around, each pulse further illuminating the
beauty of this spontaneous disruption.

At the heart of the verdant expanses and the deepest
azure oceans, lies an intricate cipher, radiant with
ethereal translucence. A complex and tiered construct,
it manifests as a mirror to the cosmos, carrying the
essence of all biodiversity within its nebulous depths.
Endowed with the noble task of imbuing life, it
spreads its vibrancy across the sphere of our
existence, a marvel spanning from the tiniest microbe
to the grandest leviathan. Spectacular in spectacle, this
marvel carries the ambiance of a grand cosmic
theatre, each character playing out their role in the
ballet of life. An opalescent structure, it mesmerizes
all who dare to decipher its encrypted beauty.

Immersed in the harmonious ballet of existence,
clusters of sophisticated life punctuate an untarnished
new world. Freed from the blemishes of a bygone era,
this place thrives in the symphony of pristine balance
that orchestrates life and demise. The architecture of
these life-forms, resplendent with complexity, paints a
riveting spectacle against the untainted canvas of the
world. The crisp air hums with vitality, and the gentle

murmur of the world itself adds an evocative undercurrent, framing a vibrant scene of existential poetry. This interplay of living organisms, all participating in the cyclical dance of birth and demise, exudes an undeniable allure that enlivens the senses. Here, in this unblemished sphere, the quintessential essence of life and death waxes and wanes in mesmerizing harmony.

In the heart of the realm, a subtle shift seized the atmosphere, a profound alteration palpable to all inhabitants. This transformation marked not just the dawn of a new era but the birth of an extraordinary existence. Amid the cacophony of life, there was an almost imperceptible rustle; it was the world acknowledging its irreversible metamorphosis.

In a quiet corner of the new world, under the soft glow of dawn, the baby Pharaoh, an emblem of fresh hope and transformation, opened her eyes for the very first time. Her look, innocent but powerful, carried a silent vow of a destiny filled with splendor, dignity, and magnificence.

THE END

Made in the USA
Las Vegas, NV
14 October 2023

79059947R00174